"Will remind readers what chattering teeth sound like."
—*Kirkus Reviews*

"Voracious readers of horror will delightfully consume the contents of Bates's World's Scariest Places books."
—*Publishers Weekly*

"Creatively creepy and sure to scare." —*The Japan Times*

"Jeremy Bates writes like a deviant angel I'm glad doesn't live on my shoulder."
—Christian Galacar, author of GILCHRIST

"Thriller fans and readers of Stephen King, Joe Lansdale, and other masters of the art will find much to love."
—*Midwest Book Review*

"An ice-cold thriller full of mystery, suspense, fear."
—David Moody, author of HATER and AUTUMN

"A page-turner in the true sense of the word."
—*HorrorAddicts*

"Will make your skin crawl." —*Scream Magazine*

"Told with an authoritative voice full of heart and insight."
—Richard Thomas, Bram Stoker nominated author

"Grabs and doesn't let go until the end." —*Writer's Digest*

I

BY JEREMY BATES

Suicide Forest ♦ The Catacombs ♦ Helltown ♦ Island of the Dolls ♦ Mountain of the Dead ♦ Hotel Chelsea ♦ Mosquito Man ♦ The Sleep Experiment ♦ The Man from Taured ♦ Merfolk ♦ The Dancing Plague 1 & 2 ♦ White Lies ♦ The Taste of Fear ♦ Black Canyon ♦ Run ♦ Rewind ♦ Neighbors ♦ Six Bullets ♦ Box of Bones ♦ The Mailman ♦ Re-Roll ♦ New America: Utopia Calling ♦ Dark Hearts ♦ Bad People

FREE BOOK

For a limited time, visit www.jeremybatesbooks.com to receive a free copy of the critically acclaimed short novel *Black Canyon*, winner of Crime Writers of Canada The Lou Allin Memorial Award.

The Dancing Plague

World's Scariest Legends 5

Jeremy Bates

The Dancing Plague

PROLOGUE

THE PRESENT

I was twelve years old, and the year was 1988, when the Dancing Plague came to my town.

It was the end of September. The long, hot days of summer were a thing of the past. The leaves on the trees were turning shades of red and yellow and ochre, and it was getting dark earlier and earlier.

Nobody knew what to make of the individuals who broke out in manic, uncontrollable dancing...not at first, anyway. There were theories later on, and speculations; educated men and women attempting to jigsaw together the unexplainable, to force reason onto the unreasonable.

Nobody got it right in the end.

The truth, as I would come to discover, was stranger than fiction.

What I witnessed and lived through—if just barely—on the night that Chunk, Sally, and I went to Ryders Field has haunted me for the last thirty-one years. During that long and somewhat directionless stretch in my life, I graduated from Northeastern University with a degree in philosophy. I married my college girlfriend and divorced her three years later (her fault, I'd like to believe, not mine; but who the fuck knows?). I held all sorts of odd jobs to scrape by, including the graveyard shift as a hotel desk clerk (and if sitting behind a counter all night sounds like it would be one hell of a slog, you'd be right...except if you were a wannabe author. Because I spent many of those nights smashing out my first novel, which defied the odds to become a *New York Times* bestseller). Since that turn of luck and fate, I've released six more novels, all considered pulp horror, all deemed unimportant and unserious by the critical literati—but they now pay the bills and allow me to write full-time. I'm fine with that.

The book I'm crafting while seated at my computer in an apartment in downtown Boston, the book that you, my silent companion, are reading sometime in the future, has no doubt been billed as fiction by my publisher. But for the record, it's not fiction. No sir or ma'am. Every word of this happened, as best I can remember.

ΔΔΔ

A bit about me.

I grew up in Chatham, Massachusetts, one of the fifteen towns dotted across Cape Cod. If you view the Cape as an arm flexing its bicep, Chatham's at the elbow. To the east is the Atlantic Ocean, to the South is Nantucket Sound, and to the north is Pleasant Bay.

Chatham kicked off in the sixteen-somethings as a fishing and whaling community. By the nineteenth century it was a summer haven for wealthy Boston elites, most of whom were ditching their Victorian peacock fabrics and trimmings for more conservative costumes. Ironically, these folks flocked to Chatham for the very reasons that made life there such a bitch for the first European settlers: the town's isolation and proximity to the ocean. They came not by stagecoach or packet boat but by train, which offered service to Provincetown by 1873. In 1890 President Cleveland made his Bourne residence the Cape's first "Summer White House," cementing the Cape as the place to *be*. Soon artists and celebrities joined the party (including the likes of Humphrey Bogart, Bette Davis, Henry Fonda, Orson Welles), and like rats following the cheese, the dilettantes and tourists came next.

If you've ever visited the Cape, you know its charm and its allure. In my opinion this gangly slice of the Atlantic coast is one of the most interesting parts of the country. The wooded uplands with their wind-bent and twisted pines are straight out of a Brothers Grimm's fairytale; the clear, cold saltwater ponds are still enough to see your reflection staring back up at you; the shallow brooks and rivers are perfect for clamming during low tide; the rolling dunes and sandy beaches that frame the picturesque harbors and inlets sell postcards by the thousands.

In 1988 Chatham had a permanent population of about six thousand souls. This swelled to more than thirty thousand between Memorial Day and Labor Day, when the vacationers and other tourists arrived in droves, strangling the streets with belching cars, prickling the beaches with parasols, and injecting a good deal of money into the economy, which allowed the mom-and-pop shops to survive the off-season to the next summer.

When the Dancing Plague arrived that September, the summer crowd had already left town, leaving many of the quaint houses and cottages empty, and the once bustling streets and beaches lonely and silent.

The Captain's House Inn, which had been booked to capacity a month earlier, housed only a single guest during the second-to-last week of that month. His name was Gregory Henrickson. He was a handsome young man who kept largely to himself. A chambermaid found his remains in his room on the morning of September 16, his body on the blood-soaked queen bed, his decapitated head on the adjacent mahogany desk.

Nobody would connect Henrickson, or his savage death, to the spontaneous dancing that would creep through the town in the following weeks. But Henrickson was most definitely connected to the plague. He brought it to Chatham, and he was responsible for the horror to come.

BEN'S STORY

"A dance is the devil's procession, and he that entereth into a dance, entereth into his possession."
—St. Francis de Sales

CHAPTER 1
1988

"RUN!" Chunk bellowed, though it didn't sound like the Chunk I knew. The imperative was high-pitched and reedy, almost girlish.

I pulled my eyes off the sidewalk and spotted the Beast immediately. The guy stood half a block away on our side of the street, facing us.

My heart slipped into my stomach.

The Beast came for us, fast.

Chunk fled the way we had come. With a belated gasp, I followed. Chunk was about my height but chubby, and I quickly pulled up beside him. Everybody had started calling him "Chunk" (instead of his real name, Chuck) after *The Goonies* hit theaters a couple of years ago.

"Which way?" I wheezed.

"Main Street!"

"Too far!"

I glanced over my shoulder. The Beast was a regular Carl Lewis, his feet barely touching the pavement, his arms busting like pistons. I noticed he'd shed his backpack, which sat askew on the sidewalk behind him.

He meant business.

I considered dropping my book-filled canvas backpack as well. It was slapping my back and felt like an anchor. But then Chunk swept left onto a stone path that led up to the big, godly doors of Holy Redeemer Church.

I skidded to a stop, high-fiving the sidewalk with one hand as I changed directions. As I scrambled along the path toward the church, the Beast leaped over the three-foot-tall hedge along the church's property line. He landed awkwardly, rolled in a somersault, and then sprang back to his feet, cutting diagonally across the lawn toward us without missing a beat.

He *really* meant business.

Chunk wasted no time slowing down and slammed full-tilt boogie into the church's arched mahogany doors. Even as his pudgy hands found the black wrought-iron door handles, I knew we were toast. The doors would be locked. We'd be trapped. The Beast would make me bite the sidewalk curb and then stomp on the back of my head to shatter my teeth—

One of the doors whooshed open on well-oiled hinges. Chunk squealed in relief. Afraid to glance over my shoulder again, knowing the Beast would be right on our asses, I shoved Chunk ahead of me inside the church. We scampered on all fours up a short flight of blue-carpeted steps and burst into the nave. We ran down the aisle that split the oak pews where the churchgoers sat, jostling to get ahead of one another.

"*Stop!*" the Beast commanded from behind us.

We stopped. I don't know why. Looking back on that day, I suppose we obeyed him because there wasn't anywhere else for us to run...and perhaps because we believed we were somehow safe. We were in a church, after all. God was watching. Nobody would be stupid enough to lay a hand on us in His house. Right?

Wrong.

Chunk was panting loudly, sounding like his sister's bulldog after chasing tennis balls in their family's shit-strewn backyard. My heart seemed to be whumping just as loudly, and my legs wanted to jelly out beneath me.

We both turned to face our reckoning.

We didn't know the Beast's real name, but "the Beast" was good enough. He wasn't big or hairy or anything like that. But he appeared to be all muscle. You could see it in the way his calves bulged away from his narrow ankles, in his ropey forearms and biceps, and especially in his neck, where ugly body-builder veins throbbed. Moreover, he just looked crazy. Maybe it was due to the manic shine in his dark eyes, or yet another vein throbbing angrily in his forehead, but he reminded me of Boner in that TV show *Growing Pains*—maybe Boner's evil twin.

"You two are so fuckin dead," he growled through a smile that was also a sneer.

"We didn't do nuthin this time!" Chunk protested.

"You called me a dickhead." He was coming toward us, slowly and menacingly. His hands were balled into fists.

What he'd accused us of was indeed true. We *had* called him a dickhead, on a previous occasion...and it was justified.

Earlier in the month, on the second day of the new school year, Chunk and I had been riding our bikes to Chatham Middle School together, where we were eighth-grade students. It was a morning routine we'd started when we became best friends three years earlier. We were heading north on Crowell Road when we encountered the Beast for the first time. He was carrying a humungous branch that had likely blown down in the previous night's storm. He held it perpendicular to his body so it blocked the entire sidewalk, forcing Chunk and me onto the road. He shot us an insipid grin as we passed him, pleased by the inconvenience he'd caused.

Standing on my bike's pedals, looping back and forth to keep my balance at the crawling speed, I called him a dickhead.

He blinked, seemingly unable to comprehend insolence from a kid younger than himself. "What didja say, loser?"

Feeling confident on the perch of his bike, Chunk shouted gleefully, "He called you a dickhead, *loser!*"

The Beast's crazed eyes went crazier. He tossed aside the branch...and then kicked off each shoe, one after the other, before charging after us.

We took off. My bike was in a high gear, and I couldn't accelerate as fast as Chunk. I smashed the gear button, the bike's chain clicking rustily as it switched between chainrings. I was just starting to pedal faster when one of the Beast's hands snagged my backpack. I heard his bare feet slapping the road behind me, felt my momentum slowing. And I knew I was done, finished, ended. Like old Humpty Dumpty, nobody would be able to put me together again—

Somehow I broke away.

The Beast pursued us for another dozen yards or so before resorting to threats and profanities. We taunted him from a distance. This was not the smartest thing to do. The fact he was walking along Crowell Road at that time in the morning (likely to the high school bus stop at the corner of Crowell and Main) meant he lived somewhere close by. And the fact Chatham Middle School was on Crowell meant chances were good we would cross paths with him again, either on our way to school in the morning or on our way home in the afternoon.

It turned out to be the former.

"We were just kiddin round," Chunk told the Beast. "*Honest.*"

"Oh yeah?" the guy said, the sneer twisting his mouth. "Well, now I'm gonna beat the snot and piss outta ya both, okay?"

"You can't hit us in a church," I protested.

"Wanna bet?"

Someone behind us cleared his throat. Chunk and I spun around.

The back wall of the church was paneled in wood. A somber crucifix hung in the center of it between two equally somber stained-glass windows. To the right of the white-clothed altar, Father Burridge stood at the threshold of a door that had previously been closed. Unlike his fancy dress during Sunday morning mass, he wore black jeans and a black button-down shirt with a white clerical collar (*just one of the guys*, the outfit seemed to say...only a guy more righteous than thee). Steel-colored eyes glared at us from behind tortoiseshell eyeglasses. He clearly wasn't happy to find a trio of kids horsing around inside his sanctuary.

"He's trying to beat us up!" Chunk blurted, jabbing a sausage finger at the Beast.

"They called me a name—"

Father Burridge cut off the protest with a divine flourish of his hand. "Nobody will be beating anybody up today," he said in a stern tone. "Not in this house of worship, and not anywhere else in town. Today, or any day, for that matter. If I hear about anything of that sort, I will be sure to speak with all your parents."

"You don't even know my parents!" the Beast shot back. It surprised (and impressed) me that he had the balls to argue not only with an adult but a *priest*. He added defiantly, "My dad don't live in Chatham, and my mom don't go to church neither. So there."

"Trust me, son," Father Burridge said flatly. "I will find out who your mother is, and I will have a few choice words with her. Now, I repeat, no fighting. Do I make myself clear?"

"Yes, sir," Chunk said, bobbing his head.

"Yes, Father," I said, suddenly very glad for the existence of priests and churches.

The Beast mumbled something that suggested the priest hadn't made himself clear at all. With a vindictive glance at Chunk and me (a glance that promised there would be fighting indeed, and soon, oh yes) he stalked out of the church.

CHAPTER 2

THE NEW TEACHER

We ragged on the Beast as we continued to Chatham Middle School. For the life of us, we couldn't understand why the joker had kicked off his shoes during our first encounter and not this most recent one. Chunk figured that first time he might have had blisters of the sort you get from new shoes, or not wearing socks. On the other hand, I figured maybe his laces hadn't been tied up and he'd been worried about tripping on them (lame speculation, for sure, but it was all I could come up with).

In any event, by the time the school bell trilled and we were lined up out front of our homeroom door, I was no longer thinking about the Beast. More immediate concerns had diverted my attention, like Heather Russell, who stood in front of me, talking to Laura Holson. Despite having a minor insurrection of acne around her mouth, Heather was probably the prettiest girl in school. Her shoulder-length golden hair fell around her face like cornsilk, and her blue eyes were as enigmatic as sapphires. We'd been in each other's classes for years now, but I'd barely said a handful of words to her in all that time. I wasn't great at talking to girls in general, and I was particularly bad at talking to pretty and popular ones.

Chunk never had this problem, and he butted into their conversation now, saying, "Hey, Heather, how'd ya miss the high jump bag yesterday? Landing on your head like that musta hurt like mad, huh?"

Heather smiled at him but kept up her conversation with Laura. That was another thing about the girl. She had the heart of a saint.

Undeterred by the polite brush-off, Chunk tugged Laura's honey-colored braid, which reached down her back to the top of her butt, and said, "Hey, Laura, wanna hear a bitchin joke?"

Short and roundish (though not chubby like Chunk), Laura might have been one of the most unlikeable and scary people I knew back in those days, as she was always carping about one thing or another. My mom would have called her snobby—a word she'd used often to describe the governor of our state, who had also been the Democratic presidential candidate in 1988.

Laura scowled at Chunk and said, "Don't you have a Twinkie to eat?"

Elbowing me in the ribs, Chunk mouthed Laura's jibe, imitating her peeved-off face. I marveled at his temerity in not only talking to girls but also making fun of them. I suppose he knew he was too fat to date them, or even befriend them, so he had nothing to lose being his regular old self around them.

Me, on the other hand...well, I wasn't great looking, but I wasn't bad looking either, and on more than a few occasions I'd imagined myself marrying Heather. I'd romanticized where we would live, how many kids we would have, all that crazy stuff. That sort of explained why I always froze up around her. One wrong word and my entire contrived future could come crashing down around me.

The chatter in the line died when our teacher, Mr. Riddle, arrived with a busy keychain in one hand, a coffee in a paper cup in the other. Unlike most of the other male teachers, he didn't wear a suit and tie, or even khakis or corduroys and a button-down dress shirt. Instead he rocked high-top Nikes, sweatpants, and tee shirts. Today his sweatpants were light blue, and his tee, one of his favorites, was white with "Sir!" scrawled across the chest in slime green. That was what he insisted we call him. Not Mr. Riddle, not Teacher. Only Sir. Tufts of silky white hair stuck out from beneath a beat-up baseball cap patterned in camouflage. As usual, he reeked of cigarettes.

His keys jangled as he unlocked the classroom door. While he made his way to his big desk at the front of the room, he said, "Everyone in your seats for morning announcements!"

Chunk and I slung our backpacks on wall hooks at the back of the classroom and slumped down at our desks, which were in the back row. On the first day of class, Sir had let everyone choose where they wanted to sit, which was different than most other teachers, who made you sit where they wanted you to (so they could put the troublemakers in the first row where they could keep an eye on them). However, Sir did have the caveat that if you goofed around, you would be moved. So far he'd only had to relocate Harry Booth, though a few other students already had two strikes against them. Three and you were doing the walk of shame to the front row.

Sharing the back row with Chunk and me was a thin girl named Tania Eldredge, who had approximately zero friends, and a guy named Craig Snelly, who wasn't batting much better. Craig had a pair of elbow crutches to help him walk because he had a disease that caused his legs to go spastic if he tried to stand or walk on them unassisted (multiple sclerosis, I now figure). Everyone called Craig "Smelly" because his legs couldn't always get him to the bathroom on time. This was also why his seat was not only in the back row but right next to the door. Unfortunately for him, our classroom was on the second floor, and the boys' bathroom was in the basement, so even sitting by the door didn't guarantee he wouldn't piss himself. They didn't cut anyone any slack at CMS.

After the morning announcements crackled over the PA system, and our class recited by rote the Pledge of Allegiance, Sir scribbled the date on the blackboard.

Without needing to be told, everybody took their notebooks from their desks and copied down the date. I was getting better at a cursive script and took some small pride in keeping the letters between the feints.

Someone knocked at the door. It swung open a moment later, and an attractive woman poked her head inside the classroom. She looked a little bewildered at all the sets of juvenile eyes staring back at her.

"Ah, Miss Forrester!" Sir said, smiling at the woman. "You found us, I see? There's a desk in the corner there with your name on it."

Skirting the back of the classroom like a latecomer sneaking into Sunday morning mass, she settled into the desk and busied herself taking a notebook and a pen from her handbag.

Sir plopped down on the corner of his desk with one foot planted firmly on the floor and the other rocking in the air, and said, "Miss Forrester is going to be with us for the next...?"

She cleared her throat. "Two weeks. Um, ten classes."

Everyone was still turned in their seats to study (and judge) her. And kids were aces at judging adults, more than most adults knew. We made judgments in seconds, not hours or days. Most of us in the classroom right then were probably already snap-calculating what we could, and couldn't, get away with if Miss Forrester ever took over the reins of the class—and most of our calculations would probably be right on the money.

Physically, Miss Forrester resembled Heather Russell, I thought, only her blonde hair was curly rather than straight, and she was a lot older—though not nearly as old as any of the other teachers at the school. She wore a purple blazer with big shoulder pads over a shiny silver top. Even though the top was loose-fitting, I could see the outline of the wire parts of her bra. Chunk would say she had a great set of jugs, and he wouldn't be wrong.

I wondered who she was, and why she was lurking in the back of our classroom. From my experience this kind of arrangement wasn't a good sign. Last year a few of the girls in my class had accused our teacher, Mr. Breuninger, of massaging their shoulders while they were sitting at their desks, and waltzing into their change room during phys ed. I never saw any of this happen firsthand, and I didn't understand why it was a big deal, not then, not as an eleven-year-old kid. But I quickly learned it *was* a big deal because the vice principal took a seat in our classroom one afternoon, not at the back but the front next to Mr. Breuninger. She'd asked each of the girls making the complaints—which included Heather Russell and snobby Laura Holson—to explain in detail what had made them uncomfortable. I don't remember how Mr. Breuninger responded, except he denied everything. I thought the matter was forgotten because the next day everything seemed back to normal. But Mr. Breuninger didn't come back to school the next year, and nobody knew what school he had transferred to.

Looking back on it, the old perv had clearly been embarrassed about the whole incident and didn't want to return to Chatham Middle School. Then again...perhaps his teacher's accreditation had been revoked and he wasn't allowed to return.

Anyway, on the day that Miss Forrester joined our classroom, I had been hoping that Sir hadn't been massaging any of the girls' shoulders or peeking in on them while they were changing for gym. So far he'd been a good teacher, and I didn't want a different one. His replacement might be like Mr. Zanardo, the other grade-eight teacher at the school, who had some sort of vendetta against me.

From the front row Harry Booth asked, "Are you gonna teach us, Miss?"

"Hand up, Martin," Sir told him.

He wiped the back of his hand across his face—his nose always seemed to be running—and raised his arm lazily. "Are you gonna teach us, Miss?"

"I'm not sure," she replied. "That will be up to Mr. Riddle to decide."

"So you're a teacher?" I said, sticking up my arm.

"I'm training to be one, yes. And if Mr. Riddle would like me to teach some of your lessons, I'd be happy to do so."

"Can you let her teach us, Sir?" Harry asked, sniffling.

"I have no problem with that. But let's give Miss Forrester a few days to get a feel for the classroom and to learn some of your names. Any other questions?"

A few hands went up.

"Elise?" Sir said.

"Where do you live?" Elise Summers asked.

"Where am I from, do you mean? I'm from Provincetown, in the Upper Cape."

"So why don't you teach in Provincetown if that's where you're from?"

"A teacher has to agree to mentor an undergraduate student like myself. There's more to the relationship than allowing me to observe their lessons. And the teachers I contacted in Provincetown all had very busy schedules."

Another hand.

"Go on, Steve," Sir said.

"Why'd'ya needa train to be a teacher? Teachers don't do nothing."

"We put up with ignorant statements like that," Sir said, shushing the burst of laughter that followed. "In fact, any teacher who makes teaching appear effortless is doing a lot more than you know. Martin?"

"Are you married?" he asked.

More laughter, though not as loud this time and a bit uncomfortable. Asking a looker like Miss Forrester whether she was married was pretty much admitting you wanted to marry her yourself—and I was sure half the boys in the class wanted just that, myself included.

"She's a *miss*, not a *missus*," Elise quipped loudly. "Duh!"

"And we'll pause on that note." Sir stood. "History books open to Chapter 2. Let's go, let's go, let's go!"

CHAPTER 3

THE NOTE

C hunk flicked me a note that was folded up into a ball no larger than a marble. His aim wasn't good, and the note landed on the floor a couple of feet away from my desk. Sir was writing on the blackboard, his back to us. I glanced at Miss Forrester. She was shuffling through some papers.

I pushed my pen off my desk, then bent over to pick it up, along with the note. I unfurled the ball of paper against my chest so Miss Forrester couldn't see what I was doing (what a pisser to have a teacher both in front of you *and* behind you).

Chunk had written two words:

She's hott!

I wasn't sure if that was how he thought you spelled "hot" or if he was doing it for emphasis. You never knew with Chunk.

I shrugged in his direction. What did he want me to write back? *Yeah, she is.* I tossed the note into the open front of my desk, where about a dozen other discarded notes shared the space with my notebooks and textbooks. I resumed copying down what Sir was writing on the blackboard.

Another note came my way, this one landing on my lap. I ignored it until I couldn't any longer:

Great ass too! Bet you want to slap it!

I made a face at him. What did he know about asses, great or not? And slapping it? I figured he got that idea from one of his older brother's porno movies. We'd watched one called *Co-Ed Fever* at a sleepover at his house not too long back, and there was a lot of ass-slapping going on in it, as well as much more dirty stuff. He'd been really into all of it, while I was sort of grossed out.

The cherub smirk on Chunk's face suddenly vanished, and then he was staring at the blackboard and scribbling diligently in his notebook. I knew what that meant even before I looked up and found Miss Forrester looming behind me, one hand outstretched.

"Pass it here," she said quietly.

I flattened my hand over the note. "Pass what?"

"Right now, please."

Some of the students in the row in front of me were looking back.

"I ain't got nothing," I said lamely.

"The note."

"What's going on?" It was Sir, and I knew I was screwed.

Miss Forrester pointed at Chunk. "That young man passed this young man a note."

"Hand it over, Ben," Sir said to me. "You know the rules."

"Are you gonna read it out loud?" Harry Booth asked happily.

"Quiet, Martin."

"That's the rule—"

"*Quiet.* Ben, hand over your note to Miss Forrester. Now."

I felt my cheeks burning. There was no way I was giving the note to her. *Great ass too. Bet you want to slap it.* Forget it. No way.

Out of desperation, I popped the tear of paper into my mouth and swallowed it with a declamatory bob of my Adam's apple.

The class broke into cries of "Gross!" and "Eww!"

"I hope it tasted good, Ben," Sir said over the ruckus. "Because that stunt has earned you a morning detention with yours truly."

△△△

When the recess bell rang, and everyone rushed outside to play, I remained at my desk. Miss Forrester went to the front of the classroom to chat with Mr. Riddle. They both ignored me, and for a buoyant moment I wondered if perhaps Sir had forgotten he'd given me detention. I stood quietly and looked at the open door.

"What do you think you're doing, Ben?" Sir said.

"Getting a snack from my bag...?"

He nodded in a sign of permission. I went to my canvas backpack dangling on the wall hook and pulled out the brown paper bag that held my lunch. A peek inside revealed a peanut butter and jam sandwich, a McIntosh apple, a juice box, two Oreo cookies in a Ziplock bag, and a granola bar. I wanted the Oreos, but if I ate them now, I wouldn't have anything good left at lunchtime. Reluctantly I withdrew the granola bar, stuck the paper bag back in my backpack, and returned to my desk. I was disappointed to find the granola bar had bits of nuts and fruit instead of chocolate chips. Still, my stomach was growling, and it was better than the apple.

While I chewed on it, I opened my religion notebook to the back inside cover, where I was working on a pencil sketch of Reggie Lemelin, the new goalie for the Boston Bruins. It was about half done and looking pretty bombdiggity. In recent years, when any art went up on the classroom wall, mine was usually the best. My parents had planted the idea in my head that I should work for Disney when I grew up. That sounded like a rad job, and my future seemed on track.

Until the start of this year when a new kid from Springfield showed up at CMS.

His name was Billy Brown, and he could draw to the max. Secretly I thought he was more talented than me. He didn't draw real stuff. He did cartoons, faces with big noses and no chins and that stuff. It was just like the artwork you saw in comic books;

it was that good. I tried copying one of his faces once, and it turned out pretty good. But when I tried drawing others on my own, they bombed. That was when I realized I was only good at *copying* pictures and not *imagining* them like Billy did...and it was also when I realized I might not be able to work for Disney, after all.

I was focused on shading in one of Lemelin's goalie pads (copying it from an O-Pee-Chee hockey card when he still played for the Calgary Flames), when Sir said, "Ben?"

I looked up cautiously. Sometimes teachers would make kids in detention run errands for them, like taking the attendance sheet to the office. Once I was asked to fetch a zucchini from the school garden; to this day I have no idea what the teacher had wanted with it.

"Bell's going to ring in five minutes. If you need to visit the bathroom, you can go now."

I didn't need to go, but the bathroom sounded better than being stuck at my desk. I left the classroom and skipped down the stairs, passing Craig Snelly, who was on his way up them. He always came in early from recess so he could get back to the classroom before everybody else; otherwise he'd probably get crushed in the stampede. Not having working legs would suck at any age, but it must have particularly sucked in middle school when most kids were running around more than they were walking.

"Hey, Craig," I said as I zipped past him. I never called him Smelly; I thought that was a little too mean.

"Hey, Ben," he said, pausing to catch his breath. His legs looked like they belonged to a puppet, floppy and without strength. His upper body, on the other hand, was just the opposite, all burly muscle.

He probably wanted to trap me in a talk, so I told him, "I gotta get to the bathroom. I only got five minutes."

The school's basement had a weird vibe about it, probably because it was always quiet and empty. The only classes taught down there were shop and home ec, and those rooms were often unoccupied. Also, the faculty staffroom was in the basement, so you had a better chance of running into a teacher there than anywhere else in the school, which was why most students avoided the basement unless they were busting to pee.

The walls of the boys' bathroom were painted blue. I went to one of the urinals along the wall, realizing I had to take a leak, after all. When I was done and zipped up, I was about to leave— and heard laughter in one of the toilet stalls. Beneath the closed door I saw two sets of feet.

"Who's in there?" I said, going over.

The laughing stopped. "Nobody."

"Chris?" I said, recognizing his voice.

"Ben?"

"What're you guys doing?"

The door swung open. Chris Anderson and Ken McPhee stood shoulder to shoulder, grinning. In his hands Chris held a big paperback book, opened about halfway. He showed me the cover. The author was Stephen King. Below the title, *The Tommyknockers*, was an eerie green mist and the silhouette of a house. The biggest books I'd read were Hardy Boys, but I knew who Stephen King was. Once Chunk and I had rented one of his movies about trucks and other machines coming to life and killing people.

"Ain't it scary?" I asked, confused as to why they'd been laughing.

"Read it again," Ken said, giggling.

Chris read a passage, emphasizing each F-bomb: "'Get your mind right, Bobbi. If you want to go on doing what you like, get your *fucking* mind right and stop that *fucking* crying. That *fucking* crying makes me sick. That *fucking* crying makes me want to puke.'"

This cracked them up, and I smiled. All the cussing was sort of funny.

Ken said, "Read the part about the period."

I was wondering how you could read a dot when Chris flicked through the book to a dog-eared page and read: "'But after she had showered, put a pad in a fresh pair of cotton panties, and pulled the whole works snug, she checked the sheets and saw them unmarked. Her period was early, but it had at least had the consideration to wait until she was almost awake.'"

This totally cracked them up, and I smiled again. I didn't find it funny, but I didn't want to let on that I didn't understand what exactly *was* funny.

Chris said, "I bet you don't even know what a period is."

"I do too."

"What is it then?"

I was saved from answering by Mr. Zanardo who'd just walked into the bathroom. Scowling at us, he demanded, "What the hell are you boys up to?" Unlike Sir, Retardo (as some of us called the prick behind his back), always wore an important suit. The one he had on now was light brown with beige patches on the elbows. The knot of his red tie was pulled so snug some of the flab of his chin hung down over it. He wasn't fat though. He was...solid, I'd guess you'd say. With his puffy brown mullet and matching beard, he was a dead ringer for The Million Dollar Man Ted DiBiase.

"Nuthin," I said promptly and started toward the door.

"Stop right where you are, Ben," he told me. "Chris, what are you doing with that book? Is it from the library?"

"Nah," Chris said. "It's my brother's."

"Give it here." He held out his hand. This was something teachers always seemed to be doing—holding out their hand in want of something. A salacious note, an adult book, chewed bubblegum, whatever, it didn't seem to matter. They just liked taking stuff from kids.

"But it's my *brother's*," Chris protested. "He collects them."

"I said give it here. One, two..."

Reluctantly Chris slapped the paperback into Retardo's hand.

Retardo glanced at the cover and said, "Don't you think this is above your reading age?"

Chris shrugged. "My parents lemme read anything I want."

Ken smirked. "Even *Playboy*?"

"Knock it off, Ken," Retardo said absently. He was studying the back cover. I expected him to skim through the pages to the dog-eared ones that contained all the cussing. But he only looked at us and said, "You boys know you're not allowed to be in here."

"The bathroom?" I said, frowning.

"Let me rephrase that for you, Ben. You're allowed in the bathroom if you need to use the facilities. However, you're not allowed to loiter about in here. You're supposed to be outside at recess."

"I had to piss."

"Excuse me?"

"I had to *pee*," I amended. "And I got a detention this recess, so I can't go outside."

"Is that so?" he said, raising an eyebrow. "Well, now you have lunch detention too. All three of you. My classroom, noon—and don't make me come looking for you."

CHAPTER 4

DETENTION

I got back to my desk just before the recess bell sounded. When the rest of the class filed in, I kept my head down and worked on my goalie picture. I was too amped up to talk to anybody. Recess detentions were only twenty minutes, not a huge deal. Lunch detentions, on the other hand, were forty-five friggin minutes of unrelenting boredom. Copping one then was even worse than staying back after school. The thing with after-school detentions was that teachers usually wanted to go home too, so they rarely kept you longer than the ten or so minutes it took them to pack up their stuff and tidy the classroom.

I heard Chunk bragging about a hat trick he got in foot hockey. You couldn't not hear the guy. He spoke at twice the volume as everyone else, especially when he was out of breath or excited—like now.

"Ben, man, you missed a hella rad game!" he practically screamed at me. "Gotta stop eating those notes in class."

"Step off," I told him. "That was your fault."

"If you can't stand the heat, sucka, get outta the kitchen!"

Here's something you should probably know about Chunk. His parents were a couple of hippies that were high 24/7 and encouraged a laxity of rules at home (which likely explained why Chunk thought he could get away with anything, anywhere). More to the point, however, his parents spoke almost entirely in clichés. I'm not sure if they'd been too stoned to think of anything more original to say, or if they'd simply thought they were being funny or Zen or what. But you didn't have to be over at Chunk's place for long before you heard "Don't get your knickers in a twist, Chucky-baby" or "Cat got your tongue, buddy-o?" or "Only time will tell, cool cat" or "Love you more than life itself, butterking" (yeah, Chunk's parents often called him butterking). Now here's the thing: Chunk took up his parents' love of clichés about a year ago, and he burps them out whenever he has a chance. This used to bug the hell out of me—especially since the clichés he chose rarely fit the moment—but now I hardly noticed; they were just *him*.

Sir clapped his hands together to quiet the class down, and we spent the next period figuring out the lengths of geometric shapes. Geometry wasn't my thing. Not for lack of trying; I was giving the six questions Sir had assigned us my best try. I just wasn't any good with numbers and angles. Eventually I got so frustrated I simply made up the answers. Seeing that I'd "finished," Sir told me to write the first answer on the blackboard. Needless to say, he wasn't happy with it. I do believe he'd called it twittershit—and that was decades before the closely named social media platform was invented.

At a little after 11:00 the class filed down to the gymnasium for phys ed. Sometimes we had to do boring crap like hula-hooping or rope climbing. But today was soccer. We divided ourselves into two teams (I was picked third for mine), and then we dragged four orange pylons from the storage room to mark the goalposts for the imaginary nets. Nobody could find a soccer ball, so we ended up using one of those bouncy red balls better suited to dodgeball. Being larger and lighter than a soccer ball, it was harder to control with your feet, but you could kick it to the moon if you wanted to. Harry Booth didn't pass up the opportunity. Each time the ball came to him he'd boot it all the way up into the roof (where a few balls—including the missing soccer ball—were lodged in the rafters).

His latest wild-man kick ricocheted off one wall and zinged Miss Forrester right in the face. The whistle screamed, the game stopped, and then Sir was escorting Miss Forrester from the gym, her cheeks red, her eyes shimmering with tears. When some of the girls chided Harry, he was quick to point out that Miss Forrester shouldn't have been standing right next to one of the goalposts. I sort of agreed with him. There were plenty of better places she could have been standing.

Anyway, that was that. The game never resumed, and we ended up back in the classroom prematurely, where Sir made us sit silently at our desks doing nothing until the lunch bell rang. While I was taking my lunch from my backpack at the back of the room, Chunk appeared next to me and said, "George is being lame and not letting us use his tennis ball. Wanna come look for one with me?"

"Can't," I told him. "I got detention with Retardo."

"Another detention!" he crowed. Another person's misfortune was always Chunk's great fortune. "What didja do this time, man? Eat another note?"

"Chris and Ken were reading a Stephen King book in the bathroom. Retardo thought I was reading it too."

"You got detention for *reading a book*? Man, that dude majorly hates you."

"Tell me about it." I shrugged. "Anyway, I gotta motor. If I'm late, he'll freak and gimme another one after school."

Mr. Zanardo's classroom was at the end of the second-floor hallway. The door was ajar, but nobody was inside. I considered slinking off to the playground, but I knew he would come looking for me, so I slumped down at a desk in the middle of the room.

Ken and Chris arrived a minute later.

"Where's Zanardo?" Chris asked.

"Beats me," I said.

"Maybe he forgot we have detentions?" Ken said hopefully.

"Take a seat, boys!" a deep voice echoed up the hallway.

Chris and Ken dropped into the desks to my right. Mr. Zanardo strolled into the classroom a moment later, chewing an apple. In his other hand he carried a Tupperware container filled with food.

"No, I don't think so," he said, around a full mouth. "Ben, front row, move it. Chris, you can stay where you are. Ken, back row."

I switched to a desk in the front row, and then took my math textbook and notebook from my backpack.

Retardo settled into the chair behind his big desk and crossed his ankle over his knee. "What are you doing, Ben?"

I stopped digging through my pencil case for a sharpened pencil and frowned at him. "My math homework?"

He smiled at me. "I don't think so, pal. You're in detention."

"Other teachers lemme do my homework in detention."

"Well, I'm not another teacher, am I?"

"What are we supposed to do then?" Chris asked.

"Sit there and think about why you're here."

"Because we were reading a *book*?" Chris griped, making his answer sound like a question.

"Are you that dense, Chris?" Retardo took another crunch of the apple. "Didn't I make myself clear in the bathroom? You're here because you were somewhere you weren't supposed to be —"

"Sir told me I could go to the bathroom," I said.

Retardo slapped his hand on his desk with frightful force. "Shut your mouth, Ben! You know damn well you were up to no good in there!" He took the Stephen King book from a drawer in his desk, opened it to one of the dog-eared pages, and read the paragraph with all the swear words.

I was shocked. I'd heard teachers swear before. Mr. Riddle probably did it the most. But his swearwords were always silly and harmless, like twittershit. Retardo was reading the swearwords in the book with real vitriol—and even though he wasn't directing them *at* me, the situation felt not only uncomfortable but threatening too.

When he finished his eyes swept over each of us—lingering on me the longest—and he added, "Now you boys are going to sit there silently and think about why you were reading this trash and decide whether it was worth losing your lunchtime over. Hear me?"

For the next while the only sounds in the classroom were Retardo eating his lunch (some kind of pungent-smelling curry) and kids playing games outside, shouting and having fun.

I glanced up at the clock on the wall: 12:10. Another thirty-five minutes. I folded my arms together on the desk and rested my forehead on them.

This was turning into the worst day ever.

△△△

At 12:30 Mr. Zanardo said, "Chris, Ken, you can both go now."

They jumped to their feet and darted from the room.

"Walk, don't run!" Retardo called after them.

"What about me?" I asked, lifting my head from my arms and blinking stars from my vision. I think I'd fallen asleep.

Retardo had his feet up on his desk with the Stephen King book propped open on his belly. He appeared to be reading it from the beginning. "What about you?" he said without looking up.

"Can I go too?"

"You can sit right there." He turned a page.

"But you let Chris and Ken go."

"What would your mother think of you reading a book like this?" he asked, finally looking at me and raising an eyebrow.

I sighed. "It's *not* my book, and I *wasn't* reading it. I went to the bathroom to take a...pee, and Ken and Chris were already there reading it. I just wanted t'see what they were laughing at."

"Are you ratting out your friends?"

"I'm just telling you what happened."

"What was your morning detention for?"

I didn't feel like that information was any of his business, but I knew if I didn't answer he'd just get more pissed off at me.

"Someone passed me a note in class."

"And Mr. Riddle gave you a detention for that?"

I shrugged.

"Do I have to talk to Mr. Riddle myself?"

"I ate the note," I told him, trying to keep cool.

Retardo laughed, a deep-throated bark. He didn't ask why I ate the note, and I wouldn't have told the asshole if he had. He simply shook his head as if he were disappointed in me and said, "Two detentions in one day, Ben. I wonder what your mother would think about *that*?"

She would think you're the biggest turd on the planet for giving me a detention for nothing, that's what, shit-for-brains.

He said, "Perhaps I should mention this to her at tomorrow's Curriculum Night?"

I stared at him. Would he really speak to my mom? He wasn't even my teacher!

"She will be attending, won't she, Ben?"

I nodded reluctantly.

"With your father?"

I shook my head. "He doesn't get home from work until six usually."

I felt Retardo watching me, but I couldn't bring myself to meet his gaze. I really hated the guy right then.

"Get out of here, Ben."

I blinked at him in surprise but didn't linger. I left the classroom—making sure to walk, not run.

CHAPTER 5

THE PRESENT

"What a cocksucker," I said, standing up from my computer desk in the center of my little Boston apartment. I tossed the Bang & Olufsen headphones I'd been wearing onto the desk without pausing my playlist. John Lennon continued singing *Stand By Me*, his voice now shrunken and tinny.

I carried my empty coffee mug to the kitchenette, clicked on a burner on the gas stove, and placed a half-filled kettle on it. Leaning against the counter, I surveyed the studio apartment. There was my Office Depot computer desk, on which sat my laptop; a black executive chair made of heavy-duty materials (not because I was overweight but because of the amount of time I spent every day sitting in it); and a foldable cot with a foam mattress and pillow. I'd only slept in the flimsy bed on a few occasions, and my unrested body never thanked me the following morning.

I owned a three-bedroom townhouse in Back Bay. I rented the studio to serve as an office because there were too many distractions around the house that often prevented me from reaching my two-thousand-word daily writing quota. That was the reason I kept the studio unembellished. No television, no books, hardly any food in the cupboards (a big meal in the middle of the day could put me straight to sleep). I had an internet connection, yes, but I only used it for research and to stream music.

The kettle whistled. I removed it from the burner and poured steaming water into my mug. I mixed in a spoonful of Nescafe instant coffee and opened the refrigerator. The top shelf held half a dozen plastic jugs of full-cream milk. The lower shelf held an equal number of bottles of Jim Beam bourbon whiskey. The stockpile obviated the need for frequent trips to the supermarket, as I drank seven to eight milky coffees each morning, which was when I got most of my original draft writing done, and two or three whiskeys in the afternoon while polishing the morning's work. Add a peanut butter-slathered banana for breakfast, a hotdog from a vendor down on Atlantic Avenue for lunch, and a dry aperitif and frozen meal for dinner, and that was my daily diet.

Not very healthy maybe, but it got the job done.

I poured a good dollop of milk into my coffee, returned the jug to the fridge, and was about to sit back down at my computer when there was a knock at the door.

I had only ever had one visitor to the studio, so I knew who it must be before I answered the door. And so it was—Nessa Nader, an Egyptian-American woman with a pleasing Arabic-influenced accent. The best way I could describe Nessa was Deanna Troi from *Star Trek* minus the uniform and telepathic abilities.

I would guess her to be approximately forty, not because she looked that age (thirty, thirty-five tops), but because she'd told me her son had started college last year, just before I'd moved into the building. Since we were neighbors, we'd often encountered one another in the hallway or the elevator. Over time the nods of acknowledgment or banalities about the weather evolved into friendly chitchats. Things changed dramatically when she invited me to her place for a coffee—and we somehow ended up in her bed. That had been six months ago, and we'd continued getting together once a week or so, sometimes at her place, sometimes at mine. She told me she was married but she and her husband no longer lived together and rarely spoke. I believed her as I had never seen the man entering or leaving her apartment.

Nessa wore a white cardigan over a flowery dress and all her typical gold and silver jewelry. She held a Roche Bros. plastic bag filled with groceries. It was the same supermarket where I bought the milk and whiskey.

"Hey," I said, pleased to see her. "You didn't have to buy groceries for me."

"You only eat hot dogs, I thought?"

"We've gotten to know each other too well."

"How's the writing going?"

Everybody asked me this as an icebreaker. It was the equivalent of asking somebody who didn't write books for a living, "How's it going?"

"Pretty good," I told her. "I've started a new book."

"I haven't seen you around here for a while. I thought maybe you'd moved out?"

"I was in-between books last month. I didn't have any reason to hang around here." I realized how insensitive that sounded, given she and I were casual sex buddies. "What I mean is—"

"What's it about?" she asked, saving me from the sloppy explanation. "The new book?"

"It's a coming-of-age thing. Kid stuff."

"And how are you finding that—writing about kids? Must be different than writing about adults?"

"It is," I admitted. "They talk and think in their own way, so there's that. I'm trying not to use too many big words. It's tougher than it sounds."

"Are you ashamed of using little words?"

I shrugged. "Sort of, sure. It feels like I'm not trying or something."

"Keep them small," she told me. "Your readers will thank you." She switched the bag of groceries to her other hand. Tins rattled against one another. "Do you, um…have time to take a break from your work?"

"Yeah—sure." I cleared my throat. The sex with Nessa was

always free and natural; getting to it was the awkward part. "Um, do you want to come in then?"

"Let me drop these groceries off at my place. There are a few things that have to go into the freezer. I'll be right back."

Leaving the door open, I sat down at the computer and reviewed what I'd written so far that morning. Nessa returned five minutes later. She'd changed into an emerald lace teddy, a garter belt, and sheer black stockings.

One of the best perks of sleeping with your next-door neighbor, I'd discovered, was that she could do things like pop by at any time during the day in her undergarments.

Nessa closed the door behind her and flicked the wall switch to turn off the overhead lights. I got up and drew the curtain across the window, leaving a gap to allow in some dregs of daylight so we weren't stumbling around in the complete dark.

I'd barely pulled my shirt over my head when I felt her lips on mine. We backed toward the cot and dropped down onto the thin mattress. The cot wobbled and squawked.

"You really should have gotten a larger bed," she said, her voice throaty and warm in my ear.

"I never figured there'd be anybody else in it but me."

"You sure I'm not interrupting your writing?"

She was, of course. But I wasn't complaining.

CHAPTER 6
STALKERS

After the last bell of the day, while exiting the school into the cobalt-blue afternoon, Chunk said, "You wanna come over to my house?"

"I guess," I replied, knowing it was either that or having him come over to my place. "But maybe we shouldn't go the normal way."

Chunk looked at me. His eyes were perfectly round, like two pennies pushed into cookie dough. "The Beast? You think he might be waiting to *ambush* us?"

"I dunno, but he's mental. He might have asked a bunch of his high school friends to wait with him too."

Chunk blanched. "We've totally stepped in it now. Man, we're never gonna be able to take Crowell Road again."

We unlocked our bikes from the fence we'd chained them to and started home. Instead of continuing down Crowell Road, we turned left onto Stony Hill Road, then right onto Bell Road. When we got to Old Harbor Road, Chunk braked on the corner in front of an old white house and said, "Coast looks clear."

I said, "I doubt he lives this far over anyway."

"You don't know jack shit, man. He could live anywhere round here." Chunk shot me a crafty look. "Maybe we should carry a gun?"

"Yeah, right."

"Your dad's got one."

This was true. My dad kept a .38 Special revolver in a plastic box in the furnace room beneath our house. I found it when I went looking for some spray paint to freshen up my skateboard last year. I don't think he knew that I knew it was there. I never mentioned it to him certainly. But I showed the gun to Chunk once.

I said, "I ain't bringing my dad's gun to school."

Chunk chuffed. "You don't hafta *shoot* anybody. Just seeing it would be enough to make the Beast shit his pants."

"Hey, is that Justin?" I pointed down the block to a kid tying his shoelaces.

Chunk shrugged. "Looks like him. So what?"

"Maybe we can get some free french fries?" Justin's parents operated a hamburger joint on Main Street. Justin had held his birthday party there in March, and we were allowed to eat as many cheeseburgers and dogs as we'd wanted. I had three of each just because I could, plus a big plate of fries and one of onion rings. I'd never been so disgustingly full in all my life.

Chunk's eyes lit up at my suggestion. I didn't know anybody who got as excited about food as he did. "Justin!" he shouted, waving one hand over his head, the bottom of his tee shirt crawling up his fish-white belly.

Justin turned and half-heartedly waved back.

"Wait up!" I called, cupping my hands around my mouth.

When we caught up to him, he began walking without saying anything. He was shy like that and never said much unless you were asking him questions. He was shorter than both Chunk and me, but not as skinny as me, and not as fat as Chunk. His black hair fell in front of his eyes all the time, and he was always flicking his head to get it out of the way so he could see. His blue tee shirt featured a big yellow Pac-Man, and his jean shorts were neatly hemmed instead of frayed at the cut-offs (which looked nerdy, if you asked me). His worn-in baseball glove, creased in the wrong place so he was always dropping tennis balls, dangled by a strap from his canvas backpack.

"Justerino!" I said, hopping off my bike and pushing it beside me.

"Justina!" Chunk said.

"What are you guys doing?" he asked us.

"What's it look like we're doing, Sherlock?" Chunk said. "We're heading home."

"A bully might be waiting for us on Crowell," I explained. "So we're going the long route."

"Playing it safe," Chunk agreed.

"Why are you going this way?"

Justin shrugged. "I just like it better."

Chunk finally hopped off his bike and began pushing it too. The sidewalk wasn't wide enough for the three of us to continue abreast like this, and I was squeezed onto the two-lane road. As with all the roads in Chatham at this time of the year, however, there was little traffic to worry about.

"Thanks for letting me copy your answers in math today," Chunk told Justin.

"I didn't *let* you. You stole my book."

"Why are Chinese people so good in math anyway?"

"I'm not Chinese," Justin told him crisply. He'd probably told Chunk this a hundred times before.

Justin was Korean and the only Asian kid in middle school (he used to be one of two but his older sister, Kate, started high school this September). And it wasn't just Chunk who called him Chinese. A lot of kids did. When we were still in Chatham Elementary School, kids would go up to Justin and hold up their hands side-by-side and say, "Open the refrigerator." And when Justin opened one of their hands, they'd say, "Take out the pop and drink it." And when Justin pretended to do that, they would burst into the rhyme: "*Me Chinese, me play joke, me put pee in your Coke!*" Justin, the good sport, always laughed at this. I used to think he was a wimp for not pushing back. But with age comes wisdom, as they say, and I now believe he was outsmarting the other kids back then. You see, he knew that if he let on that the rhyme bothered him, he would keep getting ragged. That's just how these things worked. But by pretending he was cool with everything, the kids got bored of the teasing and forgot about him.

Chunk, of course, was the opposite of Justin. In grade three (and this is about as far as my memory stretches back with any real accuracy) I was with him in the playground when some kids in grade four cornered him and sang, "Open your mouth and close your eyes and you'll get a big surprise!" Maybe he thought he was going to get a Twinkie or Ding Dong because he happily closed his eyes and opened his mouth. What he ended up getting was a stout piece of dried dog shit that the kids had found on the grass. Everyone in school heard about this, and they taunted Chunk with the rhyme relentlessly. The reason? Because each time they said, "Hey Chunk!" in a sing-song way, and "Open your mouth and close your eyes, and you'll get a big surprise!" Chunk absolutely lost it. If the kids were smaller than him, he'd bellow in rage and chase after them. If they were bigger or older, he'd usually just burst into tears.

The moral? Well, there were a few, depending on your perspective. The bottom line was that Chunk wasn't exactly the sharpest knife in the drawer or a quick learner.

Not finished with his race-baiting, Chunk said, "Why're there so many phonebooks in China?"

I'd heard this one from Chunk before. Justin had too and didn't offer a response.

Chunk sang, "Because people always *Wing* the *Wong* number!"

"I'm not Chinese," Justin repeated.

"*Gee*, I didn't know that."

Gee was Justin's surname. "Give it a rest, Chunk," I told him.

"I know Justina ain't Chinese, fuckface. I'm just kiddin round."

"Justin could make fat jokes about you. How'd you like that?"

"I ain't fat," he said.

"You ain't skinny."

"Fuck you, dipstick."

"Bite me."

We went on like this until we reached Main Street five minutes later. We stopped out front of the Christian Science Reading Room, a dinky little building where I'd once gone for Bible lessons. It was directly across the road from Seaview Street, which led to where Chunk and I lived.

Justin said, "I'll see you guys at school tomorrow."

"Hey, ho. Not so fast," Chunk said. "Where's the fire, buddy? Whatcha doing now? Can we come over?"

Justin looked surprised. "Why do you wanna come over?"

Chunk shrugged his beefy shoulders. "To play."

"You never wanna come over."

"Well, buddy-ole-pal, like my pop says, there's a first time for everything." He hooked his arm around Justin's shoulder. "Whadya say?"

Justin shrugged off Chunk's arm and said, "I dunno if I'm allowed to have two friends over at the same time."

"Can't hurt to ask?" I pressed.

"Well...all right."

We continued down Main. The trees that shaded the street in the summertime were already turning orange and red, reminding me that Halloween was next month. In fact, reminders of Halloween were everywhere. Bales of hay and stalks of dried Indian corn decorated the porch of a cookware shop. A scarecrow sat in a rocking chair out front of a gift shop. "FALL SALE!" signs in the shape of pumpkins covered the windows of a clothing shop.

We were passing a toy store, the entrance steps piled high with pumpkins and squashes, when Chunk froze mid-step. I froze too, immediately on high alert. I'd almost forgotten about the Beast.

"There's *Miss*," Chunk said, pointing.

I resisted the temptation to smack him across the back of the head for scaring me. But he was right. Miss Forrester was half a block away, walking in the same direction as us. You couldn't mistake her curly blonde hair or her purple jacket.

"What the hell's she doing so far from school?" he added.

"Probably walking home too," Justin said.

"When do you ever see teachers outside of school?"

I knew what he meant. I'd seen my grade-six teacher, Mrs. Karlsson, at the supermarket once when I was with my mom, and I'd seen Sir and his wife at the Gloucester Waterfront Festival the summer before I joined his class. But those were the only two occasions I could recall running into any of my teachers outside of school. It was fun to think they turned into a bunch of ghouls after the students went home, sliming around in the basement and faculty room all night, knowing they'd burst into ashes if they tried to leave the school grounds. But the mundane truth was that most of them likely lived in Harwich or Yarmouth or some other Cape town so they didn't have to run into the kids they taught every time they left their houses.

Miss Forrester glanced back at us, almost as though she could hear us talking about her.

She fluffed her hair with a hand and kept walking.

"Maybe we should slow down," I said. "I don't really wanna catch up with her."

"Why not?" Chunk said. "Maybe she'll invite us over to her place? Maybe she'll let us watch her take a *bath*?"

"You wish, retard."

Miss stopped at a set of traffic lights and pushed the pedestrian crossing button. She glanced back at us again and then looked away as if trying to not see us.

"Why does she keep doing that?" Chunk said.

"Doing what?" I asked.

"Looking at us."

"Maybe she's got a crush on you? Maybe she likes fat kids?"

"Maybe she wants you to *slap her ass*?"

"Keep it down, will you?" I told him. He was getting excited, and his voice was rising. Sometimes I wonder if he'd known just how loud he could get. "She's gonna hear you."

We kept walking, getting closer and closer to her. When it became inevitable that we were going to have to walk past her and say something, my mouth went dry. I could speak to adults fine—especially if they were my friends' moms or dads—but I barely knew Miss Forrester and we weren't in school and she was pretty...

"Heya, Miss!" Chunk said loudly before burping out one of his parents' cliches: "Working hard or hardly working?"

I cringed. Miss Forrester frowned at us. "Are you boys following me?"

The three of us stopped dead. Chunk and Justin appeared as surprised as I felt. *Following her?* Did she think we'd followed her from school? I guess it might look that way. Then again, she didn't own this part of town. We could go anywhere we wanted. Just because she happened to be there too didn't mean we were following her.

The accusation made me angry, and I was going to tell her we were going to Justin's house when Justin spoke up first. "We're just walking home. That's my dad's restaurant there." He pointed down the street to a rundown restaurant bookended by a florist and a dry cleaner. The big yellow-and-red sign read TED'S DINER. "My family lives in the apartment on top of it."

The cross expression melted from Miss Forrester's face and pooled in rose puddles on her cheeks. "Oh. Well then. I— I'll see you boys tomorrow." The signal light had turned green, and she crossed Main Street.

Chunk and Justin and I continued down our side of the road and stopped in front of Ted's Diner. Justin said, "Wait here while I ask if you guys can come over." He pushed open the door to the restaurant, the bell above it jingling cheaply, and disappeared inside.

Chunk and I dumped our bikes against a street pole. While I locked them up with my chain, I watched from the corner of my eye as Miss Forrester stopped in front of a clothing shop. I thought she might be contemplating going inside when she took a key from her handbag and stuck it into a door next to the shop's entrance. She opened it, stepped inside, and closed it after her.

"Well, whadya know?" Chunk said from behind me. "Miss

lives right cross the street from Justin!"

CHAPTER 7
FRENCH FRIES

The door to Ted's Diner opened. The bell tinkled. Stepping outside, Justin said, "My mom says you guys can come over."

"Whoa, whoa, whoa," Chunk said, pressing a hand on Justin's chest, preventing him from fully exiting the restaurant. "Hold your horses, buddy-ole-pal. We don't gotta go up to your house right away. Shouldn't we say hi to your parents first?"

Justin frowned. "Why do you wanna say hi to my parents?"

"Cause it's the polite thing to do."

"You're not polite."

"He is when he wants to be," I told Justin. And it was true. Chunk was like Eddie Haskell when he was around people's parents. He'd fooled my mom so completely that she kept telling me, "Why don't you act more like Chuck? He's such a sweet and well-behaved boy." Yeah, right. Maybe I should tell her about all the *Playboy* magazines he kept buried in a hole in his backyard, or how he spied on his neighbor—a mom with three kids—while she changed into her pajamas every night.

"If you wanna say hi," Justin told him, "go say hi then."

"That's the ticket," Chunk said, patting Justin on the shoulder and slipping past him inside the restaurant.

"I better go say hi too," I said, and followed.

The interior of Ted's Diner made my dad's funeral home feel cheery. The hanging lights were a sickly yellow, and the walls were narrow and paneled in a dark wood, which shrank the already small and cave-like space. But who cared about any of that when the joint smelled so great? The greasy, tasty aromas of fried food and onions made my mouth water.

A counter ran the length of one wall. Six stools lined it, the padded orange seats torn, exposing the yellow foam beneath. Two old men sat next to each other, picking at the food on their plates like a couple of ancient tortoises.

Justin's mom, a skeletal woman with a big black perm, stood by the cash register, checking receipts and counting money. She shot us a curious look and said something to Justin in Korean.

"Hi, Mrs. Gee," Chunk said with a winning smile. "It's real nice to see you again."

"Hi, Mrs. Gee," I added.

"Ya, ya, hello, hello," she said before turning her attention back to her receipts.

"Can we go now?" Justin asked.

"Not without saying hi to your dad," Chunk said. He continued along the counter to where Justin's dad was flipping thick beef patties on the grill. "Working hard or hardly working, Mr. Gee?"

Frowning, Justin's dad said, "Huh?"

"Hello, Mr. Gee," I said.

"Ah, hello...you are...?"

"Ben Graves. I was at Justin's birthday party in March, and you had me over for dinner once last year."

"Ya, ya, I remember. You good friend. Justin, he good friend, right?"

Justin shrugged.

"I'm Justin's good friend too," Chunk said. "It's Chuck, remember me? I was at Justin's birthday party too. And, boy, do you ever make some good french fries, Mr. Gee."

"Justin, you go play with friends," he said before turning back to the grill.

"Let's go," Justin said.

Ignoring him, Chunk squeezed his hand into one of the tight

pockets on the front of his corduroy pants. "Since we're already here, I think I might just buy myself some fries..."

"You're hungry?" Justin said.

"He's always hungry," I said. "Hey, is your dad's name Ted?"

"No."

"So who's Ted?"

He shrugged.

"Hmmm..." Chunk said, checking a different pocket. "I gotta have some money somewhere..."

I realized that if Justin didn't offer us free french fries, I was probably going to have to fork over the dough to buy some. Chunk might offer to pay me back, but I knew he never would. Whenever he had money—which was often as he got five bucks allowance every weekend for doing nothing (hard work was an anathema to him)—he spent almost all of it the same day on candy and joke books and comic magazines. Concepts such as "savings" and "debts" mattered little to him.

"How much does a box of small fries cost, Justin?" I asked.

"Jeez, guys," he said, clearly suspecting what we were up to. He spoke to his dad in Korean. His dad said something and shook his head. But then he dumped a scoopful of fries into the deep fryer. The oil exploded in bubbles and hisses.

"My dad's gonna make you guys some," Justin told us.

"Atta boy!" Chunk exclaimed happily, slapping Justin on the shoulder. "Hey, Ben, you got a quarter for the video game?"

"You must have one," I told him. "You were gonna buy french fries, remember?"

His lips twisted. "Yeah, but I musta left my money at home. In my other pants. So whadya say? It's gonna be a couple of minutes until the fries are good and ready."

My dad didn't give me a weekly allowance like Chunk's dad gave him—I guess he wanted to inspire in me entrepreneurship or something—so I made all my money myself by raking leaves in the fall, shoveling snow in the winter, and cutting grass in the spring and summer. I worked hard at these jobs and didn't blow the dough, so I always had a few bucks on me...a fact Chunk was well aware of.

I fished a quarter from my pocket and gave it to him. He plopped into a chair at the sit-down arcade in the back corner of the restaurant and dumped the quarter into the slot. A graphic of Wonder Boy and his green-haired girlfriend appeared, and then "PUSH!! START BUTTON ONLY ONE PLAYER."

As the game got underway, Justin and I pulled up chairs to either side of the machine and watched Chunk's caveboy character hustle through a forest, jumping over obstacles and throwing stone hatchets at oncoming enemies. Chunk and I had played the game for the first time back at Justin's birthday party, and even after spending almost two dollars we never got past the second level. Chunk didn't achieve that feat now either, losing his last life when he leaped off a moving cloud and plunged into the ocean.

He was begging me for another quarter as the thirty-second blinking timer to CONTINUE? ticked down, and I was refusing when Justin's dad set the box of french fries on the flat, glass top of the arcade machine.

When Justin's dad retreated out of earshot, Chunk mumbled, "What? No gravy?"

"Tough luck," Justin said. "I'm not asking my dad for gravy too."

I grabbed a bottle of ketchup from a nearby table and slathered the fries. I didn't bother with vinegar because I knew Chunk would throw a fit.

The french fries were piping hot but smelled so good we didn't bother waiting for them to cool down. I stuck one into my mouth, trying to keep it on my teeth so it didn't burn my tongue. Chunk had no such restraint and shoved three fries into his mouth at the same time. He flapped a hand in front of his face, and I could almost see smoke coming from his ears like in the cartoons. Finally he swallowed and blurted, "Jeezus, Justerino! Your dad trying to kill us or what? You better go ask him for three cold Cokes."

Before Justin could tell him to piss off, he was already stuffing more fries into his mouth.

CHAPTER 8

THE WOMAN IN THE WINDOW

After we chowed through the box of fries, we thanked Justin's parents and left Ted's Diner. The entrance to Justin's apartment was right next door. We climbed a steep staircase and entered a room as gloomy as the restaurant had been. The furniture, simple and sparse, was different than the antiques and stuff in my house, and there was a strange smell in the air. Every house had its own smell. Mine smelled of floor wax and old wood and vacuumed carpets. Chunk's smelled of cigarettes and pot and air freshener. Justin's smelled of…the unknown. At least, that's how I'd thought of it back then. Today, I'd wager those "unknown" smells had been things like sesame oil and fish sauce and ginger root and other Korean staples.

An old man sat on an elegant leather sofa watching the bunny-eared TV. He turned his head to look at us, seemed perfectly unimpressed, and turned back to the tube.

"Hi, *hahl' bee*," Justin said, slipping off his shoes. I slipped off mine as well.

The old man lifted a hand absently.

"Hiya, Halbee!" Chunk said.

Justin punched him on the shoulder.

Chunk frowned. "What gives?"

Shaking his head, Justin led us to his small bedroom and closed the door.

"What gives?" Chunk said again, rubbing his shoulder.

"Why'd'ya punch me?"

"Cause you were rude to my grandfather.'"

"Halbee isn't his name?"

"It's Korean for 'gramps.'"

"You called him gramps."

"Because he's my grandfather! And you have to take off your shoes when you're inside."

Chunk glanced down at his dirty Reeboks. "I ain't taking off my shoes."

"It's the rule!"

"Who's rule?"

"My parents. And you're in their house."

"Fuck the rule! It's stupid. I ain't taking them off." He looked around the barren bedroom. "Where's all your stuff?"

"What stuff?" Justin asked, still staring annoyedly at Chunk's sneakered feet.

"You don't have your own TV?"

"Nope."

"So no Nintendo?"

"Sorry."

"Sega?"

"Sorry."

Chunk seemed exasperated. "What the lame-ass hell are we supposed to *do*?"

Justin shrugged. "I dunno. You're the one who wanted to come over."

I asked, "Can we jump on your parents' bed?"

Chunk frowned. "Why'd we wanna do that?"

"It's a waterbed. It's a lot of fun. Justin let me jump on it last time I was here."

Chunk's eyes brightened. "How about it, Justerino? Can we?"

He shook his head. "Sorry."

"C'mon, hose-head! You let Ben last time."

"My parents got mad when they found out. They told me not to do it again."

"We'll make the sheets after."

"They'll know."

"We'll make em real good."

"Forget it. They'll just *know*."

Chunk cursed creatively and looked like he was about to announce his departure, which would have likely served Justin fine.

I spotted a stack of *MAD* magazines on the windowsill, went over to them, and picked up the top one. I flipped immediately to the back page Fold-In, which was marked with two vertical creases. The picture showed a bunch of horny-looking men on a pink landscape. At the bottom of the page it read: "Millions of supposedly normal people in our shameless society can turn on to anything. Sometimes, they pick sex objects that would even make Cupid turn groggy." When I folded the page so "A" met "B," the picture turned into Miss Piggy.

"Got any *Playboys* stashed under your bed?" Chunk asked Justin.

"I can show you my Garbage Pail Kids cards?"

"They'll hafta do, if we're stickin round. Ben, we stickin round?"

"For a bit," I replied.

Justin opened a desk drawer and withdrew an acrylic case that must have held over a hundred Garbage Pail Kids cards—way more than I owned. He handed it to Chunk and told him not to bend any of the cards. Chunk opened the case and quickly skimmed through the pile. I knew he was looking for a card with one of our names on it.

Justin pressed Play on a red radio cassette player and Brian Johnson's nails-on-a-blackboard voice began screeching out "Hells Bells." I used to have the same tape, but I'd traded it with a friend for *Diesel and Dust* by Midnight Oil because the cover looked cool. The tape was pretty good, especially "Beds Are Burning," but I thought I got gypped in the deal. Nowadays my opinion has flipped due to songs like "Put Down that Weapon" and "Dreamworld" and "The Dead Heart"—concept stuff on salient issues I didn't understand when I was a kid. Hindsight, huh?

As the music played, I continued perusing the *MAD* magazine until I found the comic strip *Spy vs Spy*. I began "reading" it, even though there were no words. I always hoped the White Spy would win their confrontations, and this time he did by tricking the Black Spy into thinking he was dead. When the Black Spy went to a bar to celebrate, he drank poisoned wine—served to him by the White Spy wearing a face mask.

Suddenly Chunk cried out, "Bent Ben!" He thrust a Garbage Pail Kid card in the air that depicted a hunchbacked freak. "Kinda looks like you too, Ben," he added and laughed in that wheezy, honking way of his, which sounded like a car motor trying to catch.

"He's got orange hair," I remarked.

"They got the face just right though. Nice and ugly."

I was about to return my attention to the magazine when I happened to look out Justin's window, which offered a view of Main Street. Across the road, in the second-floor window of the building directly across from Justin's, was Miss Forrester—in her underwear!

I did a double-take to make sure my eyes weren't tricking me. They weren't: it was Miss, all right. She had on a pair of black panties and a matching bra and might have been dancing... before she twirled out of sight.

"Guys!" I exclaimed. "Come here! Look!"

They crowded up next to me to get a view.

"Is it the Beast?" Chunk asked anxiously. "Is he down there?"

"It's Miss Forrester!" I said without taking my eyes away from the window. "And she don't got no clothes on!"

"Shove a butt!" Chunk trumpeted, nearly knocking me over in his effort to press his nose up to the glass. "I don't see her," he said, sounding desperate. "*Where is she?* What window?"

"Stop shoving!" I cried, shouldering back into my previous spot. "And it's the second-floor window. Just wait, she might come back—there!"

Miss Forrester appeared again in the window. She was

definitely dancing, her arms floating at her sides, her head lolling about on her neck.

And she still didn't have any clothes on.

Her panties were skimpy, showing off a lot of her butt when she spun in a circle, reminding me of the panties the woman wore in *Crocodile Dundee* when the crocodile jumped out of the water and almost ate her. Her bra propped up her boobs and squeezed them together so they were almost spilling out of the cups.

"Mother frickin fracker..." Chunk said with thin rapture, as though his brain was in the midst of an orgasm.

"Lemme see!" Justin piped, and I felt his head burrowing between Chunk's side and mine. I knew Chunk wasn't going to budge, so I eased aside a little. Justin's head popped through. When he saw Miss dancing in her underwear, he giggled feverishly.

"Lookit her tits..." Chunk said, still using that thin, spent voice. "Lookit them *bounce*..."

He didn't have to tell me twice; I couldn't pry my eyes away from Miss Forrester's breasts. Even so, I was feeling bad about looking when she didn't know I was. It was a lousy thing to do (and something I had always scolded Chunk about when he bragged about watching his neighbor change into her pajamas), but I couldn't help myself. I was in love.

"Why's she dancing?" Justin asked.

"Who cares *why*," Chunk barked. "She's practically *naked*. And she's our *teacher*. Guys, I'm getting a boner."

That comment broke the spell I'd fallen under, and I sprang away from him. Justin did too.

A door banged shut and Justin's mom called out. Justin called back, then yanked Chunk by the back of the shirt. "Get away from the window! My mom's coming!"

Chunk wheeled away from the window. I could see he had a boner going on, all right: his shorts were tented out at the front.

Justin's eyes widened. "Get rid of it!"

Blushing, Chunk pulled his shirt down in front of his groin. "I can't just turn it off!"

There was a knock at Justin's door, and his mom stuck her head inside. She fired off something in Korean.

Playing it cool, Justin said, "She wants to know if you guys are staying for dinner?"

Chunk nodded while I shook my head to say no. Last year I'd been over at Justin's house for the first time, and when he'd asked if I wanted to stay for dinner, I'd immediately agreed, thinking we'd be eating cheeseburgers and french fries and onion rings and maybe drinking some chocolate shakes. But dinner turned out to be Korean food. Everyone sat on cushions on the floor and ate off a low table. The only food I recognized was a big bowl of white rice, and that was mostly what I had, even though I didn't like rice. Also, there was nothing to drink but cold tea. Pretty much, it was one of the worst dinners that I'd ever had. To top everything off, Justin's grandfather let out a monster burp at the end of the meal...a sign that he'd enjoyed the food.

"I, uh, can't stay," I told Justin. "My mom's already making dinner."

"How'd you know that?" Chunk challenged. "You haven't even called home yet."

"She told me this morning. Said she's making macaroni and cheese, and I hadda be home by five."

"So you're not staying, either, Chunk?" Justin asked hopefully.

"Not if Ben ain't, I guess..."

After Justin's mom left, we all went back to the window, but Miss Forrester was gone. We waited a few minutes, but she never returned, and I said, "She must be finished dancing..."

"Don't jump the gun, fuckface," Chunk said. "Let's give it a bit longer..."

CHAPTER 9
THE PHONE CALL

C hunk and I left Justin's house fifteen minutes later. Miss Forrester had never returned to the window, and Justin had to go downstairs to lend a hand in the restaurant so his parents could prepare their family dinner. Chunk was bummed—he would have sat at that window all night if it had meant seeing more bare flesh—but Justin was adamant he wasn't welcomed any longer. If Chunk were guilty of any of the Seven Deadly Sins, gluttony would surely take the top spot, though lust would be a close second, as you might have guessed by now.

The strip of Main Street outside Ted's Diner (now doing a brisk early dinner business) was empty except for two women fast-walking in sneakers and Lycra tights, and a man walking a schnauzer in a doggy sweater. Unlike the lucky mutt, I was only wearing a long-sleeve shirt and felt an immediate chill. It wasn't yet five o'clock, still another two hours until sunset, but the warmth had gone out of the air, another reminder that October and Halloween were just around the corner.

Chunk said, "Wanna knock on her door?"

"Whose door?" I asked, playing dumb. I wanted to go home.

"C'mon, man! She might still be in her underwear. She might *answer the door* in her underwear."

"You're a pervert, you know that?"

"You don't wanna see her tits up close and personal?"

"You're warped."

"I know you wanna. C'mon, dude, let's go knock. *I'll* knock."

That was rather brave of him, as he often deferred to me the stuff that could get you in trouble. "No way," I said.

"Yes way," he said.

"And tell her what, Chunk? That we weren't following her home, but we were spying on her from the window across the street? That'd go over really well, doofus."

"We could think of something else…"

"I ain't knocking on her door." Seeing he was about to object, I added, "*You're* not knocking on her door. Nobody's knocking on her door. All right?"

We started walking toward our houses, speculating as to why Miss Forrester was dancing in her underwear in the first place.

Chunk suspected she might be practicing for one of the strip joints outside of town, where his brother had told him, nearly nude women danced on tables. He reasoned that teachers didn't make much money, so maybe they needed to earn a buck on the side—especially a teacher-in-training. I didn't buy it. I couldn't picture Miss Forrester dancing in one of those places. I didn't know why I thought that; I didn't know anything about her. She very well could have been moonlighting as a stripper. Hell, she could have been a hooker. I just didn't think so. Partly because she *was* a teacher, at least a wannabe teacher, and that meant something. But also because she didn't seem like the type. I might not know her well, but I thought I knew that much at least. Besides, some of the dads of the students at our school probably frequented the local strip clubs now and then. What if they recognized her as their kids' teacher-in-training? In a place like Chatham, it would be front-page news the next day. She'd be run out of town faster than Hester Prynne.

I told Chunk all of this, which irked him. I think he wanted her to be a stripper, or at least he wanted to cling to the fantasy that she was a stripper. So when he challenged me to come up with something better, and I told him Miss Forrester was likely dancing because sometimes that's what people do when they don't think anybody is watching, he scoffed and delved into different stripper scenarios.

A short time later we turned right onto Library Lane, named after the Eldredge Public Library on the corner. I said goodbye to Chunk when we reached his house.

"Call you later?" he said.

"Sure," I said.

I continued down the street, pushing my bike and avoiding stepping on the sidewalk cracks, a ritual I followed when I was on my own. I turned left onto Seaview Terrace, where my house was halfway down the single-lane road. It was a small three-quarter Cape, boringly practical, with a front room and living room on the first floor modeled after an English-style hall and parlor. Upstairs there were three attic-like, slanted-ceiling bedrooms. The biggest belonged to my parents, while the smallest had been Brittany's, my little sister. But even after she'd died, my mom wouldn't get rid of any of her stuff or let me or my brothers move into it. So the three of us—Ralph was three years younger than me, and Steve was three years younger than Ralph —continued to share the same bedroom, which was crowded with two bunk beds and one large dresser with nine drawers.

I guess my dad got tired of hearing me complain about the arrangement because that summer he had paid some men to renovate the garage, putting in real walls and a ceiling and carpet. Now it was my bedroom, and it was dope. Not only was it about twice as big as my old room, but I also had it all to myself. The best thing was that I could sneak outside whenever I wanted. And I had my own key to the door, so Ralph and Steve couldn't get in and screw around with my stuff when I wasn't there.

I went up the driveway, rested my bike against the usual tree, and used my key to open the garage door. I dumped my backpack on the floor, flopped onto my bed, and turned on the TV that sat on a desk at the end of the bed. I'd found the TV on the front lawn of a house at the end of my street. It had been garbage day, and a piece of paper with the word "FREE!" had been taped to the screen. I didn't expect the thing to work when I got it home, but it did, and depending on the weather and the position of the antenna, I could usually pull in ABC, NBC, and CBS.

One of those channels was currently playing *The Cosby Show*. I watched it for a bit, got bored, and turned off the set. I flopped onto my back and folded my hands together beneath my head and stared up at the *Nightmare on Elm Street* poster I'd taped to the ceiling. I thought about the scene with the girl in the bathtub when Freddy Krueger's clawed hand comes up out of the sudsy water between her legs and yanks her down into an underwater cave or something. That was friggin scary, but it was also friggin awesome because you could briefly glimpse the girl's boobs as she struggled to get back to the surface.

And then I wasn't thinking about that anymore; I was thinking about Miss Forrester dancing in her underwear. Closing my eyes, I nodded off and began dreaming that Chunk and I had knocked on her door, after all. Miss answering wearing a smile and little else. Inviting us upstairs. Puttering around doing stuff without her clothes on like everything was normal. Chunk asking her if she was going to take a bath, then asking if we could watch. Miss telling him yes she was going to take a bath, and yes we could watch, but only if we got permission from our parents.

That was when the dream got warped because Chunk ended up in the bathroom with Miss, and I remained stuck out on the sofa because I knew my parents wouldn't allow me to watch anyone take a bath, especially our teacher-in-training... but neither would Chunk's...so what the hell was up with that? Why was he allowed in the bathroom and not me...?

I opened my eyes. My mom was knocking on the garage window. She saw me sit up and said, "Dinner time, Ben."

I nodded, feeling guilty about the dream.

I entered the house through the back door, which led straight into the kitchen. Ralph and Steve were already seated at the table, Ralph with his Transformer that turned into a Lamborghini, and Steve with three He-Man action figures (including a Skunk-man that smelled musky). My brothers sort of looked like me, but Ralph's face was longer and thinner than mine, and Steve had satellite ears. Not to mention that while my hair was brown, both of theirs was bright blond and styled in a bowl cut (my mom literally whacked a bowl over their heads and snipped away whatever hair dared poke out below the rim).

I sat in the chair across from them. To my right was where Brittany used to sit. I could almost see her in one of the girly dresses she liked, brushing her My Little Pony's yellow mane with a toy comb, or talking to her pink Care Bear with the rainbow on its tummy.

Seeing her chair empty always gave me a pang in my chest. I hoped she was in heaven. I wanted to believe she was. But I wasn't so sure. I didn't think heaven was in the clouds, and I had a hard time picturing where else it might be. Maybe Brittany was just dead and not anywhere. This thought made the pang hurt even more, and it scared me too. Because it meant sometime in the future I would be dead and not anywhere either. I couldn't understand this, not really, and I tried not to think about it much.

"What's for dinner, Mom?" I asked.

"Mac and cheese," she replied, and I remembered she'd already told me that in the morning. She stood in front of the stove in a pair of high-waisted acid-wash jeans and a blue sweater. Her hair, the same brown as mine (God knew where Ralph and Steve got their blond hair from because what was left of my dad's was reddish), was corralled into a ponytail with an orange scrunchie.

"With wieners?" Ralph asked.

"I'm boiling them right now, hon." She never called me "hon" anymore. I wanted to believe that was because I was too old for stuff like that. But I couldn't help but think it was because I was the one who got Brittany killed.

"Where's Dad?" I asked her.

"I'm right here, Ben," he said, coming through the swinging kitchen door. He was wearing a pair of khaki pants and a

Hawaiian shirt instead of the jacket and tie he always wore to work, which meant he'd been home for some time already. He had a fluffy mustache like the man on the Monopoly box, only his was reddish, like the last of his hair.

He kissed my mom on the cheek, took a beer from the fridge, and sat down at the end of the table.

"How was school today, boys?" he asked all of us at the same time.

Ralph and Steve both said "Good!" without looking up from their toys.

"Ben?"

"Good," I said also, not wanting to tell him I'd gotten two detentions.

"Learn anything new?"

"Some math and history. And during gym, my friend Harry kicked the ball in the teacher's face and she began crying..." I ended there, realizing I'd said too much.

"*She?*" he asked. "Did you have a substitute teacher today?"

"No, we have a new teacher watching our class."

"Watching your class?"

"She's not a real teacher. She's training to be one..."

"What's her name?"

"Miss Forrester."

"Will she be at Curriculum Night tomorrow evening?"

I shrugged. I hoped not. What if she told my dad that Justin, Chunk, and I had been following her? What if she'd seen us watching her from Justin's window? Would she tell my dad we'd been spying on her in her underwear?

My mom set bowls of mac and cheese in front of my dad and me, then went back to the counter to fetch two more for my brothers. Then she brought her bowl over, as well as a plate stacked with boiled wieners. After my dad told Ralph and Steve to put away their toys, we dug in. With my knife, I sawed a wiener into little pieces, then mushed them into my mac and cheese. Ralph and Steve squeezed ketchup all over everything on their plates. My dad ate noisily and drank his beer. My mom ate slowly and sipped from a full glass of red wine.

Nobody spoke much, and the silence bugged me. It was *dark*, if you know what I mean. It never used to be like this when Brittany was here. My dad would tell jokes and my mom would laugh and sometimes they'd leave the radio on so we could listen to stuff like "Under Pressure" or "Eye of the Tiger" while eating. Ralph and Steve would be insulting each other (which was better than nobody talking), Brittany would be mumbling to her Care Bear (she'd been allowed to have it at the table because "It needed to eat too"). And I'd just sit there and soak it all in and not think too much about anything.

Now I was thinking too much about *everything*. The empty clinks of everyone's silverware against their bowls. How my mom never set down her wine glass but just kept it in her hand while she ate with the other. How my dad wouldn't look anybody in the eyes even when he was asking them about their days. And especially the silence that lurked just beneath and around all this. I hated that silence. I just wanted things to be how they were before Brittany died.

"Ben, grab me another beer from the fridge, will you?" my dad asked me.

"Sure, Dad," I said, getting up, happy to be useful. I opened the fridge and took out a bottle of Old Milwaukee.

The telephone rang.

"Should I get it?" I asked. Neither my brothers nor I were allowed to take phone calls during dinner, but sometimes a call might be for my dad.

"See who it is," my dad said.

I picked up the receiver. "Graves' residence."

"Is your father there, please?" a man's voice asked.

"Dad, it's for you."

"Who is it?"

"May I ask who's calling?"

"Tell him it's Sheriff Sandberg."

"Um, Dad? It's the sheriff…?"

His brow furrowed. But then he dabbed his lips with a

napkin, came over, and took the receiver from me. I returned to the table and continued eating. But like my mom, I was also listening to his conversation. We knew that whenever the sheriff called it was because somebody in town had died, and he wanted my dad to pick up the body in his van and drive it to the funeral home which also served as the town's morgue.

My dad finished his conversation with "I'll be there soon" and hung up. To my mom he said, "I have to head out for a little. Supper was delicious."

He left the kitchen.

When I finished everything in my bowl, my mom asked me if I wanted any more.

"No thanks. I'm stuffed. I had some french fries at Justin's restaurant after school."

I thought she might ask me about this, but she seemed preoccupied. I excused myself from the table, put my dishes in the dishwasher, and then slipped out the back door into the cold, black evening, glad to be on my own again.

$$\triangle\triangle\triangle$$

Chunk called half an hour later.

"Somebody died," I told him.

Because my dad was the town's funeral director, Chunk knew immediately what I meant and that I wasn't kidding around.

"*Who?*" he asked excitedly.

"I dunno. But the sheriff called my dad, and he left halfway through dinner."

"I hope it's *Ronny*." On our way home from school last winter Chunk and I had popped into a computer store on Main Street that sold used parts and games aptly named Ronny's Computer Repairs. Our backpacks were heavy with books, so we left them by the front door while we browsed the shelves of junk. Ronny —a hairy guy with bad BO—saw them and thought we'd been shoplifting. Cussing us out, he upended our bags on the counter. Even when he found nothing but our schoolbooks, he kicked us out and told us never to come back.

"I doubt it," I said. "Ronny wasn't very old."

"The shithead might've been run over by a car."

"Or one of his computers electrocuted him."

"Or his fridge fell on top of him. Squashed him so his insides came out like when you step on a bug. Man, *I'd* like to step on him like he was a bug."

"Hello?" a girl said in a mousy, prepubescent voice.

"Get off the phone, Steph!" Chunk ordered his younger sister.

"I needa call Fran…"

"No can do, barf bag. I got on the phone first."

"Who're you talking to?"

"None of your beeswax. Now scram, you little shit, will ya?"

"It's my turn! You've been on it all night—"

"Moooooooommmmmmm!" Chunk hollered. "Steph's on the phone when I'm on it!"

There was a loud plastic wham—a receiver hitting the cradle.

"Chunk?" I said, unsure who'd hung up.

"What a spaz," he said. "I betcha she's still listening. Anyway —you wanna play King's Quest?"

We both had gotten our parents to buy us a point-and-click adventure game called King's Quest III. We usually played it sitting side-by-side when I was over at his house, or when he was over at mine. But in those pre-internet days, we'd sometimes load it up at the same time on our own computers and play it together while yacking over the phone.

I didn't feel like playing the game. Chunk typed way slower than me, and I always had to wait for him to type in the commands. Besides, I wanted to be by myself.

I said, "I'm just gonna watch some TV. We can play it tomorrow. Wanna have a sleepover at my place?"

"Do you think you can sneak the Leisure Suit Larry disk from your dad's drawer?"

"I dunno… He knew we took it last time."

"But there're boobs in that game, man! I betcha we could get all those age questions right this time and see all the good bits we missed."

"Yeah…"

"And maybe we'll know by tomorrow which poor sucker bit the dust?"

"Yeah, maybe."

"Ain't you gonna ask your pop tonight?"

"He doesn't like talking about his work."

"But can't you just ask him?"

"Dunno. Maybe." I wasn't going to.

"If you don't, I'm gonna ask Tom tomorrow at school." Tom's dad was the sheriff.

"Good idea. I'm sure he'd know."

"Whatever. You're being lame, man. I'm gonna split."

"See ya, doofus."

"Later, fuckface."

I hung up and turned on the TV and watched a bit of *48 Hours*. But my mind wasn't with it. I'd had one heck of a day, and all I wanted to do right then was close my eyes and go to sleep.

So that's what I did.

CHAPTER 10

THE PRESENT

I woke at my usual hour of five a.m. However, instead of settling down in the den with a coffee and the newspapers I had delivered to the house, I busied myself showering, shaving, and preparing an atypically large breakfast of eggs over easy, bacon, hash browns, and a muffin. Dressed in loafers, comfortable jeans, and a brown merino wool sweater, I was out the front door by six-thirty. I got in my black BMW SUV and filled up the tank at a Mobil gas station before getting on I-93. The drive south through Boston was a slog, but by the time I got on Pilgrim's Highway the traffic had thinned out and I was enjoying the freedom of being on the road. The morning sky was overcast and dreary, yet this had the effect of accentuating the October colors of the vibrant turning trees that lined the margins of the highway.

It was a two-hour drive to Chatham. I listened to three chapters of an audiobook, then switched on the radio. When my Boston station became staticky around Plymouth, I opted for a Cape Cod one that played anodyne New Age music. The local news updates and community information brought me back to my childhood—which was the point of today's excursion.

I hadn't returned to Chatham since I'd moved away in 1988, and I figured if I was going to spend the next few months writing about the seaside town, it would be a good idea to visit the place.

Eventually the Mid-Cape Highway became a two-lane

freeway. When I was a kid, this section had been called "Suicide Alley" due to the high number of head-on collisions. Since those days a center berm with reflection stanchions had been installed, but I nevertheless stuck to the speed limit.

The scenery flashing past was idyllic. Tall, top-heavy pitch pine—many shaped brazenly by the wind—towered over smaller species of black and white oak, red maple, and beech. Rolling hills were dotted with kettle holes, brooks, marshes, and rivers. Dunes, wooded moraines, and sandplain grasses were all engulfed in the pervasive smell of the ocean, a reminder that it was never far away.

The freeway passed through most of the towns on the Cape but ran north of Chatham, so in Harwich I merged onto Main Street. That was when the nostalgia started to hit home. I passed the A&W my parents had taken me, my brothers, and Brittany to on special occasions, followed by the Dairy Queen for banana splits. Then there was Saquatucket Harbor where my dad taught me how to fish (and where I accidentally launched my rod into the harbor while casting). The familiar mom-and-pop shops and inns and taverns that I drove by looked as though they hadn't aged a day. The vernacular architecture of everything, from the oyster shacks to the little timber bridges to the unassuming Cape houses that were simultaneously old yet modern. The park where the Chatham Anglers baseball team played and where a sprawling flea market would pop up on summer weekends, the vendors selling everything from inexpensive antiques and tools to old books and magazines, discounted T-shirts and underwear, and Cape Cod sweatshirts. The stately Chatham Community Center where I attended Cub Scouts for several years and where I remember with vivid detail printing my name for the first time (with a backward E).

Although much of this area of the Cape had remained the same, much had changed as well. Many of the buildings on "my" side of Main Street (which I'd considered everything east of Stage Harbor Road) were as they had been, but the businesses operating out of them were new. The discount stores and tacky tourist traps and rundown realtors offices that handled summer rentals had been replaced with fancy cookware stores, upscale clothing boutiques, and ritzy galleries.

I was especially disappointed to find that Ted's Diner—the greasy spoon that Justin Gee's parents had run—was now a swanky deli that would have fit in just fine on Newbury Street in Boston.

Despite having eaten a large breakfast I was hungry again, so I parked and walked back to the deli, trying to absorb everything at once: the briny air, the ethereal light that seemed proprietary to Chatham, the quiet.

When I opened the screen door to the deli, I was greeted not with the savory smell of fried onions and french fries and fatty meats, but with the sweet smell of fresh-baked pastries. Gone was all the dark wood. Now the interior was bright and clean, outfitted with buttery wooden floor planks and beige walls. A series of shelves held staple groceries but also Camembert and Brie, marinated artichokes, and imported olives. The deli was where the kitchen had been, and the counter was in the same place, though now it was topped with white marble. The glass display showcased rotisserie chickens, smoked salmon baguettes, and a panoply of sandwiches named after famous former Chatham residents (thankfully I wasn't among them).

I bought a smoked salmon baguette, got back in the SUV, and drove to Light Beach, where I had nearly drowned to death in 1988. I parked in the mostly empty parking lot next to a white van with MAGIC FISHING CHARTERS stenciled on the side. I walked south along the beach, grassy dunes to my right, infinite water to my left. The surf was churning, the wind suddenly blustery and sharp, a reminder of how unpredictable Cape weather could be. I followed a sandy path through the dunes to a public gazebo, where I ate the baguette while gazing out at the endless blue of the ocean, remembering the night I was pulled out in a riptide, how convinced I'd been I was going to drown, how close I had been to dying.

Sometimes I wondered how I'd survived to forty-three years

of age. Even ignoring everything that had happened in 1988, I could count at least a half dozen other occasions when I'd escaped death by the skin of my teeth. Like the time in college I nearly got run over twice within seconds, first by a bus I hadn't seen coming while I was jaywalking, and second by a car that I'd leaped in front of while trying to get out of the way of the bus. Or the night I'd partied in Paddy's Bar in Bali on October 12, 2002, leaving thirty minutes before the bomb detonated. Or the night I smoked pot on the roof of my hostel in London with some other backpackers. While searching for somewhere to relieve my bladder, I plummeted down a two-foot gap between the hostel and the building next to it, saved only by an air-conditioning unit protruding from a window half a story down. And most recently, falling off a ladder in the two-story foyer of my Back Bay townhouse while I was painting the crown moldings. I broke two ribs when I hit the travertine floor and would have cracked open my skull had it not been for the bicycle helmet I'd worn in an abundance of caution.

I was like a cat with nine lives, I mused—only my nine lives must nearly be up.

△△△

After finishing the baguette, I strolled up from the beach to Seaview Street, where the multi-million-dollar coastal summer homes all featured trimmed privacy hedges. Farther up the street, the year-round residences were a more modest size. One of them was the bungalow where I once saw a woman named Margaret Flatly dancing zealously to no music. The bungalow looked just as it had all those years ago, only now a silver Toyota Prius was parked in the driveway and the oaks in the front yard were larger than I remembered.

Next I came to Sally Levine's childhood house (though in the book I'm writing she's called Sally Bishop). The house was a Colonial Revival Cape with symmetrical wings, clapboard siding, and a massive entry door flanked by double windows on each side. Sally had been my neighbor. When I was twelve, I thought her house was huge, and indeed it had been one of the larger homes around. Now, however, it was dwarfed by the three-thousand-square-foot newly built monstrosities popping up all over town.

Poking out of the center of the roof was an idiosyncratic little tower. Sally had taken Chunk and me up there one day so we could scan the town for people affected by the dancing plague. That had been right before Sally, whose parents had been out of town, had cracked open a bottle of wine. I'd gotten drunk for the first time in my life that night—and Chunk had gotten so fucked up he'd vomited in her swimming pool.

I shook my head slightly, finding it hard to believe that thirty-one years had passed since then. Sometimes those days felt like an eternity ago, yet other times they felt like only yesterday.

I turned up the one-lane road that was Seaview Terrace and stopped at the driveway that led to my old house. It was smaller than Sally's, simple and unadorned, what a child would draw if you asked them to draw a picture of a house. It had a side-gabled, steep-pitched roof to keep the snow from piling up on it in the winter and windows that touched the roofline. My dad had painted the façade white and the shutters black because that had been the classic color combination at the time. The current occupants, however, had opted for electric pink shutters and trim.

Seeing the old place hit me like a ton of bricks, and a deluge of memories came crashing back. One in particular was foremost: the last Christmas before Brittany's death. My family gathered in the living room, a cozy fire burning in the central brick fireplace. Stockings with our names sewn onto them hanging from the mantel. *Christmas Eve on Sesame Street* playing on the record player. A generous pile of presents beneath the Christmas tree dressed in tinsel, baubles, and pinecones and crowned with a star. Brittany rooting through the presents for any with her name. Her jubilation when she decided that a pathetically wrapped tricycle was for her...

I squeezed my eyes shut, blocking out the memories.

I continued along Seaview Terrace and turned right onto Library Lane, arriving at my last stop. I had expected Chunk's childhood house to have been long demolished, given how rundown it had been even thirty-one years ago. But there it was, a mid-century modern cottage hovering on stilts, with a low-slung roof and screened-in porch and glass sunroom. It had clearly seen better days: the timber shingles had turned gray from the salty air; the green accent paint was fading and flaking; and the footings, poured with sand from the beach, were crumbling, causing the entire structure to lurch drunkenly to one side.

While the house appeared abandoned now, in my mind's eye I saw it as it had been in its prime, filled with music and artists and eccentrics on a Friday or Saturday night, all friends of Chunk's parents, everybody drinking and dancing and getting high.

No wonder Chunk had been such an asshole, I thought. *His parents had been a couple of laissez-faire bohemians who'd always let him get away with saying and doing the stupid shit he said and did.*

I found myself wondering what Chunk might be doing with himself these days, and then decided I didn't give a damn. He would still be just as self-centered and greedy as he'd always been.

I started back to my car.

△△△

As I drove along Queen Anne Road toward the Mid-Cape Highway, my mind drifted through a stormy sea of memories, some good, most bad. When I reached the junction with Training Field Road, I pulled over onto the grass shoulder and stopped.

Training Field Road cut through what's known as The Triangle—forty acres of thick, uninhabited forest owned by the town. Located directly in the center of the wilderness, accessible by a single dirt road, was Ryders Field, which had once been the location of Chatham's only Drive-In theatre.

Ryders Field was also where Sally, Chunk, and I had been imprisoned for the longest, most terrifying night of our lives... a night during which five innocent people, my father included, had suffered hellish and gruesome deaths.

I told myself to put the SUV in gear and drive to Ryders Field so I could confront the long-ago fears that still haunted me every day. But I couldn't. I physically couldn't bring myself to perform the actions—shifting into Drive, footing the accelerator, manipulating the steering wheel—that were required to get me from Point A to Point B.

It wasn't until an hour later, my face and armpits and palms damp with perspiration, that I finally snapped out of the past and got moving.

Not to Ryders Field.

Back to Boston.

CHAPTER 11

THE FIGHT

A t school the next day Heather Russell asked me, "Are you coming to Vanessa's party tonight?"

We were both in the library at lunchtime. I'd recently finished *The Secret of the Old Mill* and wanted another Hardy Boys book before the sleepover with Chunk so I had something to read if he fell asleep first like he usually did. I didn't know why Heather was in the library. She was a looker but not a brainer, so I doubted she was there to study or do homework. I suppose she was getting a book too—and I found it cool that she liked to read, like me.

A red headband pushed back her golden hair from her face, and a string of fake diamonds dangled from her right earlobe. Her blue eyes held mine, waiting for an answer.

I said, "Vanessa's having a party?"

"Yeah. It's tonight at her house. So…do you wanna come?"

Of course I did—although the invitation not only surprised but terrified me. You see, most kids stopped having birthday parties back in elementary school. There were exceptions like Chunk, who still held his birthday party every June because he didn't want to give up all the presents that came with it. And Justin, who had a boss venue like a restaurant to host his. But for the most part, birthday parties were for little kids.

Party parties, on the other hand, were a different matter altogether. Last year was the first I'd heard of them: kids (only the most popular ones) getting together on a Friday or Saturday night at somebody's house just to hang out. No birthdays to celebrate. No presents or loot bags or anything silly like that. And the real game changer: *no parents*. I was never invited to any of these parties, and neither was Chunk. But we got all the juicy bits through the grapevine. Guys and girls jumping into a swimming pool in their underwear. Flora Lewis and Owen Fleming frenching on a sofa in front of everybody. And what had to be a rumor except for the fact it wouldn't die: Kelly Christgau giving John Taylor a hand job in a sauna.

"You think...Vanessa will let me come?" I asked, wondering if I was being set up for a joke.

There's no way Heather Russell is asking me to a party...

Heather nodded. "Yeah, totally. She's like my best friend. I asked her if you could come."

I swallowed. "Um, okay." *You asked Vanessa Delaney if I could come?* "What, uh, time?"

"It starts at six o'clock. Do you know where she lives?"

I had a general idea of where most of the boys in my grade lived, even if I hadn't been over to their houses. It was a territorial thing, I guess. But I had no idea where any of the girls lived.

"Wilkey Way," Heather told me. "It's the first house on the right. It has a big white porch. You can't miss it."

△△△

After stashing the book I'd checked out in my desk, I hurried outside to the playground with my lunch. It took me a while to find Chunk and my usual gang because they weren't where we played foot hockey, and they weren't on the basketball courts either.

I ended up spotting them at the baseball field playing fence ball. Justin was throwing a tennis ball as hard as he could at the backstop fence, trying to get it either stuck between the chain link mesh (five points) or through it (ten points). Neither happened. Instead, the tennis ball bounced back away from the fence, and Chris Anderson went chasing after it. When he caught up to it, he threw it against the fence. This time it bounced high into the air.

"Got it! Got it! Mine!" Chunk cried and caught the ball in his baseball glove. "You're out, motha-fucka-sucka!" he crowed gleefully. "Chris is out!"

Shrugging, Chris came over to where I'd sat down on the infield grass.

Justin threw the tennis ball sidearm, snapping his wrist as he let it off. The ball bounced diagonally off the fence and shot past Chunk before he could intercept it. By the time he'd hustled over to where it had stopped, he was all the way out past the pitcher's mound.

"Bombs away!" he shouted as he took three running steps (which wasn't allowed) and launched the tennis ball.

It missed the entire backstop fence, sailing straight over the top and disappearing into the trees on the other side. The throw had been so comically bad and ungraceful I laughed hard enough that some of the Minute Maid juice I was sucking up a straw came out of my nose.

"What the hell, Chunk?" Chris complained, springing to his feet. "Why'd'ya go and do that?"

Chunk was typically unapologetic. "I didn't do it on *purpose*, dumbfuck."

"How'd you miss the entire *fence*?"

"I was far away."

"Well, go get it."

"We're not allowed off school property."

I knew Chunk didn't care about leaving the school property if it was only to get a tennis ball (we did it all the time when the ball went *through* the fence). He just didn't want to because he was lazy and would have to go all the way around the foul line fence and come back again (not to mention he'd thrown it about a mile into the woods).

Chris wasn't having any of this. "You threw it over, you hafta go get it. That's the rule."

"Forget it. The game's over. Nobody wins."

"You owe me a ball then."

"Big whoop. I'll bring one tomorrow—"

"Nice throw, lard bucket! Ya retard!" Tom Sandberg shouted. He was hanging out over on one of the player benches with Dean Polsson and Sam Turner. Tom had an older brother in high school who got into trouble all around town despite his dad being the sheriff, and Tom had that same reckless streak in him. Sam was by far the strongest kid in school. He'd gotten an earring in his left ear this summer (which looked a bit gay, but nobody would ever say that to his face). Dean got busted last year for stealing Roy Temple's baseball glove. When Roy got it back, his name written along the thumb in black marker was crossed out and DEAN was written above it. Dean wasn't strong like Sam, but he was tough and a spaz. By that I mean he got mad at the smallest things and would go apeshit on anybody regardless of their size or age. The three of them would surely be at the party tonight, and that made me nervous about going all over again. "Go on!" Tom continued. "Shake your fat ass and go get the ball!"

Chunk should have ignored Tom, but he wasn't wired like that. He wasn't brave or anything; he just never thought things through.

"I'm no retard!" he shouted back. "You are!"

Tom stood up from the bench. "What didja call me?"

"You called me it first."

"Cause you *are* a retard. You're a fat-ass retard."

"Your mom sucks dick!"

"*WHAT?*"

"Your mom's got two cunts, and you're one of them!"

I almost slapped my forehead.

Eyes seething with anger, Tom ran at Chunk. I expected Chunk to try to run away, but he just stood there. Either he was like a fear-frozen doe caught in headlights, or a fatalistic part of him knew that Tom would catch him long before he could get to a teacher on duty.

When Tom smashed into him, he immediately got Chunk in a headlock. He appeared to be trying to judo-flip him onto the ground. The thing is, Chunk might have been fat but—and I'd fake wrestled him enough times to know this—he was a big guy and not easy to take down.

Tom was finding this out for himself now as he struggled to get Chunk off his feet.

Soon kids were coming from as far away as the soccer field to watch the fight. They circled Tom and Chunk, crying out excitedly, all of them rooting for Tom, chanting his name.

I'd left my lunch on the grass and was in the circle as well. Tom began punching Chunk on the top of his head while kneeing him in the gut. I hated seeing Chunk get beat up, but I had no dibs on getting involved. It wasn't my fight.

Roaring, Chunk suddenly grabbed Tom around his legs and heaved him into the air. I didn't know what Chunk was trying to accomplish, but it sure looked impressive.

That was when Dean rushed in and began kicking Chunk in the butt.

That wasn't fair—Dean had no dibs either—so I grabbed the guy by the back of his shirt and swung him away. I guess I swung him harder than I meant to because he went flying through the air and landed hard on his hands and knees.

One of the grade-six teachers, Mrs. Bivins, appeared before Dean could come after me. She was making a holy hell of a ruckus with her brass bell while trying to break up the kids watching the fight with her free hand.

"Chuck Archibald!" she said in a loud, shrill voice. "Put Tom down right this instant! Chuck Archibald!"

Chunk dropped Tom, who landed on his feet and whacked Chunk in the chest, to get the last hit in. I think he was mad and embarrassed that Chunk might have gotten the better of him in the end.

"Off to the principal's office, both of you!"

"But he started it!" Chunk protested.

"You heard me!" Mrs. Bivins' baggy, swollen eyes scanned the rest of us. "Ben, Dean, you boys can join them. I saw you fighting. Get going!"

We skulked off in pairs, Tom and Dean ahead, Chunk and me behind. When we reached the principal's office, Tom knocked on the door to the waiting room. Mr. Shoemaker's secretary stopped typing on her computer and said, "Yes?"

"Mrs. Bivins sent us here for fighting," Tom said.

"Have a seat. Mr. Shoemaker's in a meeting."

"Can we come back later?" Dean asked.

"Have a seat," she said tightly. "He'll see to you shortly."

Six chairs lined one of the walls. We sat, Chunk and me keeping two empty seats between us and Dean and Tom. I was working on what to tell Mr. Shoemaker—or *Shit*maker, as he was better known—when the door to his office opened and Mr. Zanardo stepped out.

He looked disapprovingly at the four of us. "What's going on here, boys?"

"Tom called me a retard," Chunk blurted.

"And Ben threw me to the ground when I wasn't looking," Dean added.

"Ben, Ben, Ben..." Retardo said, shaking his head but looking happy. "You just can't help yourself from getting into trouble, can you? Your mother will definitely be hearing about this tonight." He looked back into the principal's office. "Mr. Shoemaker, you have four students out here that have been fighting. Would you like me to send them in?"

"Oh, yes, please," came the principal's voice, and it sounded like he was smiling.

CHAPTER 12

SLEUTHING

After school Chunk and I rode our bikes home together, once again taking the long route so as not to run into the Beast. When we reached Main Street, I said, "Heather invited me to Vanessa's party tonight."

Chunk looked over at me in either a thoughtful or cunning way, I couldn't tell which. "Van's party?" he said. "Why'd Heather invite *you*?"

I shrugged. "Beats me. She just asked."

"She was probably joking."

"I don't think she was."

Now he looked petulant. "But you're not even their *friend*."

"I talk to them sometimes."

"Yeah, but you're not—" He hardened his jaw. "You said we were gonna have a sleepover tonight, man."

"We still will. The party starts at six. It probably won't go longer than two hours. I'll be home by eight-thirty."

Chunk was quiet. I could tell he wasn't happy that I was going to be having fun without him.

"Why'd Heather invite *you* and not *me*?" he said finally. "Or why didn't she invite *both* of us together? She knows we're friends, right? And it ain't even Heather's house. You sure she can just invite you over to Van's house like that?"

"She said she asked Van and Van said it was okay."

"Motherfuck." Chunk stood on his pedals, his belly jiggling as

73

he pedaled. "Maybe I can just show up?" he said, glancing at me expectantly.

I'd known he was going to suggest something like this—you couldn't be best friends with a guy for three years and not anticipate his moves—and I already had an answer planned. "You know Tom's going to be there, don't you?"

"Big whoop, man. I'll just beat him up again."

"You did do pretty well against him…"

"I did, right? I lifted the loser right up in the air. Fuckin call me a retard. So he tries anything, yeah…I'll just beat him up again. Right?" The hint of desperation betrayed the bravado.

I pressed on. "Dean and Sam will be there too. They might try to triple-team you."

"What about *you*? You're the one Dean hates. Maybe they'll try to triple-team *you*?"

I had wondered about this, but I didn't think they would try and jump me or anything. I wasn't the one who'd demeaned Tom's mom, after all. I just pulled Dean off Chunk because it wasn't his fight. They had to know that was only fair. Worst case, Dean would talk trash to me. Best case, he wouldn't mention anything because he knew kicking Chunk when he was helpless was a rat thing to do.

"They might," I said. "But they'll definitely do you in first. You told Tom his mom sucks dick."

"And that she has two cunts and he's one of them," he added proudly.

"And you think he's going to let that pass?"

"Probably not…"

"There's no way he's not. You're number one on his most wanted list."

"Fuckin bogus, man. I've never been to a cool party…"

"I'll tell you what goes down. Probably won't be anything special anyway."

"Bullshit. You heard what goes on at them parties. Hand jobs, man. And that was last year. Maybe this year Kelly Christgau will be giving out *blow*jobs."

We had reached the Christian Reading Science room and were waiting for some cars to pass before crossing the street. I had an idea and said, "Wanna go check on Justin?"

Chunk frowned. "Whadya mean?"

"Didn't you notice? He wasn't at school today."

"So what?"

"Miss Forrester wasn't at school either..."

I could tell Chunk was trying to figure out what I meant and not getting it. It was like you could look right through his eyes and into his head sometimes.

"Miss wasn't at school today," I told him slowly, "and Justin wasn't either. You don't find that a bit suspicious after yesterday? With him living across the street from her and all...?"

"Why's it—?" A sly grin spread across his face as what I was saying finally sunk in. "Fuck a duck! You don't think the weasel went over to her house, do ya? You don't think he's been *boinking* her all day, do ya?"

I guess I gave him too much credit. "I think, you moron, that if Miss was dancing in her underwear again this morning, and Justin saw her through his window, maybe he decided to keep watching her instead of coming to school."

"Ah!"

"And maybe," I added, "she's been dancing all day long, and he's been watching her all day long, and that's why he didn't come into school after lunch either."

Chunk bobbed his head in agreement. "I betcha you're right, dude! But why would Miss be dancing all day? You'd think she'd get tired."

"Maybe she's practicing for something?"

"The titty bars!"

"Well, something. I dunno what. So do you wanna check on Justin or not?"

"Fuckin A I do! No reason he gets to keep Miss all to himself!"

$$\triangle\triangle\triangle$$

75

When Justin answered the doorbell, he only opened the door a crack and said suspiciously, "What do you guys want?"

"To play again," Chunk said.

"I can't today."

"Why not?"

"I just can't."

"Why weren't you at school?" I asked.

"I'm sick."

"You don't look sick to me," Chunk said, trying to push open the door farther. "You look like you've been watching Miss dance around in her skivvies all day."

Justin's eyes flashed with surprise. Then he threw his shoulder into the door and slammed it closed in Chunk's face. Chunk rattled the handle but wasn't quick enough. The deadbolt shot home with a dull *clunk!*

"Come on, dude!" Chunk cried, banging on the door with his fist. "Let us in! Just a quick look!"

"Go away!"

"Come *on!*"

"I'll tell my parents you're bugging me!"

"Oh yeah?" Chunk said. "Maybe I'll just go say hi to your parents right now." He paused. "Tell em what you've been up to..."

Chunk grinned sideways at me. I nodded. It was a good bluff.

And Justin fell for it because a moment later the door opened and he said, "You guys can come up and look, but you can't stay long. I'm supposed to be sick."

CHAPTER 13

THE PARTY

Back outside on Main Street, Chunk rambled on about Miss Forrester as we peddled along. I had too many thoughts buzzing inside my head to pay him much attention.

Miss had been dancing again, all right. It had taken her a few minutes before she'd appeared in her window, but when she did it was just like yesterday—too much like yesterday. Because she was not only dancing the same way as before—a mix of ballerina and Woodstock acid-tripper—but she had on the same underwear too. You'd think she'd get sweaty doing all that twirling and hopping around. So why not change into some new underwear in the morning? Or *clothes*, for that matter? Even Chunk and I changed our jockeys and clothes every day, and girls were supposed to be sugar and spice and everything nice.

When we reached Chunk's house, he tried one last time and said, "You sure I can't come with you to Van's party?"

"I'll come by at eight-thirty," I told him. "We'll rent a movie."

"Ah...all right, man. But don't be late."

A few minutes later I entered my house through the back door and called, "Mom?"

"Yes, Ben?" She was upstairs.

I went to the base of the staircase and said, "I was invited to a party tonight. It's at six o'clock. Can I go?"

"A party?" She appeared a moment later at the top of the stairs, pressing an earring into her earlobe. I barely recognized her. She usually wore jeans and sweaters around the house and tied her hair back in a ponytail. Now she had on a snug knee-length dress and was all dolled up with makeup and fancy hair. She'd even put jewelry on.

"Are you and Dad going out?" I asked.

"I'm heading over to your school shortly to speak with your teachers, and Ralph's."

"Oh, right." I'd forgotten about Curriculum Night. I thought about Mr. Zanardo and his threat to tell my mom I'd been fighting. I knew he was going to lie about me, make things worse than they were, so I decided to get out in front of it. "I got in a fight today. It wasn't a big one. I was just helping Chunk because he was getting beat up."

"Were you hurt?"

"No."

"That's good. But you shouldn't be fighting with your school friends, Ben. What's this party you mentioned?"

I didn't want to tell her it was at a girl's house, so I just said, "It's on Wilkey Way. I can walk there by myself."

"When will you be home?"

"Eight-thirty? I invited Chunk over for a sleepover. Is that okay?"

"That's fine. I didn't have time to make you or your brothers dinner. Can you whip together something before you go to your party?"

"Sure."

"Have fun then." She went back to getting ready.

△△△

In the garage I changed into black jeans and a black Iron Maiden tee shirt. I didn't have any of the band's tapes, and I couldn't name any of their songs. But the zombie on the shirt had looked sick, so I'd chosen it when my mom had taken my brothers and me to the Cape Cod Mall to get new clothes for the upcoming school year.

I watched TV for a while and then went inside the house to make dinner for Ralph and Steve. I could tell right away that my mom had already left. The house felt different when neither of my parents was in it. I went to the bottom of the stairs and called, "Whadya guys want for dinner?"

"Pizza!" Ralph called back.

"Mom didn't leave us money for pizza."

"Pizza!" Steve yelled.

I went back to the kitchen and opened the fridge. I studied the contents, trying to figure out what I knew how to make. I ended up taking out the pack of wieners my mom had opened for dinner last night, as well as the bottles of mustard and ketchup. I dumped four wieners into a bowl, decided Ralph might want two, and added another. I sliced them down the middles so they didn't explode, then set the bowl in the microwave and punched one minute into the timer. While they were cooking, I opened a loaf of white Wonder bread, placed a slice on a plate for Steve, and two more on another plate for Ralph.

The microwave beeped. I took out the wieners, grabbed the two for myself (I liked eating them without bread or sauces when my mom wasn't around), and called out, "Dinner's ready!"

△△△

I was almost to Vanessa Delaney's house, going over what I would say to Dean if he challenged me to a fight when I heard someone behind me. I turned around. It was still an hour before sunset, and in the queer, burnished light of dusk I easily spotted the person ducking behind a parked car.

"I saw you, Chunk!" I shouted. "Come out!"

He stepped back onto the sidewalk. His hair was slicked back with Dippity-do styling gel, and he wore his favorite jean jacket with the brown corduroy collar turned up, like he was The Fonz or somebody. "Funny bumping into you here, Ben."

"What the hell are you doing, man?" I demanded, although I knew exactly what he was doing. He was following me to find out where Vanessa lived so he could crash the party.

"Nice night for a walk," he said, hurrying to catch up.

"You ain't coming to the party," I told him.

"You don't own the sidewalk," he stated stubbornly. "I can be here if I wanna be."

I shook my head. "You can't come with me."

"I won't. I'll come *after* you. You go first, I'll come later. Don't worry, man. It's all cool."

"It's *not* cool. Everyone will still know I brought you."

"I'll tell them I came on my own."

"C'mon, Chunk! Please? I'm gonna be late."

He slapped me on the shoulder. "Then you better book it, buddy-ole-pal. Don't wanna miss the cake."

"Jeezus fuckin shit," I mumbled sullenly and started walking.

I had a really bad feeling about this.

ΔΔΔ

Vanessa Delaney answered the door to her house (which was about three times the size of mine and so close to the ocean you could hear its steady drone) in baggy jeans and an oversized white sweater sporting colorful diagonal lines. Her chocolate hair was puffed up with hairspray so her head was way bigger than normal.

"Oh, hi, Ben." She smiled, showing off her expensive braces. "Glad you could come by."

"Heather invited me," I said, to make sure there had been no miscommunication.

"I know. She's been waiting for you. Do you wanna come inside—?"

"HELLO!"

Vanessa squinted past me. I turned, feeling sick to my stomach.

Chunk was hustling up the walkway toward us, his canvas pants making a swishing sound as they rubbed together between his beefy thighs. "I was just walking on the street and saw you guys. I really didn't know this was where you lived, Van."

Have you ever noticed that people who emphatically deny something inadvertently reveal the opposite to be the truth?

"As *if*," Vanessa told Chunk, not buying his schtick. Then to me: "You invited *him*?"

I shrugged awkwardly. "He kinda followed me."

Chunk bounded up the porch steps and stopped next to me, panting a little. "Hey, is that music I hear? Are you having a party or something, Van?"

"You're not coming inside, Chunk," she stated. "No dorks allowed."

"But I'm already *here*," he said. "What's the damage?"

"Seriously, get lost."

"Come *ooooon*. Ben, ask her for me."

"He *is* already here," I said. "Can't he come in just for a bit?"

Vanessa folded her arms across her chest. "How long?"

"Half an hour?"

She considered this and said, "Half an hour, that's it. And Chunk, you better not break anything."

△△△

The party was in the basement, a sprawling space featuring rustic furniture and wall-to-wall lime carpet that smelled of shampoo. A Madonna tape was playing on a boombox somewhere. Kids from my grade were standing everywhere, some holding Red Solo cups. On a table were plastic bottles of Coca-Cola, Dr. Pepper, 7-Up, and Orange Crush. Next to these were several bowls filled with potato chips.

When Chunk and I came down the stairs, I almost expected the music to stop and everybody to stare at us like the rumpots do when a stranger enters a saloon in an old Western flick.

As it turned out, some of the kids did look our way, but nobody made a big deal about our arrival. I figured everyone was having too much fun to bother being mean.

"What should we do?" I asked Chunk quietly.

"I'm gonna get me a soda," he said. His beady eyes were giddy with delight as he took in the party. "Want one?"

"Sure," I said.

He went over to the table and poured Dr. Pepper into two cups, the fizz spilling over the rims.

Roy Temple, standing nearby, tilted back his head and bellowed, "Chunnn-keeeee!"

Some kids laughed, but that was all.

Beaming, Chunk came over to the empty corner where I'd gone to stand.

"Nobody even cares that I'm here!" he boasted, handing me a red cup. "How hellacious is that?"

"It's pretty good."

"You see that douchebag, Tom, anywhere?"

"Not yet."

"Me neither. Maybe he pussied out and didn't come?"

"Because he knew you were coming and were looking to mop the floor with his face?"

"Exact-de-mondo!" He finished half his soda in a single gulp.

I kept looking around the basement, trying to loosen up. It felt a bit unreal to be hanging out down here with so many of the popular kids. Seeing everybody getting along and acting nice to each other was weird but good. It wasn't like this at school where somebody was always goofing off or teasing somebody else. I suppose it was because here no rules or teachers were telling us what we could and couldn't do. We could do whatever the hell we wanted, and because of that freedom, there came responsibility too: if we did something stupid, or acted like dickwads, there was no one to blame but ourselves.

What I'm trying to say, I guess, is that that party was the first time in my young life that I'd stepped out of the moment and understood that I was growing up, that all my friends were growing up, little by little, every day.

"This party is gnarly," Chunk said, wiping his mouth with the back of his hand after taking another big gulp of soda. "I ain't never been inside a girl's house before. Wanna go check out Van's bedroom?"

"Please don't do anything stupid," I said. "If you do, I'm gonna be the one who cops it."

"Chill, dude. I was just joshing. Have you seen Van's parents anywhere?"

"They're probably at Curriculum Night—"

Chunk elbowed me in the side. "Yo, look!" he hissed. "There's Tom! And he just came outta that room with Brenda!"

Chunk wasn't the only one who'd noticed. Everyone started oohing and tiss-tissing.

Hubie Pendleton yelled out, "Tom and Brenda sitting in a tree, K-I-S-S-I-N-G—"

"First comes love," Sylvia Heaton sang, "then comes marriage—"

Everybody together, Chunk included, concluded: "Then comes a baby IN A BABY CARRIAGE!"

Vanessa held up the now-empty Coca-Cola bottle and said above the laughter. "Who wants to play Spin the Bottle?"

Hoots and hollers answered in the affirmative, and all the kids made a big circle in the middle of the floor.

"C'mon, Ben!" Chunk said, yanking my arm. "Spin the Bottle, man!"

"Nah…" I said, shaking free.

"Don't be lame, dude! You might get to *kiss* someone."

That was what I was afraid of. I'd never kissed anyone before, and I didn't know how.

"You go," I told him. "I'll just watch."

"Your loss, Ponch." He often called me Ponch, after Officer Frank Poncherello from the TV show *Chips*. He hurried over and plopped down on the carpet between Dean and Sylvia. Sylvia immediately got up and went to the other side of the circle, leaving a telling gap next to Chunk, though he didn't seem to mind or notice.

Vanessa set the plastic Coke bottle in the middle of the circle and gave it a twirl. When it stopped moving, the neck pointed at

Lou Malone, which got the girls giggling because Lou was pretty good-looking. Vanessa gave the bottle another twirl. This time when it stopped the neck pointed at Sam.

"Woot!" Lou said, throwing his arms in the air. "Pucker up, Sam, my man!"

"Bite me," Sam said, clearing his long blonde bangs from his eyes with an expert flip of his head.

Vanessa redid the spin. The bottle selected Shelly Randolph.

Everyone went nuts.

Lou and Shelly got reluctantly to their feet. Both of them pretended they didn't want to go into the closet, but everyone knew they were faking it. They'd had a crush on each other since grade six.

Lou entered the closet first. Face crimson, Shelly went in next, barely looking up from the floor as she pulled the door closed behind her.

"Thirty seconds!" Vanessa announced, glancing at the fluorescent pink Swatch on her wrist and counting the seconds out loud. When she reached thirty, Lou and Shelly emerged from the closet, and now *both* their faces were bright red. Everyone wanted to know whether they'd kissed or not, but they wouldn't tell.

Vanessa spun the bottle again.

It stopped on Chunk.

"Oh yeah!" he cried, jumping to his feet and pulling his tee shirt down where it had crept up over his belly. "Spin it, Van! Let's see who the lucky lady's gonna be!"

Vanessa spun the bottle. All the girls in the circle appeared terrified of it stopping on them. Some locked their arms together with their neighbors in fright. Others peeked through splayed fingers.

The bottle stopped. The neck pointed toward Elise Summers, even though she tried to shimmy out of the way. "In your dreams!" she cried above the uproar. "I'm not going!"

"You hafta!" Chunk replied, practically shouting. "No backing out if you don't like who the bottle chooses! That ain't how it works! Guys, tell her she hasta!"

"He's right!" Sylvia said, laughing.

"No backing out!" Shelly said.

"You have to *make out* too!" Margaret Wallach said.

Elise pretended to vomit. "Gag me with a spoon!"

Nevertheless, she got to her feet and went to the closet with Chunk. You could tell she really, really didn't want to go. There was no faking anything this time. But in she went anyway. Chunk followed—but not before he turned to the circle of kids watching and pumped his groin three times.

You had to give it to the guy, he was a showman.

Vanessa began counting the seconds out loud again, but this time she only got to five because Elise screamed and the closet door burst open. She dropped down behind Vanessa, using her as a shield. "He grabbed my butt!" she shrieked. "He *squeezed* it!"

Chunk came out of the closet looking dazed and cheated and said, "What gives, Leese? It's *Spin the Bottle*! I'm *allowed* to cop a feel."

△△△

Chunk's antics made him a bit of a hero with some of the guys at the party, and they seemed happy to let him hang out with them. I filled one of my hands with sour cream and onion potato chips and sat down on a large pirate chest. I was halfway through the chips when Heather Russell came over and said, "Can I sit with you?"

I nodded, wishing I hadn't stuck so many chips into my mouth.

"Are you having fun?" she asked me.

I chewed quickly and swallowed. "The party's rad. Thanks for inviting me."

"I'm glad you came."

"Me too."

"How come you didn't play Spin the Bottle?"

"I, uh…" The question caught me off guard. "I didn't know the rules."

"There are no rules, silly! You just spin the bottle and whoever it picks goes into the closet together."

"What do you do in there?"

"I dunno… Whatever you want…"

She had gone in the closet with Neal Joyner earlier, and I asked, "What did you and Neal do?"

"Nothing!" For a frightful moment I thought I'd insulted her. But she softened and said, "You only do something with someone you like…"

Her knee touched mine. I pretended not to notice. But my pulse was suddenly racing because she had to know our knees were touching, and she didn't move hers away, which meant she probably liked me—

She does not! a voice in my head told me. *She's the prettiest girl in school! No way she'd pick you!*

I tried to think of something to say. "Are you liking Sir's class this year?"

"It's okay. Way better than getting put in Mr. Zanardo's class."

"You're telling me. That guy hates my guts."

"Why?"

"I dunno. He just does."

"He hates everyone. He's mean."

"Yeah, but he hates me more. He tries to give me a detention every time he sees me."

"You should tell your parents on him."

That reminded me that my mom was supposed to speak with Retardo tonight. Maybe she was speaking to him right now. I shook my head. "It's not worth it. He's a teacher. My mom would believe him over me."

Heather shifted on the pirate chest—closer to me—so now our elbows were touching too. I had no idea what to do. Put my arm around her shoulder? That would look corny. It would be awkward and uncomfortable too. Kiss her? With everybody watching? They'd think we were dating. *Would* we be dating? Was this how it started, touching knees and elbows?

I was doing everything I could to simply sit still and act normal, and I knew I was going to have to make a move sooner or later—

"CHUNK!"

I jerked my head toward the stairs.

"That was Vanessa," said Heather.

I groaned. "Sounds like Chunk's gone and done something. I better go check on him."

"I'll come too."

Everyone in the basement was heading for the stairs. We found Chunk and Vanessa in the large kitchen. Vanessa looked majorly pissed, and Chunk was looking how he did when he knew he'd screwed up.

"He stole three cupcakes!" Vanessa said, pointing to a plate of cupcakes on the counter.

"I told ya, I'll put this one back," Chunk said, raising the one squished in his hand.

"You've already eaten two!"

"So I won't have one later. Lemme put this one back, then I'll only have had one extra."

"Don't bother. It's already got your germs all over it."

"Whad'ya want me to do?"

"Go home."

"Awww, c'mon, Van!"

"It's already been longer than half an hour. You promised. Half an hour."

"But I'm having *fun*."

"This is my house, and I'm telling you to leave, Chunk!"

"You heard her, lard-ass!" Tom Sandberg shouted. "Go home!"

Some of the other kids mimicked Tom and told Chunk to hoof it. All the friendly behavior in the basement had vanished, and it was like we were back at school again, Tom and his coterie in the cool group, Chunk in the not-cool group.

The churlish taunts continued, growing louder and meaner. Tears shimmered in Chunk's eyes.

"Aww, you gonna cry?" Tom teased. "Is the lard-ass gonna

run home to mommy and cry?"

That did it. Chunk hollered "I'm gonna kill allaya cunt-licking dick-sucking mother fuckers!" and rushed out the front door, slamming it behind him.

Everybody burst into hysterics at his dramatic exit.

I started toward the front door.

Heather whom I'd forgotten about stopped me with a touch. "Where're you going, Ben?"

"I hafta go get him."

"Forget about him. He's a loser."

My anger got hotter. "He's my friend." I continued to the door.

Heather followed me outside and said, "Ben! Wait!" She lowered her voice. "Don't go. I was… I was going to let you…kiss me."

I paused for a moment, not sure what to make of this. I mean, I wasn't totally surprised. The knee-touching, the throaty timbre in her voice. She'd made her intentions pretty clear. And I wanted to kiss her, regardless of whether I knew how to or not. She was Heather Russell, the prettiest girl in school. But that meant turning my back on Chunk, and I couldn't do that to my best friend, even if he did deserve what he got.

I mumbled "Sorry" to Heather and skipped down the porch steps into the night.

CHAPTER 14

THE DEAD MAN

I caught up to Chunk on the next block.

"Yo, Chunk! Wait up!"

He turned around. Surprise and confusion and bovine anger all found space on his face in the moonlit night. I understood the surprise and confusion at seeing me, but I didn't know if the ire was directed at the kids at the party or me for coming after him. He didn't like people feeling sorry for him, most likely because people were *always* feeling sorry for him. That was his fault though. If you did stupid stuff, you were going to get your ass ragged off. You were going to get ostracized. If he didn't want people feeling sorry for him all the time, his best bet was to simply stop being a shit.

His eyes narrowed. "What're you doing out here, Ben?"

"Going home." I shrugged to feign indifference. "The party was lame."

"Fuckin A it was. But you didn't hafta leave just for me."

"I think it was almost over anyway. No skin off my back."

"Well...thanks, man." He wiped one of his cheeks with the back of his hand, and I realized he had been crying.

"Tom's a total wastoid," I told him. "Don't listen to anything he says."

"But it wasn't just Tom calling me names. It was *everybody*."

"Why'd'ya hafta go and eat the cupcakes, man? What were you even doing up in the kitchen anyway?"

We started to walk again in a slow shuffle. "I hadda go to the bathroom," Chunk said. "All that soda, right? So I asked Van where it was, and she told me upstairs by the front door. I went and was coming back and saw the cupcakes just sitting there on the counter. I knew they were for later, but I figured I'd have mine right then."

"Van said you had three."

"Because sometimes you can't have just one when they taste so good. And I woulda put the third one back but she didn't let me. You saw."

"Where is it?"

"I ate it."

I pictured Chunk walking along the dark sidewalk on his own, crying because everyone had made fun of him, and still stuffing his mouth with a smushed cupcake—the very thing that had gotten him into trouble in the first place! To cheer him up, I said, "You shoulda taken the whole plate of cupcakes on your way out."

Grinning, he said, "Yeah, man, that woulda been dope! Van would have totally wigged out."

"We coulda eaten as many as we wanted tonight..."

Chunk stopped. "Wanna go back and get em? Everyone will be in the basement. We can sneak in, sneak out. That would show em!"

"Jeez, Chunk," I said. "You just don't learn, do you?"

∆∆∆

When we were farther up Main Street, almost to the video rental store, Chunk said, "Hey, look, it's the sheriff. Wonder what he's up to?"

I couldn't see the sheriff anywhere, but his brown car was parked at the curb beneath the yellow cone of a sodium-vapor streetlamp. The lights on the roof alternated between red and blue.

As we got closer we could hear a dispatcher speaking over the two-way radio in staticky bursts. The door to the antique store on our right was open, and the lights were on. All sorts of useless knickknacks occupied the display window, along with a shelf full of porcelain figurines of the kind my grandmother collected.

"Wanna go in and check things out?" Chunk said.

"No way," I told him. "The joint was probably robbed. The guy might still be in there—"

"Keep walking, boys," the sheriff said, appearing from around the corner of the building. The brim of his Stetson hat was pulled low over his eyes, pooling his hard-boned face in shadows. His starched and creased tan uniform fit tightly on his well-built frame, and his big handgun hung importantly on the side of his duty belt. A cigarette dangled from between his thin lips.

"Hiya, Sheriff Sandberg," Chunk said, waving. "Catch any lowlives tonight?"

The sheriff took a puff of his cigarette without responding, exhaling the smoke into the night. He frowned at me. "You're one of Stu's boys, aren't you?"

It was always strange to hear someone call my dad by his first name. I was used to hearing Mr. Graves, but not Stewart or Stu. I nodded. "I'm Ben."

"Shouldn't you boys be at home at this hour?"

"We're going to the video store to rent a movie."

"Best get a move on then. Your father will be here shortly. He wouldn't be happy to see you nosing around."

"Ben's dad's coming?" Chunk said, surprised. He peered into the antique shop. "Did somebody *die* in there?"

"Who are your folks, son?"

"Mr. and Mrs. Archibald, Sheriff. My dad's an accountant. His office is just down the street, beside the bookstore."

"Wally, huh? Sure, I know him. He does my taxes. Now like I said, best you two get a move on."

We started walking again. Chunk turned around so he was shuffling backward and said, "Um, Sheriff? Tom was at the party with us. He gave me a beer. I didn't wanna drink it, but he told me

I still hadda pay him back for it. So do I still hafta pay him back if I never drank it...?"

"My son gave you a *beer*?" the sheriff said evenly.

Chunk bobbed his head. "He had a whole case, enough for everyone. But my dad don't lemme drink beer. So I ain't gotta pay him back, do I—?"

I yanked Chunk around by the arm. We picked up our pace, but not enough for it to be obvious we were trying to get out of there as quickly as possible. From the corner of my eye I saw the satisfied smirk that had crept across Chunk's face. I knew his stunt was going to come around to bite him in the ass—they always did—but right then I couldn't help but smile too.

ΔΔΔ

"Tom's gonna deny it," I said.

"His dad might not believe him," Chunk said.

"Tom's gonna know it was you."

"How's he gonna know that? I never told the sheriff my name."

"You told him who your parents are. Anyway, all he gotta say is the fat kid at the party said—"

"I ain't fat!"

"The *big* kid at the party."

Chunk shrugged. "I don't care if Tom finds out it was me or not. The dipshit ain't as tough as everybody thinks." Changing topics, he added, "So who d'ya think died in the antique store? Cause if the sheriff called your dad, then somebody definitely croaked."

"That'll be two stiffs in two days."

"If it was the owner of the store, he wasn't even that old. I've been in there with my mom a few times. I said hi to him. That's messed, huh? Saying hi to a corpse?"

"He wasn't a corpse when you said hi to him. And maybe the person who died wasn't the owner."

"I wish you'd asked your dad who died yesterday."

"Why do you care so much about who dies or not?"

"Cause shit is going down around town, man! First that sucker gets his head chopped off two weeks ago in the Captain's Inn, and now everybody else is dying?"

"Everybody else isn't dying. Two people have died."

"*Two* people in *two* days."

"People croak. It happens. My dad wouldn't have a job if it didn't."

"But the sheriff never caught the person who cut off the guy's head. So maybe the killer's still round? Maybe he killed whoever died yesterday, and then killed the antique store owner tonight?"

My stomach knotted tightly because what Chunk was saying made a bit of sense. I said, "If someone was going around town killing people, the sheriff would say something. He wouldn't keep it a secret. My dad wouldn't either."

The discussion was dropped when we arrived at the video store. We rushed up the wheelchair ramp and stepped through the automatic sliding door into the brightly lit interior. Right away I was hit with the movie theatre smell of buttered popcorn. We rounded the counter and went to the popcorn cart.

Like he always did, Chunk filled two of the little bags for himself. He stuffed a handful of popcorn into his mouth, a few kernels falling to the floor, and said, "Whatcha wanna rent?"

"Something scary?"

We went to the horror section and searched both sides of the aisle, moving the top videos to see the ones hiding behind. Eventually we picked three each. My choices were *Forbidden World*, *Creature*, and *The Kindred*. Chunk's were *Slaughter High*, *Chopping Mall*, and *Trick or Treat*. From the six we settled on *Trick or Treat* because of the gnarly cover that showed a rock star playing the guitar superimposed over a burning jack-o-lantern.

"It's R-rated," I told Chunk hesitantly.

"Check out who's at the counter. She's the one who let us rent the Stephen King flick."

"We just got lucky that time."

"It's worth a shot. If she doesn't let us, we'll come back and find something else."

We got in line at the counter. When it was our turn, I set the movie facedown on the counter so the woman couldn't see that it was R-rated. I set my five-dollar bill and membership card beside it and crossed my mental fingers.

The woman was chewing bubblegum and talking on the phone to a customer, so she wasn't paying much attention as she took the cassette tape from beneath the counter and stuck it in the empty display case. She dumped change in my hand and kept talking on the phone as she put the movie on the other side of the counter for us to pick up.

Chunk and I walked quickly through the exit alarm gate, grabbed the movie, and booked it outside.

"We got it!" Chunk said, grinning from ear to ear. "She didn't even give it a second look!"

"Lucky she was on the phone. She musta been distracted."

"I betcha there's gonna be some major boobs in it! There's gotta be, right?"

"Beat you back!"

Dead people and murderers forgotten, we raced through the brisk September night toward my house, thinking only about cheap scares and cheesy nudity, two kids without a care in the world.

CHAPTER 15

THE PRESENT

"WAAANNN-WAAANNN-WAAANNN—"

I leaped up from my desk in a panic. My thighs slammed its underside, and I flailed backward. The executive chair, on wheels, shot out from beneath my grasping hands. I smacked the floor, striking my tailbone.

For a perplexed moment I thought the ear-splitting horn must be coming from a car down on Atlantic Avenue, maybe an obnoxious driver enraged at being cut off. I immediately dismissed this possibility and remembered the fire alarm notice taped to the inside of the elevator cab a few weeks back. It mentioned that during the last fire alarm in July the firefighters who'd responded had noted that only a small number of residents had vacated the building, even though there had been a fire on the 10th floor. The notice concluded with a reminder that fire alarms should always be treated as genuine until the firefighters announced the cause.

So, a false alarm? I wondered. A real one? A drill?

The alarm going off so shortly after the notice was put up made me suspicious that it was a drill, and I had half a mind to remain where I was...only I knew I wouldn't get any writing done with all the damn racket. Deciding to be a good resident and comply with expectations, I pushed myself up off the floor, grabbed my keys, and left the apartment at the same time Nessa was emerging from her place next door.

I was going to wait for her until a man followed her into the hallway. She caught my eyes and looked away shyly.

I went to the emergency stairwell at the end of the hall and quickly took the six flights of stairs down to the lobby. I tried not to think about Nessa and the guy she was with. She and I weren't dating. She was free to see whomever she wanted. It was none of my business.

Nevertheless, emotions lacked diplomacy, and I found myself irrationally jealous. This was exacerbated by the fact the guy had been bloated in the face, paunchy in the gut, and dressed in a cheap suit. Was she really choosing him over me?

Two dozen or so people were milling about in the lobby. I joined the crowd and kept an eye on the stairwell until Nessa and Below-average Joe emerged. They appeared to be engaged in a heated discussion, speaking loudly over the fire alarm.

"He's in university now," the man snapped, "and he should get a job to pay his way. Why the hell should we keep doling out for his education?"

"Because he's our *son*, Rudy," Nessa replied tightly. "And if he's not working, he'll be able to devote more of his time to his studies."

Ah ha, I thought, my jealousy going up in smoke. *Rudy the deadbeat husband.* Now I could understand why Nessa wanted nothing to do with the guy. Not only had he let himself go physically, but he also sounded like he was an asshole to boot.

"Studies?" he said. "You know what kids do in university, right? They party. Nobody studies. I don't want us blowing our money on him. He's not worth it."

"*My* money," Nessa said. "It's my mother's money, and my inheritance, and I'll spend it how I wish."

The alarm stopped. A moment later a male voice announced over the loudspeakers, "This is your Fire Safety Administrator, folks. Good news is the alarm you heard was a test."

Groans and moans broke out in the lobby, as though the news the building wasn't on fire was a bad thing. Some people made their way back to the stairwell.

The Fire Safety Administrator continued, "However, bad news is I pressed the wrong button down here at the call box. What you just heard, those short blasts, that was actually the alarm for a gas leak. You'll be hearing the proper fire alarm shortly. So thanks for vacating your apartments and please bear with us."

Wonderful, I thought, regretting not remaining in my apartment, after all.

Nessa and Rudy resumed their argument. I was no longer interested in it and was about to head back to my apartment when Rudy said, "Are you fucking somebody?"

I froze.

Nessa said, "What are you talking about?"

"I'm not an idiot. I can tell these things."

"You can just tell them, is that right?"

"Yes, I can. And don't deny it. I saw the new lingerie you bought."

"You went *looking through my stuff*?"

"You're still my goddamn wife, ain't ya? I can do whatever I want."

"No, you can't! And I should never have agreed to see you today. I don't want you coming over again."

Nessa tried to leave; Rudy grabbed her wrist.

"Get back here, we're talking!" he growled, yanking her toward him.

"Hey," I said, shoving past the people standing before me and grabbing him by the shoulder. "Take it easy, will you?"

He scowled at me. "Who the fuck are you?"

"Ben, it's okay," Nessa said.

"You know this asshole?"

"He's my neighbor."

"Well, neighbor," he told me with a mirthless smile, "butt out, how bout that?"

"Let her go."

"It's okay, Ben—"

"Fire Safety Administrator here again," the man said over the loudspeakers. "I just had a look at my work order, and it says I actually have to test the gas alarm today too. How bout that? The thing is, when I tested it a few minutes ago, I didn't know I was testing the gas, you see? And I spent all that time figuring out how to turn it off instead of paying attention to whether it was working properly or not. So I'm going to need to perform another gas-alarm test."

More moans and groans from those still gathered in the lobby.

"Sorry bout that, folks," the Fire Safety Administrator went on. "Let me bang out that fire-alarm test first. Won't be a sec. Please bear with us."

As soon as he signed off, Rudy said, "Are *you* the guy she's fucking?"

"Watch your language," I told him.

"Watch my language? You my fuckin mother? What are you going to do about it?"

"Do you want to step outside with me?"

"Damn right I do—"

"Me again, folks!" the Fire Safety Administrator said. "I've been discussing things here with some people, and I want to make clear to everyone that in the event of an emergency, you folks shouldn't feel the need to stop and wonder what type of alarm is being sounded. What you should be doing—if you hear anything that sounds like an alarm—is get out of the building as fast as you can. I hope I haven't confused you. Over and out."

Rudy said, "What are you waiting for, tough guy?"

I waved an arm toward the front door. "After you."

"Ben!" Nessa said. "Stop this!"

"Leave us alone, dammit!" Rudy said. "I'm gonna take this loser to the cleaners." He shoved her hard enough that she left her feet and landed on her rear in a tangle of skirts.

Snagging a fistful of his jacket in my left hand, I threw a right cross that rocked his jaw.

In all my adult life, I had never before punched anybody

in the face. However, I boxed for half an hour every Monday afternoon at my gym with a personal trainer, and it seemed like the training was paying off. The asshole dropped straight to the floor like a wet noodle.

People in the crowd cried out at the violence and gave us space. I went to help Nessa, extending my hand. She ignored it and got back to her feet on her own.

"Sorry for getting involved," I said, "but he pushed you..."

Her dark eyes burned with anger as she moved past me to her dazed husband, who was trying to get to his knees with uncooperating legs. She crouched next to him, issuing some soft words.

"WAAAAAAAAAAANNNNNNNNNNNNNNNNN—"

The fire alarm—a rising, fainting wail, like the second phase of a car alarm—drowned out the commotion that had picked up around me. I took it as my cue to leave.

I exited the lobby into the clear November morning and went down the street to buy a hot dog.

CHAPTER 16
THE NEIGHBOR

We watched the movie in the garage with the lights off, me on my bed, Chunk in a chair he had pulled over, his feet propped up on my mattress. The story was about a kid who gets his revenge on a group of bullies, and I think Chunk appreciated that since he could relate to getting bullied all the time himself. But what he liked best (as did I) was the scene in which the ghost of the dead rock star undoes the blue silk dress of a woman listening to his music without her knowing—and then brainwashes her to take off her bra. Chunk made me rewind that scene four times before I told him I wanted to watch the rest of the movie.

After debating and ranking some of the other good scenes (the gunshot from the end of the rock star's electric guitar; the kids spinning the record backward to hear the hidden message; the guy getting blasted across the bedroom by the melting record), Chunk asked me if I wanted to watch the movie over again.

"Not right now," I told him. "Maybe tomorrow when we get up."

"So whatcha wanna do?"

"Final Fantasy?"

"We can play Nintendo any time. What about sneakin out?"

"Where do you wanna go?"

Chunk shrugged. "Dunno. The beach?"

"I ain't allowed going to the beach at nighttime."

"And you ain't allowed sneakin out neither, dipshit. So what does it matter *where* you go? Nobody's gonna know."

I suppose he was right. And if we did get caught—say, my mom or dad came to the garage looking for me for some reason while we were gone—I could tell them we were playing in Veterans Field or Gould Park. They wouldn't be happy we were at either of those places after nine o'clock, but they wouldn't be as mad as they would be if they knew we'd been at the beach.

"All right," I agreed. "But we can't go in the water."

Chunk raced to the door. "Last one outside's a fart on a log!"

He always said this when leaving the garage, knowing he could get out first because I had to find the key to lock up. I stepped outside into the cool night and locked the door as quietly as I could. I put my finger to my lips.

Whenever we sneaked out during sleepovers, we didn't go down my driveway to Seaview Terrace. It would probably be safe—I didn't think my parents stood around looking out the windows at nighttime (and if they did, I'd be more than a little concerned for them)—but you never knew. A random glance out the living room window and, bam, our night would be finished. Chunk would be sent home, and I'd be grounded for a week.

So to play it safe we hopped the fence at the farthest part of my backyard. The property on the other side was as big as all four backyards on my street lined up in a row. The house was one of the mega ones you found here and there in Chatham, probably just as big as Vanessa Delaney's had been. And because the backyard was almost a small field, Chunk and I could easily sneak across it to Fairway Drive without anybody in the house catching us. The only risk was the damn dog. In early spring when there had still been patches of snow on the ground, we had been creeping across the yard late at night when out of nowhere came a frenzied, ululating *woo-woo-woo-woo-woo*. I'd thought we were being ambushed by a goddamn Indian. Chunk had shouted "Haul ass!" and we booked it as fast as we could to the fence along Fairway. There was a tree there you could climb up to get over the fence, which was taller than the one bordering my backyard. I shot up it first and leaped over the fence, crashing to my hands and knees. Chunk cried "Argh!!!!" Standing on my tiptoes, I peeked over the fence and saw Chunk in the tree, a poodle savaging the hem of his pants with its teeth. Its black fur was shaved close to the skin except for poofs around its head, feet, and tail. And as ridiculous as its haircut was, it was nevertheless large and threatening. I was torn between hysterics and terror as I urged Chunk to jump. He finally managed to yank his leg free from the dog's jaws. Quick as a treed cat, he stepped onto the top of the fence and jumped down, crumpling to his knees. He was panting for breath, his eyes were wide and watery, and I thought he was going to lose his shit. But he calmed himself down and we got the hell out of there. The whole thing had been a pretty terrifying experience for us. It had taken Chunk two more sleepovers before he would risk cutting across the yard again.

"Don't hear that fuckin mutt anywhere," he whispered.

"It's probably inside," I said, searching the black yard.

"We shoulda brought one of your hockey sticks—"

"Hello? Who's that?"

Chunk and I dropped flat to our chests. It had been a girl who'd spoken. I hadn't heard her voice for a long time, but I recognized it as Sally Bishop. A year older than me, she'd started at Chatham High School this year. We used to be quasi-friends when we were younger because my parents were friends with her parents. Sometimes Sally's mom would watch me at her house when my mom needed to go out, and sometimes my mom would watch Sally at our house.

She always came to my birthday parties. She usually gave me the best present out of all my friends because her parents were rich. I went to her birthday parties too. The last one I was invited to was when I was in grade three. After that we got too old to remain friends, and I hadn't spoken to her in the last four years. I saw her around when she was still at Chatham Middle School, but we pretended we didn't really see each other. You didn't talk to kids in the grade above you...or the one below you, for that matter.

"Ben?" Sally said. "Is that you?"

Busted! And I was sure if I didn't say anything in response, Chunk was going to make a break for it, and I'd have to follow him. We'd look like two silly little kids, and I realized I didn't want Sally to think of me like that.

I pushed myself to my knees and said, "Sally? Hey. Um, this is my friend, Chunk."

We both got to our feet. Sally's brown hair used to be straight but now was wavy, resembling the hair of the girl who took off her bra in *Trick or Treat*. I'd always thought she had pretty brown eyes, and she still did. Her GUESS shirt hung off one shoulder, revealing the strap of a leopard-patterned leotard beneath. The shirt was so big it almost looked as though she wasn't wearing any shorts, except I could see the tiniest bit of red beneath.

"What's crackalackin?" Chunk said.

"I know you," Sally told him. "I saw you around when I was in middle school."

"You know me, huh?" he said boastfully, and his chest might have puffed out a little.

"What are you guys doing?"

"Sneakin out," he told her.

"My dad moved my bedroom to the garage," I explained, "so it's easy now."

"Where're you going?"

"The beach," I said.

"Are you allowed to go to the beach at nighttime?"

I could practically hear Chunk rolling his eyes. "We're *sneakin out*," he said. "That means nobody knows we're gone. We could go to the moon and come back, and nobody would be the wiser."

"If you had a rocket ship," Sally said.

"A fast one to get to the moon and back in one night," I added.

She smiled, and I did too. Sometimes serving Chunk some of his own medicine was fun, especially when you were doing it with an attractive girl.

Chunk saw the exchange and said, "Are you guys gonna do it or something?"

"Yeah, we are," Sally said. "Do you wanna *watch*?"

I was speechless. I knew she was kidding around, but it still embarrassed the hell out of me.

Chunk, of course, loved this kind of back-and-forth and challenged, "You gonna do it right here on the grass?"

"Right here, under the stars."

"Your parents will hear you."

"They're away. Do you think I'd be out here having a cigarette if they were home?"

My eyes went to her hand. I hadn't seen the unlit cigarette pinched between her finger and thumb until now.

"So you really *are* serious about boinking Ben—?"

"Chunk!" I said, knowing I was blushing but unable to help myself. "Drop it, will you?"

"Be cool, man. I just wanna know because maybe she'll let me get some action after."

"Oh my," Sally said, biting back a smile. "You're something, aren't you?"

"You know it."

Now she laughed. "You guys are funny." I was happy she included me in the statement because I'd barely said anything yet, and certainly nothing funny. "So what're you gonna do at the beach?"

She was looking at me when she asked the question.

"Just walk around, I guess," I told her. "Maybe see if any crab pots have washed ashore."

"Can I come?"

"You wanna come with *us*?" Chunk said.

"Why not?"

"You're older than us."

"Only by a year." She was looking at me again.

"Um, yeah, sure," I said, shrugging like it was no big deal. "If you really wanna come with us, you can come. We don't mind."

CHAPTER 17
THE DANCER

We showed her where to climb the tree to get over the fence. When we were all on the other side, she said, "You guys seem to know my property better than I do."

Chunk said, "We only cut through during sleepovers."

"Cut through whenever you want."

"Ever think about getting a leash for your crazy poodle?"

"Goldie? Has she chased you? She's only playing."

"Why's her name Goldie?" I asked. "She's black."

"My parents bought her for me after my goldfish died. My goldfish's name was Goldie, so I decided to call my dog the same thing."

"So original," Chunk said.

"Shut up, Chunk," I said. "Like you're so original."

"I could think up a better name for a dog than fuckin Goldie."

"Like what?"

"Midnight."

"So original," Sally said.

"Jabba the Mutt?"

"I don't like *Star Wars*."

"Meatball?"

"How bout we call *you* Meatball?" I said.

We kept up the banter as we turned right onto Seaview Street. Most of the houses we passed had lights on inside, which made me uncomfortable. What would the occupants think if they glanced out and saw Chunk and me walking to the beach at ten o'clock at night with a girl? This was the street we took to the beach in the daytime, so although we didn't know the people who lived in the houses by name, we recognized a lot of them, and they probably recognized us. Some of them might know our parents. They might have their phone numbers and be calling them right now.

However, we didn't have any other good options. There were no nearby streets that led to the beach. We could cut across the sixth hole of the Seaside Links golf course to Bars Avenue, but the last time Chunk and I tried that someone in a buggy raced us down and almost caught us. So we were stuck with Seaview Street.

As we walked Chunk kept asking Sally questions, and she kept answering them. It surprised me how chill she was with hanging out with us.

Feeling like I was being left out of the conversation, I asked her, "What's high school like?"

"It's okay so far, I guess," she said.

"Better than middle school?"

"I'd say so. But a lot more homework."

"Are you really gonna smoke that cigarette?" Chunk said. "Or you just gonna keep holding it like a poser?"

"I'm gonna smoke it, but not in the open on the street."

"Got an extra?"

"You don't smoke," I told him, figuring he was showing off.

"First time for everything, Ponch."

"Maybe you should try a puff on mine before you waste a full one?" Sally suggested.

"You'd let me try yours?" Chunk elbowed me in the side, getting off on the idea of having his lips on the same part of the cigarette that Sally's lips had touched, maybe even tasting her saliva. In his books, that would qualify as a kiss.

"How's your brother?" I asked her. "Kevin, right?"

Sally shrugged. "I haven't seen him in years. He was in the

Army for a bit but was court-marshaled for something and discharged. He spent a stretch in jail for something different, criminal assault, I think. Last I heard he was in Baltimore with a kid."

"A *kid*?" Chunk said. "How old is the freak?"

"He's not a freak, and he's twenty, I think. Maybe twenty-one."

I sensed she didn't like talking about her brother—and with a rap sheet like that, I could understand why—so I changed the topic. "Why'd your parents go away?"

"My grandma died earlier this week. They flew down to Florida for her funeral."

"Jeezus on a bike!" Chunk said. "You're full of cheery news, aren't ya?"

"You guys are asking."

"So you skipped out on your *gran's* funeral?"

"I wanted to go," she said, "but my dad didn't want me to miss any school."

"I'd say your gran's funeral is more important than missing school."

"It wasn't my choice, Chunky, okay?"

Chunk scowled. "It's just Chunk, no y—"

"Hey!" I whispered, pointing across the street. "Over there!" Through the front bay window of a gray-shingled house, a woman in a peach-colored dress was dancing by herself.

"Holy moly!" Chunk said. "Another one!"

"Another what?" Sally asked.

"Dancer!"

"Huh?"

I would have preferred not to tell her that we'd been spying on Miss Forrester, but Chunk was already recounting what had happened at Justin's house yesterday. Thankfully he didn't mention that Miss hadn't had any clothes on.

Sally frowned. "So what does that woman over there have to do with your teacher?"

"Nuthin, I guess," I said, feeling foolish for making a big deal over it. "I just thought...it's weird to see someone else dancing by themselves like that."

"Like what?"

"Like…she totally doesn't care. Look at her. Have you ever danced like that in your living room?"

"I don't dance in my living room," she said flatly, "and we shouldn't be standing here watching *her* dance. It's what Peeping Toms do. Come on, the beach is just ahead.

CHAPTER 18

THE BEACH

We followed a sandy path through the dunes to Chatham Light Beach. The chilly wind gusted on every side of us, mussing our hair and flapping our clothes. The foaming surf lapped up against the beach, leaving swampy-smelling deposits of decaying seagrass on the hard-packed sand. We took off our shoes and socks and carried them in our hands as we walked along the high tide line.

Some people find the ocean to be soothing. I've always found it to be overtly menacing, and this was the case even before it nearly took my life that night with Chunk and Sally. It wasn't like a freshwater lake whose deceptively calm surface could lure inexperienced swimmers to their deaths. The ocean was unapologetically ferocious, roaring, crashing, smashing, mammoth—almost taunting you to step on in.

"We shoulda brought a bag of marshmallows," Chunk said, patting his belly hungrily. "We coulda made a campfire with driftwood and roasted them on sticks."

Although roasting marshmallows over a fire sounded like fun, I was glad we didn't have any. I didn't want to draw attention to ourselves. I didn't know what my punishment would be if my parents found out I was here past dark, but it would be worse than a grounding, I was sure of that.

"If you're hungry," I told him lightly, "you should have eaten more cupcakes earlier."

"We shoulda gone back for the lot," Chunk said. "We'd have em to eat right now."

The surf frothed around our ankles and Sally said, "Water's nice and warm."

"Too bad we can't go in," I said.

"Why not?"

I looked at her. "We can't go swimming when it's dark."

"And we don't got our trunks," Chunk pointed out. "Unless... you wanna go *skinny dipping*?" This seemed like a grand idea to him.

"I don't mean *swimming*," she said. "I mean we can walk deeper in it. Up to our knees."

I was pretty sure that was still against the rules, but I didn't say anything. I didn't want Sally to think I was a wimp-o-rama. Chunk didn't say anything either. Not that he was trying to impress Sally; he simply got off doing stupid and risky stuff. Sometimes I envied his impulsiveness. It must be nice to do whatever you wanted, whenever you wanted, and not worry about the consequences.

Sally took our silence as acquiescence and went in the water first, angling deeper until it reached her knees. I went in next, the legs of my jeans turning wet and heavy, the sand squishing between my toes. The water was cold enough to scare my testicles back up inside me. An ambitious wave splashed above my knees. I sucked in a sharp intake of air. When I glanced at Sally, I was alarmed to see the water came to her waist. Holding her shoes and socks at shoulder level, she was having a blast, twirling this way and that.

I told her, "You're gonna be completely soaked when we get out."

"Just my shorts. No biggie."

"Maybe you should take them off?" Chunk suggested. He was still only about shin-deep.

"You wish, Chunky."

"I told you it's just Chunk!" he snapped. "You braindead or something?"

"No problem, Chunky."

Sally and I giggled.

Chunk splashed water at her.

"Hey!" she said, frolicking away from him. "Not cool."

"Call me Chunky again and I'll end ya!"

"Yo, check out the stars," I said to change the topic. I didn't know what Chunk meant by ending Sally, but you couldn't put anything past him, even going berserk on a girl. "Think there are some aliens out there?"

"I'm not so sure," Sally said. "If there were, wouldn't they have visited us by now?"

"Outer space is pretty big. They'd hafta come a long way. We haven't even gotten past our moon yet."

"I don't think I'd want to meet an alien."

"Guess you've never laid eyes on the Orion slave girls in *Star Trek*," Chunk said, back to his old self. "Just gotta oil up their green skin and—"

"Forget about him," I told her. "He's a perv."

"You said you'd like to see them oiled up too!"

"Wave! Jump!" Sally squealed as the wave crashed into her.

Chunk and I instinctively turned our backs on it and jumped. It soaked us to the waists. When Chunk landed, he stumbled and grabbed my shoulder, tugging me off balance. I stumbled backward, arms pinwheeling, and plunged neck-deep into the frigid water.

"Chunk!" I shouted, splashing back to my feet. Somehow I'd managed to keep my shoes dry above my head.

"Shoulda watched where you were going, Ponch."

"You pushed me over!"

"Not on purpose—fuck! My hat!" One hand slapped the top of his head. "Where'd my hat go?"

"Serves you right."

"There!" He pointed. "It just floated past you! Grab it, Ben!"

"You get it!"

"You're already all wet! C'mon, man. It's *fitted*."

That meant the world to him. He always ragged on me

because all my baseball caps either had snapbacks or Velcro to adjust the sizes. I could buy a fitted cap if I wanted with my raking/shoveling/mowing money, but I didn't see the point; at our age, our heads were still growing.

"Please, man!" Chunk begged. "It's getting away!"

"Aw, fine…" I launched my shoes onto the beach, then turned to face the ocean.

"Are you sure, Ben?" Sally said. "It might float back in on its own?"

"Hurry!" Chunk said.

I swam front-crawl toward the hat. I had almost reached it when a wave submerged my head, plastering my hair to my skull. I burst through it, scanned the roiling surface for the stupid hat. I spotted it only a little distance away.

"Come back, Ben!" Sally said. "You're getting too far out!"

"Get it, Ben!" Chunk said. "You almost got it!"

Their voices sounded farther away than I would have thought. I gave one last push for the hat. My fingers brushed the brim, then I had it in my hand.

"Got it!" I shouted, waving the hat in the air and trying to keep my head above the surface with only one arm working to keep me afloat. I clapped the hat on my head so I could use both arms and started swimming back to shore.

And I knew something was wrong right away.

For one, I was so far out Chunk and Sally were just small black shadows on the shore. And two, even though I was paddling my arms and kicking my legs, I didn't think I wasn't getting anywhere.

In fact, I was still moving *away* from shore…and one word filled my head.

Riptide.

△△△

Chunk and Sally were calling to me, but I couldn't make out what they were saying. It sounded like I had the roar of the ocean inside my head. I'd stopped trying to swim to shore and focused on treading water. I'd never been so scared in my life. I was getting sucked out to sea and I was going to drown. It was just a matter of time until my lungs and limbs gave out.

This made me breathe faster. My arms turned heavy and I began struggling to keep my chin above the waterline. The black ocean seemed to be sucking at me from beneath.

How far was it to the bottom? I wondered dimly. Would anybody find my body? Were there sharks down there? Would they eat my remains? If they did, I'd definitely never be found. My grave would be the belly of a fucking shark. What if there was one circling below me right now? What if it hit the buffet before I was good and truly dead? Christ Jesus, I'd rather drown than get eaten alive!

Good going, Ben. You let Brittany get eaten by a dog, and now you're going to get eaten by a shark. No wonder Mom hates you so much...

Squeezing my eyes shut, I floated and bobbed in the water —and saw myself lying in a bed in Cape Cod Hospital, my dad sitting in a nearby chair, a magazine in his hands, staring at it without seeing it.

"Dad...?" I said.

He looked at me like he was looking at the magazine: without seeing me.

"Dad...?" I said again.

"Your sister's dead," he told me flatly. "Brittany's dead, Ben."

Although he didn't say it then, I could hear it in his voice: *And it's your fault.*

My mom and dad had gone to a car dealership that morning to look at an 87 Plymouth Reliant that my dad had had his eye on. They left me in charge to babysit my brothers and Brittany. Around lunchtime we were getting hungry, and I decided to go to the Penny Candy Store on Main Street to pick up some snacks. I was allowed to leave Ralph and Steve at home by themselves if I wasn't going to be gone somewhere for long, but I had to take Brittany with me wherever I went.

My mom had left me two dollars to spend. I picked out a pouch of Big League Chew bubble gum for me; Razzles for Ralph (the box reading *First It's Candy...Then It's GUM*); Gobstoppers for Steve (he liked them because they lasted forever and made him feel like he got more bang for his buck); and some Fun Dip for Brittany. When the cashier handed me my change, I realized I had enough for a pack of Candy Sticks, so I got those too (choosing the red pack with KINGS written across the front because it looked boss).

We didn't take Seaview Street home. Instead I led Brittany down the dirt path behind the jewelry store. Although this way was longer, I liked it better because it cut through woodland and felt like an adventure. When we were a little way into the summer-green trees, I searched in the brown paper bag for the Candy Sticks so Brittany and I could pretend to smoke cigarettes on the walk. However, they weren't in the bag. I checked my pockets. They weren't there either, and I realized I must have left them on the counter of the candy store. Brittany didn't want to go back with me, and she would have only slowed me down, so I told her to wait where she was until I returned. To my relief the Candy Sticks were still on the counter where I'd forgotten them. While hoofing it back through the woods, I heard a dog barking. My heart did a quick Texas two-step because the barking sounded like it was coming from where I'd left Brittany.

And then Brittany screamed.

I'd heard Brit scream a lot over the years. She screamed when the sprinkler water got her, or when she fell on the sidewalk and scraped her knees, or when Steve took one of her dolls and wouldn't give it back. She probably screamed at least once a day.

But she'd never sounded like she did right then.

Knowing the dog must have gotten her, I ran faster. I leaped over a log that had fallen across the dirt path, rounded a corner, and skidded to a halt. Ahead, my little sister was lying facedown on the path with a black-and-brown dog hunched over her. She wasn't moving or kicking or trying to fight back. The dog wiggled its head, and Brit wiggled with it like she was a stuffed toy. In an instant of slow-motion horror I realized the dog had its teeth around the back of her neck.

I shouted at it at the tops of my lungs, hoping to scare it away. It lifted its blood-painted snout. My eyes searched for a broken tree branch or something to serve as a weapon. I settled on a nearby rock. Yelling, I approached the dog with the rock thrust upward in my hand. The dog lowered its head. It raised its hackles and growled. Any other time this would have been enough to send me running, but not now. It would keep

(*eating?*)

biting Brittany.

I launched the rock. It whizzed past the dog's ear. I scrambled for another rock. The dog sprang at me. I kicked and got lucky, my foot connecting beneath its jaw.

It yelped and twirled in a confused circle, allowing me to scavenge another rock, bigger than the last one.

I hefted it above my head. The dog barked twice at me, sizing up the situation. Then it turned and fled down the dirt path, disappearing into the woods.

I crouched next to Brittany, dropping both rock and the brown paper bag that contained our candy. Ragged teeth marks punctured the back of her neck and blood seemed to be everywhere. I knew there would be no hiding this from my parents; I was going to have to fess up.

I turned Brit over—and my stomach flipped upside-down.

The front of Brit's throat was torn out. I mean, it was *gone*, if you can dig that. I could see right into the pipe where her food went down. Her eyes were wide open and looking blankly at me (how my dad would look at me later in the hospital room) and I couldn't understand why she wasn't more frightened. Her mouth was open too like she was trying to sigh or scream, I couldn't tell which.

Oh boy, you're going to get it now, I thought. *She doesn't have a throat! She can't talk anymore. She might never be able to talk again. Oh boy—you're going to get the belt for this one, Benny-boy.*

I tried to sit Brittany up, but her body was floppy like she was sleeping. I tried talking to her, but she wasn't hearing me. And while I sat there, holding her, begging her to wake up, I came to the dumb realization that she was dead and wasn't going to be waking up ever again—

My head dunked beneath a wave. Saltwater filled my mouth and stung my eyes. I kicked my legs until my head broke back through the surface. Eyes bugging out of my face, I coughed and flapped my arms to stay afloat.

Suddenly I wanted to cry. I didn't know whether it was because I'd let Brittany die, or because I was about to die myself.

And all because of a stupid hat!

I should never have gone after it. My mom told me every summer to be careful about riptides because they were invisible and would pull you out into the ocean.

I heard her voice now as if she were right beside me: *If you ever get caught in one, Ben, don't try to swim back to shore. You'll get exhausted and drown. Just stay calm and tread water until a lifeguard can come and get you.*

And if there's no lifeguard? I'd asked her.

There will always be lifeguards around. But if they don't see you, you can try swimming in the same direction as the shoreline until you're out of the current...

I gave it my best shot.

CHAPTER 19

YOU AGAIN?

When my feet touched the squidgy, sandy bottom, I had never felt so mortal and glad to be alive. Unable to muster the strength to stand, I struggled up onto the beach on my hands and knees. When the hard-packed sand turned loose beneath me and I was no longer in danger of being dragged back out to sea, I flopped flat onto my chest and recited a litany of prayers.

Eventually I stood on matchstick legs. I looked down the beach. It was too dark to see Chunk and Sally—if they were still where I'd left them. They'd most likely gone to get help. I cursed, my brush with death already fading behind more pressing matters, namely not getting busted by my parents. They would go nuclear if they found out I'd not only gone to the beach after dark but had gotten dragged out a hundred yards in a riptide. And they would surely find out if Chunk and Sally had sought assistance from a nearby resident, or worse, the police.

I ran down the beach in a drunken kind of sprint, though my footing became steadier with each stride. And then I saw Chunk and Sally...or at least I thought it was them. There appeared to be at least three people, maybe four, huddled together.

They had *gone for help*, I thought with deflated certainty.

"Hey-ho!" I said, waving my arms as I approached. "It's me! I'm okay!"

"Ben!" Sally cried, and then she was running toward me.

We caught each other in a hug and spun in a clumsy circle, almost falling over. She felt so good in my arms, so real, I would have done this forever.

"Oh my God, Ben. *Oh my God*," she mumbled into my shoulder, not caring that I was drenched. "You kept going out deeper and deeper...we were gonna try to find somebody to help, but *those* two assholes didn't let us. They just started beating up Chunk."

"Huh?" I said, stepping apart reluctantly and looking past her.

"If it ain't the *dickweed* back from his swim," one of the shapes down the beach called, and I recognized his voice immediately.

△△△

Chunk lay flat on the sand on his stomach like a lumpy black pillow. In the silvered light of the nearly full moon, I could see that tears streaked his cheeks and blood blotted his chin. His eyes looked up at me, big and white and pleading. The Beast stood on his back, pinning him down. Another guy stood a little distance away next to two mountain bikes collapsed on their sides. I didn't know his name but recognized him from Chatham Middle School. He'd been in the grade above me and was presumably in high school now.

I found it hard to believe it had only been yesterday morning that the Beast had chased Chunk and me into the church. And I also found it hard to believe how scared of him I'd been. Because right then I wasn't scared at all. I was furious, maybe the maddest I'd ever been in my life. I had been a hairbreadth away from drowning to death in the ocean, and here this guy was, this total poser, concerned only with getting revenge on Chunk because we'd called him a dickweed once.

What a *douchecanoe*. What a *fuckshitter*. What a major-league *pisswizard*.

I began to laugh.

The Beast snarled. "What's so funny, *dickweed*?"

The insult made me laugh harder. It seemed so toothless and petty. At the same time I was feeling great. I wasn't scared of him. Not one bit. The tables had somehow turned on him. I knew it. He knew it. And that scared him big. Bullies didn't like having the tables turned on them because they were spineless weasels who only preyed on those they perceived as weaker than them.

"You better scram, loser," he growled at me. "You got three seconds or I'm gonna break your face—"

I ran—directly at him. Drove my shoulder into his chest and sent him careening backward. He landed on his back with a deflated "*Oomph!*" and was turtling to get up when I dropped on top of him. I leaned my weight through my arms, drilling his face sideways into the sand, which got in his eyes and ears and nose and mouth. He went ballistic trying to buck me off him. I rode him like a rodeo bull and heard myself cackling crazily. I guess I scared him as much as I was scaring myself because he began wailing, on the verge of tears.

I got hold of myself. I boxed his upturned ear for good measure, then pushed off him. Chunk was back on his feet and staring at me like he didn't recognize me.

Coughing sand from his mouth and rubbing more sand from his wet eyes (and refusing to look at me), the Beast lumbered to his feet and straddled his bike. He and his friend wheeled off into the night without so much as a parting zinger.

CHAPTER 20
THE DANCER

"Here," I told Chunk, removing his sopping baseball cap from my head and offering it to him.

He wiped some blood off his hand onto his shirt, then took it. "Thanks, man." He was still staring at me in that weird way.

"What?" I asked.

"You just beat up *the Beast*, dude..."

I hadn't thought of what happened like that, but I guess I did beat the guy up.

I smiled. "It wasn't even that hard."

"You kicked his fuckin ass!"

"He deserved it."

"You bet he did," Sally said. "He wouldn't let us go for help when you might have been *drowning*. That's almost like murder, isn't it?"

Chunk touched the blood on his chin. "The shit-for-brains sissy-punched me in the face."

"He slapped you," Sally said.

I'd thought the blood on Chunk's chin might have been from a bloody nose, but now I saw it was from a split lip.

"It still hurt," Chunk said. "Let him slap you and see how you like it."

"I wouldn't like it, and I'm glad Ben beat him up too. But we should probably get going. Everyone knows Frankie's crazy. He

120

might come back."

"That's his name?" I said. "*Frankie?*"

She nodded. "I go to school with him. He just moved to the Cape this year. Nobody likes him because he's such a spaz. He's already had like three temper tantrums in class."

"You think he'd still come back after Ben beat him up?" Chunk asked, looking toward the dunes as if they might be crawling with commies.

"If he brought a knife, maybe—"

"A *knife*? I'm outta here!"

"Lemme find my shoes," I said.

△△△

As we walked back along Seaview Street we passed the house where the woman had been dancing in the front bay window. She was still there, still dancing, only now a man stood by her. He was yelling and waving his arms angrily. She kept dancing as though he didn't exist.

"We can hear him from way over here," I said.

"He sounds majorly pissed off," Chunk said.

"What I mean is, we can hear him easily, but we can't hear any music..."

"Guess she didn't turn any on—" And then Chunk seemed to recognize how odd it would be for someone to be dancing as zealously as that woman without any music playing. He frowned. "You mean...she's dancing around like that to *nothing*?"

"Sorta creepy," I said.

"Mega creepy," Sally said.

CHAPTER 21
SALLY'S PLACE

"Didja guys wanna come over?" Sally asked us.

We were standing on the sidewalk in front of her house. Rosebushes lined the white-picket fence. A mass of flowers climbed up and over an impressive entrance archway.

"Hell yeah!" Chunk said. "That's *two* girls' houses in one night."

"Two?" Sally said, raising an eyebrow.

"We were at a party earlier," I told her.

"If you're all partied out..."

"I'm still wet, and I'm getting cold..."

"Duuuude!" Chunk said. "C'mon, man. Don't leave me hanging. *Two girls' houses.*"

"I never said I didn't wanna come over," I told him. "I just needa change first."

"You can borrow some of my brother's clothes. He left most of them behind when he went off to the Army."

"Cool beans!" Chunk said, bustling under the archway and up the walkway to the large house, which featured two big wings and about a dozen shuttered windows facing the street.

Sally and I exchanged amused looks and followed him.

"Your family really digs Halloween, huh?" Chunk said, eyeing the crows and bats and cobwebs and other spooky props festooning the porch.

Sally nodded. "We put even better stuff out on the front lawn closer to Halloween. Ghosts, witches, tombstones, all that. We hang a scarecrow in a noose from that tree over there." She pointed to a nearby elm.

"So that is *this* place. Ben and me came here last year."

"You were trick-or-treating last year?" she said, surprised. "Aren't you too old for that?"

"Chunk made me go with him," I admitted. "He wanted the candy."

"Fuck yeah I did," he said. "And I got two pillowcases full of it, motherfuckers."

"You swear too much," Sally told him. "Do your parents know that?"

"Where do you think he gets it from?" I said.

She pushed open the front door—nobody locked their places in Chatham, not even wealthy families—and we stepped into an airy foyer with a soaring ceiling and a fancy staircase.

"Wow," I said, craning my neck to look up to the open second floor. "I forgot how big your house was."

"Your dad must be mad rich," Chunk said.

"Actually, my mom makes way more money than my dad. Come into the living room. You can wait there while I get Ben some dry clothes."

Sally led us into a living room with a sunken floor. The sofas and chairs were all white with zebra-patterned throw pillows, which matched a large rug on top of the beige carpet. A wall-to-wall bookshelf was crammed not only with books but also small statues and what looked like expensive knickknacks. In a corner, perched on a fluted plinth, was a marble bust.

"Oh, man, lookit your TV!" Chunk hurried over to the giant Mitsubishi TV set housed in honey-colored wood. It was almost as tall as him. "Ben, check it out! It's even got a built-in VCR!"

"My dad bought that this year," Sally told him. "So don't break it. Be back in a jiff with some dry clothes."

"Why does everybody always think I'm gonna break something?" Chunk complained. He started pressing random buttons on the front of the TV.

"Because you *do* break things," I said. "So leave it alone. And, seriously, don't break anything. If you do, we'll have to pay for it, and then we'll have to tell our parents we were here."

"So—you gonna bone her or what?"

I stiffened. "What're you talking about?"

"She invited you into her house, man. Maybe she'll invite you up to her bedroom too?"

"Maybe you're a world-class idiot."

"Like you don't wanna bone her..."

My cheeks burned. "Would you stop saying that?"

"If you don't, maybe I will instead?"

"Yeah, fine, go for it," I said, knowing he didn't have a chance...but did I?

No, that was crazy. Sally and I were friends when we were little kids. She didn't like me in the way Chunk thought. She was just being nice hanging out with us. Besides, she was in high school and I was in middle school. No way she'd like someone still in middle school.

And you didn't think Heather Russell could like you either...and she said she wanted to kiss you...

"Hey, look," Chunk said, going over to the sliding doors that opened onto the back deck. "She's even got a swimming pool! This house is boss, man! *Boss!*"

You couldn't see the swimming pool from the backyard because it was built into the deck, but I'd known it was there. We used to swim in it at Sally's birthday parties.

I noticed a framed photograph of Sally on the bookshelf and went to check it out. It looked like the ones they took of you at school on Picture Day. She was wearing a green headband and matching earrings and smiling in that way I liked—

"Ben?"

I whirled around. "Oh, hey."

She held a folded pair of grey sweatpants and a sweatshirt in her arms. "Kevin's not much bigger than you, so these should be okay."

"Uh, thanks," I said, taking the clothes from her. "Where should I change?"

"There's a bathroom that way." She pointed down a hallway. "First door on the right."

I changed quickly in the bathroom, leaving my wet Jockeys on. I hung my sodden jeans and Iron Maiden tee shirt over the sink, then returned to the living room.

"Raiders, huh?" Chunk said, noting the logos on the sweatsuit. "Didn't they come in last place last year?"

I didn't watch NFL, and I didn't know. I didn't care either. "They're comfortable," I said to Sally. "Thanks for letting me borrow them."

"You look good."

I might have smiled but didn't, fearful that Chunk might make another "You gonna bone her?" crack.

"So are we smoking that cigarette or what?" he asked.

"We'll have to go outside," Sally told him. "But first, didja guys want something to drink?"

"Whatcha got?" Chunk asked, joining her in the kitchen, which opened off the living room.

She checked the fridge. "Orange juice, lemonade, chocolate milk, wine…?"

"*Wine?* Are you for real?"

"I've had some before. It makes you feel good."

"Fuckin A!"

I joined them as Sally took a bottle of white wine from the fridge and showed it to us.

I tried looking impressed but probably failed. Smoking cigarettes and drinking wine? Things were getting out of control rather quickly.

Getting out of control? a voice shot back. *You almost drowned half an hour ago! Smokes and booze are nothing in comparison to that.*

Chunk was grinning at me.

"You first," I said.

△△△

"I can't find the stupid corkscrew," Sally said, fussing through the silverware drawer.

"Maybe your parents hid it so you don't drink their wine?" I offered.

"Yeah, right. If they knew I drank their wine, they'd have a cow and probably kick me out of the house forever."

"Won't they know this bottle has been opened?"

"We'll just hafta drink the whole thing," Chunk suggested sagely, "and feel *really* good."

"We'll pour what we don't drink down the drain," Sally told me, "and I'll get rid of the bottle somewhere."

"Okay...but won't they know the bottle's missing then?"

"Not a chance," she said. "They have a wine cellar in the basement with about a thousand bottles just sitting there. I'm going to try something. Someone gimme a shoe."

"Why do you want our shoes for?" Chunk asked.

"Just one will do."

He looked at me expectantly, and I figured he didn't want to take off one of his shoes for the same reason he didn't take them off back in Justin's place: his socked feet always smelled like vinegar that had gone bad.

I took off one of my shoes and gave it to Sally.

"Thanks," she said. "But we better go outside for this."

Chunk and I followed her outside onto the porch, neither of us having any idea what she was up to. She stuck the bottom of the wine bottle into my shoe and said, "I saw someone do this at one of my parents' parties." After double-checking to make sure the bottle was snug, she slapped the sole against the wall of the house. Chunk and I stuck our noses close to the bottle.

"Hey!" Chunk exclaimed. "The cork came out a bit! Whack it again. Whack it good!"

"You guys better move back in case the bottle breaks."

It took four more wallops before the cork popped out of the

neck of the bottle. Chunk whooped and Sally gave me back my shoe and said, "Let's get some glasses."

ΔΔΔ

In the kitchen Sally poured a little bit of white wine (though it was actually yellow) into three glasses with stems—the kind adults used. That made what we were doing feel even more serious and wrong, but I wasn't about to ask Sally if I could pour mine into a mug. She handed a glass to Chunk and one to me. I sniffed and wrinkled my nose. It smelled sharp and fruity.

"So it really makes you feel good, huh?" Chunk said, eyeballing his greedily.

"Try it," Sally told him.

He took a baby sip. I could tell by his face that he thought it was gross even though he was trying not to show it. But then in typical Chunk fashion he tilted back his head and dumped everything in the glass down his throat.

"Yum!" he said, wiping the back of his hand across his mouth, which was twisted in a puckered smile. "Tastes just like fruit punch. Your turn, guys, you gotta drink too."

I sipped and scrunched my nose. It tasted as heinous as it had smelled.

"You gotta drink it all, man," Chunk protested. "You promised!"

"I never promised anything," I said. "But I'll finish it, don't worry. I wanna take my time."

"Take however long you want," Sally said, sipping hers and appearing okay with the bitter taste.

"I oughta have some more," Chunk said, grabbing the bottle. "I don't feel anything good yet."

"Whoa, slow down there, McFly!" Sally said, snatching the bottle away from him. "It takes a little time to kick in."

"How long?"

"I dunno. Just be patient. Why don't we watch a movie? My dad has a lot of videos on the bookshelf."

After Sally and I finished what was left in our glasses, we searched through the movie collection for a good one to watch. We settled on *Die Hard* because Bruce Willis was hardcore. By then everything was starting to seem...filmy, like I was looking in at the three of us through a dirty window. Sally and Chunk were giggling a lot. I figured this was what wine did to you, made things blurry and funny, and it wasn't so bad, after all. Now I knew why my mom liked it so much—only she never seemed to giggle or laugh, so maybe it affected adults differently.

In fact, I *knew* it affected adults differently, at least some of them. Like Chris Anderson's dad. Everybody knew he was a drunkard who turned as black as thunder when he was juiced up. During some of his darker benders he'd lash out at anybody who was around, and unfortunately for Chris, that was often him. Chris would show us his bruises and lumps at school on Monday morning, almost as though they were badges of honor. But you could tell he wasn't proud of them; he simply wanted to get through the explanations as quickly as possible so we'd stop ragging him about what a tosspot his dad was. One weekend he got so lamed up he stayed at home for all the following week, and the rumor (courtesy of Tom Sandberg) was that his dad was spending time in the county jail.

Sally flopped onto the floor in front of the TV and said, "I have no idea how to use this stupid VCR. Can you help me, Ben?"

I sat down beside her, liking it when she called me by my name. "You just shove the tape in the slot there."

"Oh," she said, giggling. She slid the *Die Hard* cassette into the front-loading slot. The machine whizzed and sucked in its prize greedily.

"Tubular," I said.

"Did you just say *tubular*?"

"So?"

"Nobody says that anymore."

"I do."

"Poser."

"I'm a poser?"

"You are if you say stuff like *tubular*."

We began laughing again and Sally fell against me, dropping her empty wine glass onto the carpet. I was going to reach for it but didn't. I didn't want to move her off me.

I noticed Chunk in the kitchen pouring more wine into his glass.

"Chunk!" I yelled.

"Did he break something?" Sally said, pushing off me, and I wish I hadn't said anything.

"This stuff is great!" he said and filled his glass nearly to the rim.

"You're bonkers!" Sally said. "I dare you!"

"You know he's gonna do it, right?" I said. "He never turns down a dare."

"You know it!" Chunk said, raising the glass to his lips. "Bottoms up!"

All he managed was a single, sloppy sip.

"Lame!"

"Let's see you do it!"

"Wuss!"

I figured he was going to wimp out again, but incredibly he gulped down every last drop.

"Tubular," I said, and Sally laughed.

ΔΔΔ

Most of what happened over the next hour or two was a disjointed haze. We decided to turn off the movie—partly because Chunk kept cackling "Yippee-ki-yay, motherfucker!"—but mostly because sitting around and staring at the TV seemed like the most boring thing ever right then.

Sally and I had a bit more wine—not nearly as much as Chunk had guzzled, but enough to keep us feeling silly. Sally put on a Led Zeppelin cassette tape and cranked the volume.

At one point Chunk sneaked outside with Sally's cigarette and lighter. We only caught him because we heard him coughing up his lungs, which had been loud enough to hear above the music.

Sally flicked on the light switch for the porch, bathing him in a guilty white radiance. He was doubled over and hocking a loogie, holding the cigarette away from him, maybe hoping for someone else to take it.

Sally snatched it from his fingers, and he blurted, "I gotta ralph…"

And so he did—right into the swimming pool.

△△△

That killed our fun a little bit because Sally and I spent the next ten minutes trying to get as much of the disintegrating puke out of the water as we could. When we gave up on the smaller bits and went back inside, Chunk was lying spread-eagle on the carpet, passed out. Sally flipped the cassette tape back to Side 1 and fast-forwarded to "Stairway to Heaven." She asked me to dance, and I said okay. I placed my hands on her sides, and we started moving around in a slow, small circle. At one point she took my hands and moved them down to her hips. Then she leaned her head against my chest, so my nose was in her hair. Its scent made me think of the Apple Harvest Fair I went to every year.

She mumbled, "You're pretty handsome, you know that, Ben?"

I mumbled back, "You're pretty…pretty."

We kept moving in a circle. I tried my best not to step on her feet. I was feeling dizzy but good, and I didn't want the song to end.

Sally suddenly pressed closer to me, so our private parts were touching. That was probably the best moment I'd ever had in my life—until I started to get a hard-on!

I didn't know what to do but to keep dancing like nothing was happening down there. I knew Sally was going to leap away any second when she noticed—only she never did.

And she had to have noticed; there was no way she couldn't have.

For some reason the idea that she was okay with this made me feel better than ever...until I realized I was about to have an accident of the sort that had started happening recently in the middle of the night.

Doing that all over her would be deadly embarrassing. Doing it in her brother's sweatpants would make it even worse.

Thankfully these thoughts made the hard-on go away...and I was both relieved and oddly disappointed.

Sally lifted her head from my shoulder and looked up at me. Our eyes met. There was nothing in hers accusing me of being a pervert. Actually, I was pretty sure she wanted me to kiss her right then. And I wanted to kiss her too, I *ached* to kiss her...but for some reason I just kept looking into her eyes and hoping she would try to kiss me first.

I was still hoping this when "Stairway to Heaven" ended.

The silence seemed louder than the song had ever been. Sally smiled and poked a kiss on my cheek (which wasn't anywhere near as good as kissing on the lips would have been).

"How are you feeling?" she asked.

"Okay," I said, and I was. I was still feeling a bit goofy from the wine, but most of the funny feeling had worn off. "What time it is?"

"Pretty late."

"I guess Chunk and I should be getting home."

We looked at him. He remained in the exact position on the floor he'd been in earlier.

"Good luck moving him."

"Chunk?" I said, going over and toeing him in the side. "Wake up. We're going."

He didn't move.

"What am I gonna do?

"You'll hafta let him sleep there."

"But my mom's gonna knock on my window for breakfast. She'll see he's not there, and I'll hafta tell her he slept here." My good mood deflated. "Man...when she finds out everything, she's gonna hate me more than she already does..."

"Your mom doesn't hate you."

"Yeah, she does."

"Why?"

"Because...you know what happened to my sister, right?" Sally nodded; everyone in town knew. "My mom thinks it was my fault."

"How was it your fault? A dog killed your sister."

"But I was supposed to be watching her."

Sally was quiet before adding, "I think you're wrong, Ben. Moms can't hate their kids."

"Maybe," I said reluctantly, not wanting to talk about it anymore.

"Anyway, you'll just hafta let Chunk sleep on the floor there for now. By the time the sun comes up, you should be able to wake him. Then the two of you can sneak back into your garage."

"I guess..." I said, although I wasn't happy about the plan. Sneaking out at night was one thing. Sneaking back *in* at first light was totally different and a lot worse.

Sally said, "You can sleep on the sofa and keep an eye on him. I'll get you a blanket."

She disappeared upstairs. I was hoping she might return with the blanket from her bed, but the one she held was made of patches stitched together and was probably from a guest bedroom.

"Thanks," I said, and took the blanket to the sofa. I hesitated, looking back. "Um, and thanks for having us over. It was a lot of fun."

"Yeah, it was," she said, smiling. "G'night, Ben."

"G'night," I said, settling down on the sofa and pulling the cover up to my chin.

She turned off the lights on her way out of the living room, and the black night pressed down and around me like a heavy weight.

I fell asleep a few minutes later imagining that I had kissed

Sally on the lips, after all.

△△△

I slept restlessly, drifting beneath my consciousness, sometimes bubbling up through it. But my throat was parched and my bladder stung and I didn't want to deal with any of that—not to mention the hazy, distant whispers that I wasn't in my bed, that I was somewhere I probably shouldn't be— so I concentrated on sinking again, down, down, into the dark below.

And that was where I ran into Brittany—at least, a dream about her.

Before going to bed each night, I had about a fifty-fifty chance of dreaming about her, and I always hoped I didn't. The dreams were usually nightmares, and even the few good ones left me feeling homesick and missing her more than ever when I woke up in the morning.

Tonight's dream was a bad one.

Brittany and I were building a sandcastle together, using green and blue plastic buckets and matching shovels. It was the middle of July, the sun beating down on our backs. All around us came the familiar noises of the beach: the squawks of hungry seagulls; the squeals and laughter of kids; the hoots and hollers of teenagers playing frisbee and volleyball. When I looked up from the castle for my mom, I couldn't see her anywhere among the summer crowd. I supposed she had gone to find my brothers, who weren't in sight either.

Which meant I was in charge of Brit.

For a while I leaned back on my elbows and watched the goings-on. Bronzed sunbathers soaking up the rays. Parents wading in the surf with their children, some wearing arm floats or lifejackets, others kicking behind bodyboards. Couples walking side-by-side or holding hands as they strolled the waterline. About a thousand other people lounging beneath parasols, eating Devil Dogs and salted french fries and melting ice cream cones.

When I grew bored of doing nothing, I turned my attention back to the sandcastle and discovered that Brittany was gone. A panicked moment later I spotted her out on the ocean, far from shore, somehow staying afloat even though she didn't know how to swim. In place of the tomato-red swimsuit and rainbow tutu she'd had on only moments before was the pink and blue lederhosen (one of her favorite play outfits) she'd been wearing on the day the dog had torn out her throat.

I glanced around for a lifeguard. The beach was suddenly deserted. I shouted at Brittany to come back. She ignored me and went right on floating on her back. I splashed into the water to rescue her—and in the next moment I was next to her, both of us floating lazily on our backs, the sun blazing down on us. I should have taken her hand and led her back to the beach, but I decided it was nice and relaxing right where we were.

The calm water made it easy to see the dorsal fin that cut through the surface like a hot knife through butter. It was moving in a circle around us, ripples trailing behind it.

I wanted to warn Brittany, but I couldn't speak. I tried to swim to her, to protect her, because I never died in my dreams, only Brit did, so if I could get to her, I might be able to save her this time.

It was too late. It was always too late. The shark's head emerged from the water like a huge gray bullet. A mangle of arrowhead teeth filled its gaping jaws, far too many even for a monster from the deep. It almost appeared to be grinning as it barreled down on my little sister, who didn't know she was in danger.

I threw a rock that had appeared in my hand. It bounced harmlessly off the shark's armored skin. I screamed at it to stop. The beady black eye staring my way seemed to say, *You gotta do better than that, Benny-boy, if you wanna save your sister.*

Yet there would be no saving her in this dream. The shark's pink gums pushed out of its maw and its rows of daggers chomped together, taking half of Brittany with them. Her head and shoulders and arms (which ended in pulpy stumps) were all that remained of her—and they continued to float lazily, intolerably, on the sun-spangled blue water that was quickly turning bright red.

From the beach I heard my mom yelling hysterically, telling me to *do* something.

It was too late to do anything, of course. Brittany wasn't sick in bed, her chest smothered with Vicks VapoRub. She wasn't going to rush down to breakfast the next morning with only a mild case of the sniffles. She didn't have chicken pox or bronchitis or whooping cough. She wasn't sleeping or pretending to sleep, squeezing her eyes shut tightly to convince onlookers. She wasn't doing any of this, folks, and she never would be. A doctor couldn't fix her. I couldn't. The Good Lord couldn't.

Brittany was dead, and she wasn't coming back.

CHAPTER 22
THE PRESENT

With glass clinking in my backpack and a plastic bag hanging from my left wrist, I unlocked and opened the door to my apartment. I tossed the plastic bag onto the cot, then swung the backpack off my shoulders and set it on the kitchenette counter with a rattle. I'd managed to squeeze into it three jugs of milk, three bottles of whiskey, and a bottle of Chardonnay.

I put the kettle on the stove to boil, then went to the cot and upended the plastic bag onto the mattress. Out came the seven picture frames I had picked up at a gift shop on my walk to the apartment. I tore off the flimsy plastic packaging and carried them to my desk. A few days ago I'd flicked through my mother's photograph album that had been willed to my grandmother after my mother's death, eventually finding its way to me. The 4 x 6 photos were all dated and faded and pressed behind glassine sheets. They progressed in chronological order, starting the year after my birth in 1978 and ending in 1985 (my mother had annotated the date and occasion on a piece of masking tape next to each photo). The last one showed Brittany on a swing that had hung from the maple in our backyard. More than a dozen empty pages remained at the back of the album. My parents stopped taking photographs altogether after Brittany died.

The photos of Brittany that I had selected to display were in a pile on the computer desk, and I went to work housing them in the new frames. Once complete, I stood the frames up on the desk, three on one side of my monitor, four on the other.

I studied my handiwork, pleased to have Brittany resurrected in my daily life. When the kettle whistled, I returned to the kitchenette and made a coffee. Then I produced my star purchase of the morning from the backpack.

The five-dollar bottle of Chardonnay.

I rarely drank wine, and I had no intention of drinking the Chardonnay, which was why I'd selected the cheapest corked bottle I found in the liquor store on Cambridge Street.

I slipped off my right suede Oxford and surveyed the small apartment. Any wall would do; there was nothing to ruin in the event the bottle smashed.

I decided on the wall that faced Atlantic Avenue so I didn't bother Nessa or my other neighbor. I tore the foil from the wine bottle and wedged the bottom in the shoe. It was a snug, almost perfect, fit.

Holding the neck of the bottle in one hand and the toe of the shoe in the other, I banged the sole of the shoe against the wall.

The cork didn't budge.

I gave it another shot, this time banging the sole against the wall with much more force.

The cork shimmied out a little.

Five whacks later it zonked free, along with a spurt of wine.

"I'll be damned," I said, grinning.

CHAPTER 23

THE MORNING AFTER

I woke to faint gray-orange light bleeding through the windows. I immediately knew I wasn't in my bed. It took a bit longer to realize I was on the sofa in Sally's living room. Fragmented memories of the night before assaulted me, and I had a tough time believing that any of them were real. Had a riptide really sucked me out to sea? Had I really beaten up the Beast? Had I really danced with Sally—*and why the hell didn't I kiss her when I had a chance?*

I pushed aside the patchwork quilt I had slept beneath and sat up. I groaned as I took stock of my body. My brain had grown too big for my skull and seemed to be whumping in tempo with my heartbeat. My mouth tasted like cotton balls, and no amount of swallowing seemed able to lubricate my shriveled throat. But my stomach was the worst. It felt slimy and foul as if it were filled with a quart of fish oil. For a moment I feared it would rebel and cast its gooey contents up my throat and out my mouth. Thankfully all that came up was a grody burp.

Chunk was still lying prone on the carpet like a beached starfish, and I might have worried that he was dead except for the fact he was snoring loudly.

"Hey," I said quietly, not wanting Sally to know we were awake. It wasn't that I didn't want to see her; I did. But I felt like we had totally overstayed our welcome. Last night had been fun and all, but this morning was a new day, and we were still camped out in her house like a couple of hangers-on.

Chunk didn't respond. I nudged him in his flabby side with my foot, told him to get up (in case he was semi-conscious), and then went to the bathroom. I relieved my bladder and flushed the toilet, wincing at the sound of rushing water as it rumbled through the house's old plumbing. I changed into my own clothes, which were still damp but no longer soaked. I folded Sally's brother's sweatsuit neatly and left it on the lowered toilet seat.

Back in the living room I shook Chunk's shoulder. "Hey, man," I said. "Get up. We gotta split."

"Don't..." he mumbled into the carpet.

"We hafta go, man."

"Nuh-uh."

"My parents are gonna be awake soon..."

Chunk said nothing, and the silence needled me with panic. What if I couldn't get him up? There was no way I could carry him on my own.

I went to the kitchen, filled a glass with cold water from the tap, then returned to the living room and dumped the water over his head.

"Aargh..." he said but didn't get up.

I rolled him over onto his back. He squinted and blinked.

"Where're we?" He sounded like he'd eaten a handful of rusty nails.

"Sally's house."

He groaned and said, "I don't feel so good."

"Because you drank half a bottle of wine, you moron."

"Huh?"

"You don't remember what happened?"

"Aargh..."

"I'll tell you later. But we needa go."

"Five minutes." He started to roll over again.

"*Now*," I said, yanking him to his feet.

ΔΔΔ

Once we were back in my garage, I said, "You barfed in her swimming pool."

"Aargh..." Doubling over, he rushed to the small bathroom.

I heard him puking his guts out. When I went to check on him, the throat of my shirt pulled over my nose to shield against the foul stench, I found him slumped down next to the toilet, his face resting on the seat, his eyes closed.

"What's *wrong* with you, man?" I asked, getting worried.

"I'm sick..."

"Like dying sick?"

"Yeah..."

"You can't stay there like that. My mom's gonna come get us for breakfast soon. She sees you like that, she'll know something's up."

"Can't move..."

"Yes, you can. You can sleep on my pillows. Maybe when you wake up later you'll feel better?"

That turned out to be enough of a motivation to get him to move. I took two pillows from my bed and set them on the floor. He collapsed on top of them, and I think he was out as soon as he closed his eyes.

He didn't look so terrible while he was sleeping. I could tell my mom he just wanted to sleep in. She might be suspicious that he would pass up breakfast—especially because she always cooked bacon and eggs on Saturday mornings—but I doubted she would try to wake him herself.

So we were good for now.

I only hoped he got better soon.

ΔΔΔ

He didn't.

Even when I set a plate of scrambled eggs and crispy country bacon next to him, he rolled the other way, turning his back to it.

That was when I knew he was *really* sick.

I let him sleep. In the interim I cleaned up my bedroom, made my bed (minus the pillows) then finished my homework at my desk. Doing stuff I was supposed to do made me feel better about last night and all the stuff I did that I wasn't supposed to do.

I tried not to reflect on my near-death experience. The briefest recollection of the cold black water and the faraway shore made me shiver all the way to my bones. Whenever my thoughts trended that way, I would promptly think about Sally instead, goofing around with her, dancing with her, what happened *while* dancing with her...even how I chickened out and didn't kiss her on the lips.

At a little past noon the telephone rang. I picked up the receiver and said, "Graves' residence."

"That you, Benny?" It was Chuck's mom. Her smoky voice was instantly recognizable. "What're you kids up to?"

I glanced at Chunk lying motionless on the pillows on the floor.

"We're, uh, just playing in my garage."

"Playing in the garage. I hear ya, Benny. I hear ya. How was last night?"

I stiffened. "What do you mean?"

"What did you whack-a-moles get up to?"

"Oh." I relaxed. "We, uh, watched a movie."

"Did ya? Are you going to keep me hanging...? Details, details..."

I was about to tell her we'd watched *Trick or Treat* because she was usually cool with us watching R-rated movies as long as they didn't keep us up all night, but I decided to play it safe and said, "*Die Hard*. It just came out...you know, with Bruce Willis?"

"'Yippe-kay-yay, mother trucker!' Am I right? Now would you be a doll and send Chuck home? We're having some friends by this afternoon, and I'd like him to be around to meet them."

"Yeah, okay."

"Thanks, Benny."

She hung up.

Chunk opened one eye. "That my mom?"

"She says you have to go home now."

He groaned and sat up. "What am I gonna tell her? She's gonna know I'm sick."

I'd been giving this some thought and said, "You can tell her you ate something bad and got food poisoning."

Chunk seemed hopeful. "You think she'll buy that?"

His mom had sounded high enough to buy whatever he fed her. But I only said, "I had it once. I got majorly sick like you—except I had diarrhea too."

"What should I tell her I ate that was bad?"

"I dunno. An egg?"

"An egg has never made me sick before."

"I don't know, man! Think of something on your way home. Just don't tell her it was half a bottle of wine."

He got slowly to his feet. He didn't look very good at all.

"You ain't gonna hurl, are you?"

He shook his head, clapped his Red Sox baseball cap over his head, and crossed the room. "I hadda dream about that woman who was dancing in the window," he said, pausing at the door. "She came outta her house and chased us down the street with a sword."

"Yeah?" I said.

"Yeah," he said, shuffling outside and adding over his shoulder: "Seemed like she really wanted to get us."

CHAPTER 24

THE LOWDOWN

The phone rang again two hours later. I had an uneasy feeling it was going to be Chunk's mom asking to speak to my mom because Chunk had blabbed everything. Chest tight, I picked up the receiver and heard my dad say, "Hello?"

"Hi, Stu. It's Keith. I tried getting you at work. Cal said you went home for lunch. Sorry to disturb you there."

I hadn't known the sheriff's first name was Keith, but I recognized his voice.

I should have hung up, but my dad didn't know I was on the line, so I kept listening.

"I needed a breather," my dad replied. "Preparing old people for the other side is one thing. When it's young people, it's disheartening."

"You're telling me. And that's why I'm calling—I got another body for you."

"Mary mother..." My dad groaned. "Who?"

"Jody Gwynn. Worked at the post office."

"I know Jody. Her husband, Dwight, passed last year from cancer. She was, what, mid-forties?"

"Somewhere around there, ayuh. Her neighbor found her about half an hour ago."

"That's three people in three days, Keith. Three people under fifty, two of them in their thirties. Shit, I'm used to doing five funerals a month, maybe one or two more than that in the wintertime. But three people in three days—and *young* people?"

"I'd like to know what the fuck is going on too, Stu. I have a pair of reporters from the *Chronicle* hounding my ass. I've agreed to hold a press briefing this afternoon at five. You think I don't wish I had something to say?"

"What *are* you going to say?"

"Natural causes—Dale and Lin passed from natural causes. Straight from your mouth. Sounds like a heart attack or stroke got Jody too. The neighbor found her lying facedown in the middle of her living room, purple as a lilac."

"What about their feet, Keith?"

"What about their fucking feet?"

"If it was just Dale's, fine. But both his and Lin's, swollen and bleeding? What do Jody's look like?"

"I haven't seen them yet. I'm heading over there now."

"And if they're swollen and bleeding too?"

"What are you getting at, Stu?"

"I don't know. Fuck, I don't know, but I don't like it."

"Don't like what? I don't see how any of these deaths are related, Stu. And if I suggest they are, everybody's going to be talking about Henrickson and a faceless killer, and I'm not having any of that shit in Chatham again. Whoever killed that transient is long gone. These were natural deaths. No decapitations, no foul play. The Gwynn's place is the last one on Northgate Road. I'll see you there soon."

I silently replaced the receiver and stared at the phone, thinking.

CHAPTER 25

THE CONFESSION

After dinner—shepherd's pie, which I hated—I returned to the garage and called Chunk's house.

His mom answered. "Chuck's in dreamworld right now, Benny. You'll have to hang tight until tomorrow."

"He's gone to bed already?" I said, surprised. It was only 6:30 p.m.

"Not already. He hit the sack as soon as he got home this afternoon. Seems the butterball ate something at your house that put him under the weather, though he can't remember for the life of him what it might have been…"

"I'll call him tomorrow," I said quickly and hung up before I had to start making up what Chunk might have eaten to make him sick.

I paced back and forth in my room. I really wanted to talk to Chunk. I almost *needed* to. The conversation between my dad and the sheriff had been eating at me all afternoon—especially the part about the two people with swollen and bleeding feet. The sheriff hadn't known what might have caused those kinds of injuries, but I did.

Say, if you'd been dancing for two or three days straight.

I picked up the phone and called Justin Gee.

His sister answered. "Hi, Kate. It's Ben."

"Hi, Ben. Didja wanna speak with Justin?"

I didn't know who else she thought I might want to speak to,

145

and I said, "Yeah, is he there?"

I heard her set the receiver down. Ten seconds later Justin picked up. "Ben? What do you want?"

"Hey, Justin. What are you doing?"

"Reading."

"What are you reading?"

"A book."

"Okay, well... I have a question for you. It's serious. It's not because I wanna see Miss Forrester again or anything... I just wanna know if she's still dancing in her window?"

I was expecting Justin to tell me that he didn't know, that he wasn't watching her anymore, something like that. He simply said, "She hasn't stopped."

I frowned. "She's still in her underwear?"

"You said you didn't wanna see her again!" he said in an accusatory tone.

"I don't. Honest. I'm just wondering, is all...?"

"Why?" Suspicious now.

I hadn't planned on telling Justin why I wanted to know, but I ended up saying, "Me and Chunk saw someone else dancing like Miss Forrester. And I overheard my dad talking to the sheriff, and I think more people might be dancing too. And...I just wanna make sure Miss is all right."

"Why wouldn't she be? She's just dancing."

"She's been dancing for a really long time. You said she hasn't stopped. What if she has a heart attack and dies? That'll be on us for not telling anybody nothing."

"Yeah, right. A heart attack? If she was that tired, she'd just fall down and go to sleep. She wouldn't *die*."

"But what if whatever's making her dance doesn't let her go to sleep?"

"What's making her dance?"

"I dunno..."

Justin lowered his voice. "She's still in her underwear, okay? The *same* underwear. And she's still dancing. I just saw her."

I was relieved. "And she's okay?"

"She looks okay. So don't tell anyone about her—because then they'll know you were watching through my window."

"I won't," I said, though I wasn't sure whether I had made up my mind or not. "Thanks, Justin. I'll see ya later."

"See ya. And Ben—you better not tell."

△△△

When it was dark outside, and I was sure my parents weren't going to come to check on me, I slipped out of the garage and hopped over the backyard fence. The first-floor lights were on in Sally's house.

Heart thumping, I hurried across her lawn. I climbed the back porch steps and looked through the glass door. Sally was sitting on the sofa I had slept on, watching TV, a bowl of popcorn on her lap.

I knocked on the door and quickly took a step back so she wouldn't know I was peeking in at her.

She appeared a moment later. The worried look on her face became a smile when she recognized me. She slid open the door and said, "Hey, Ben. Whatcha doing here?"

"I needa tell you something."

△△△

I recounted everything I'd heard in the phone conversation between Sheriff Sandberg and my dad. Then I told her I thought the two people with the bruised and bloodied feet might have danced themselves to death, and that whatever made them dance might also be what was making Miss Forrester and the woman in the house on Seaview Street dance. I finished by saying, "I think something bad might be going on around town, but I don't know if I should tell my dad or not."

Sally had listened to everything attentively, and I thought I'd made the right decision confessing to her. But when she spoke I could tell she didn't believe any of it.

"You really think it's all connected?"

"How else did those two dead people get bruised and bloodied feet? Maybe the third one too?"

"I don't know, Ben... Like, what would make people dance and not stop?"

I shrugged. "Drugs?"

"Drugs that make you dance for days? I guess. But who gave the drugs to them?"

"I dunno. I'm just worried about Miss Forrester. She's been dancing since we saw her on Thursday. That's three days, and I don't think she's stopped."

"How do you know that?"

I hedged, then said, "She's still wearing the same underwear as when we saw her on Thursday."

"How do you know what *underwear* she's wearing?"

"She wasn't wearing clothes, only underwear when we saw her on Thursday. She was wearing the same underwear when we checked on her on Friday. And I just phoned my friend Justin now, who lives across the street from her, and he says she's still wearing the same underwear. You'd think if she stopped dancing she would have taken the time to put some clothes on."

Sally frowned in thought. "You never told me that!"

"And I bet if you checked her feet, they would be bruised and bleeding from all the dancing."

"You're probably right..."

I was buoyed. "So you believe me?"

"I don't think you're making it up. And I saw the woman on Seaview Street dancing. I guess they could be connected. And if they're connected, I guess the dead people could be connected too..." She exhaled. "This is pretty heavy stuff for a Saturday night, Ben. So whatcha wanna do?"

"I think I should tell my dad about Miss Forrester and the woman on Seaview Street. But I don't know what to say. I can't tell him I was eavesdropping on him and the sheriff."

"You don't hafta tell him you were eavesdropping. Just tell him you were at your friend's house on Thursday and you looked out the window and saw your teacher dancing in her window across the street. And you talked to your friend again today and he said she's still dancing and doesn't look very well and you're concerned about her."

"Justin said she looked okay."

"But you don't hafta tell your dad that. You just want him to go check on her, right?"

"Well, not him. The sheriff."

"Well, if you want the sheriff to check on her, then you're gonna hafta say she doesn't look very well."

"You think he'll make the connection to the dead people?"

"If he doesn't, then he's not a very good sheriff, is he?"

"What about the woman on Seaview Street?"

"What about her?"

"If she's been dancing for a long time, then she's probably going to drop dead from a heart attack too. But if I tell my dad that me and Chunk saw her Friday night, he'll know we snuck out. He might even guess that we went to the beach."

"Easy. Just don't tell your dad you saw her Friday night. Tell him you saw her today when you were riding your bike around. It doesn't matter *when* you saw her, right?" Sally checked her wristwatch. "You better go speak to your dad before he goes to bed. If you're right that those two women might drop dead, the sooner the sheriff checks on them, the better."

"I s'pose you're right..." I hesitated, wondering how to say goodbye. If Sally had been Chunk, "Seeya fuckface" would have sufficed. But we'd danced together and almost kissed, so I felt as though I should say something meaningful before taking off, only I had no idea what.

She said, "How's Chunky, by the way?"

"His mom says he's been sleeping all day. I don't think he's ever gonna drink alcohol again."

Sally laughed. "Serves the doofus right. Hey...do you wanna come over tomorrow sometime? My parents won't be back until Monday or maybe Tuesday. We can watch a movie?"

"Yeah, sure," I said, liking that idea a whole lot. "What time?"

"How bout noon? You can tell me how things went with your dad."

ΔΔΔ

While lying in my bed with the garage lights off and the crickets and katydids chirping in the darkness outside, I played over the conversation I'd had with my father. He'd been watching the CBS Evening News with Walter Cronkite. When I'd asked if we could talk, he sensed something was serious because he muted the TV. I told him everything that Sally and I had talked about. I made sure to emphasize that Miss Forrester didn't look well and that I was worried she might drop dead from a heart attack. My dad's face remained expressionless, and by the time I was finishing up I was worried he had suspected that I'd eavesdropped on his conversation with the sheriff earlier. But if he did, he didn't say so. He only stood up and led me to his office (a shoebox space he'd cornered off from the living room), where he asked me for the addresses of Miss Forrester and the woman on Seaview Street. Then he told me to go to bed and closed the door to his office. I hovered around on the other side of it for long enough to hear him begin talking on the phone, and I guessed it was to the sheriff.

You did what you could, I told myself now, rolling onto my side. *If something happens to Miss Forrester, or the other woman, it won't be your fault. You're not keeping anything secret anymore. It's up to Dad and Sheriff Sandberg to fix things...*

These thoughts should have comforted me, but future scenarios played out relentlessly and dreadfully in my mind—the worst ones culminating in blood and death and punishment—and it took me a lot longer than usual to get to sleep that night.

CHAPTER 26

SUNDAY MASS

As we did every Sunday morning, my family attended the ten o'clock mass at Holy Redeemer Church. After the opening hymn was sung, all the little kids, including Ralph and Steve, filed out of the pews and went downstairs to the church basement for Sunday school. I used to go with them, and I missed doing that. It wasn't enjoyable exactly, but it had been better than being stuck up here for a full hour. All the standing and kneeling and "Amens" were worse than listening to Mr. Riddle bang on about the American Revolution during history class, or topographic maps and contour lines during geography. Sometimes I wondered whether adults simply didn't have anything better to do with themselves, or if at some point when they were growing up they forgot how to have fun.

When the congregation finished singing a hymn that could have made the soundtrack to *Rosemary's Baby*, Father Burridge opened his huge Bible slowly and importantly. In a serious voice he read a passage from the New Testament in which Jesus and his apostles got caught in a storm at sea that nearly drowned them. Jesus, however, woke up in time to calm the weather with his magic.

Father Burridge spread his hands wide and said, "And in this we learn to trust in the Lord our Savior and to always keep hope even when facing one of life's many storms...wise counsel in light of the devastating losses that we have all heard about and no doubt struggled with in recent days. You see, there is no guarantee against the sudden. In Mark 4, the sudden is the storm, but in the larger context of life, the sudden is the inevitability of death, which will come for us all...some sooner than others. And when that happens to a friend or loved one, you might think that God is indifferent to us, that He doesn't care about us, and you might become angry and confused. Like Jesus' apostles, whose lives were at risk in the storm, you might protest when he seems to be asleep on the job. Yet I am here to tell you we cannot let anger or fear replace our faith. We cannot respond like Jesus' apostles responded. After all, Jesus did hear their cries for help, didn't he? He did take action. He spoke and the winds and the waves of the Sea of Galilee ceased. He then asked his apostles the very important question, 'Why are you so afraid?' Because he was with them all along, even though they did not know it. He is always with us, even when we think he is not. That is why we cannot let anger and fear—of illness, of life's many hardships...and, yes, anger and fear of losing a friend or loved one—shake our faith as it did Jesus' companions. For when fear knocks at our door, we must send faith to answer—"

"Dale Francis was thirty-four years old!" a man shouted from the back of the pews. "He had three young girls who are gonna grow up without a daddy now. That's something to be angry about!"

I was shocked. I'd never heard anybody shout out like that before during mass. Everybody else was shocked too, it seemed. The church had gone completely silent except for the sounds of people turning to see who had spoken.

I caught a glimpse of a scowling man with red hair wearing a collared shirt and tie.

"Lin Loob was only thirty-six," a brunette woman next to him said loudly. "She had two boys not even ten yet."

Now people were nodding and mumbling and speaking quietly among one another.

Dale Francis and Lin Loob were two of the people who the sheriff had mentioned on the phone conversation with my dad, two of the people who'd died. And I realized: *everybody already knew*. All the adults already knew what was happening around Chatham; they just weren't telling kids like Chunk and me yet.

Father Burridge raised his hands and said, "Everyone, please, please. Let's not lose control here." When he was the center of attention again, he resumed. "Why? Yes, why? Why do bad things happen to good people? Why do bad things happen in general? Why is there war, famine, disease, death? Yes, it's a fair question. Why does a loving and powerful God allow any of these things to happen?" He shook his head slowly. "I wish I had an answer for you, but I don't. I have asked these questions more times than I can count during my lifetime, often after learning of the kind of sudden tragedies that we have all witnessed this week. But I don't have God's mind. I don't share His perspective. In Corinthians we're told, "Now we see things imperfectly, like puzzling reflections in a mirror, but then we will see everything with perfect clarity." So someday in heaven we will understand, but not at present, not from our finite perspectives. And to be frank, the people suffering the most right now, the families of those lost to them this week, don't need a theological treatise. What they need, what we all need, is the very real and comforting presence of Jesus Christ in our lives—"

"What we need," the same man with the red hair shouted, "is to know what's going on in this goddamn town!" There was a chorus of agreement. He continued, "Because three people— three young and healthy people—for them to...well, that just ain't normal."

"It is unusual, I agree," Father Burridge said. "All I can tell you is that we live in an imperfect world—and one of life's cruel realities is that tragedy is always just around the corner—"

"It's got something to do with that Henrickson!" a woman cried. "He's got something to do with this! They never caught his killer!"

The congregation was getting very agitated now. Everyone seemed to be speaking at once.

"People, please!" Father Burridge said. "From what Sheriff

Sandberg shared at his press briefing yesterday, each death was a natural—"

"Bullshit!" someone shouted. That seemed to cut through the chaos, and in the ensuing silence, the man added, "Sorry, Father —I mean no disrespect. But I was good friends with Dale. He was in fine shape. I played ball with him the other weekend. Now, could he drop dead of a heart attack? Sure, I s'pose any of us could. But him and Lin and Jody—all in a matter of days? Who's next? My wife? Me?"

There were more murmurs of agreement. I looked up at my dad. He was staring straight ahead. He was the one who had examined all the dead people and had decided on their causes of death. Was he going to say something?

"Who's next?" Father Burridge said. "I pray with you that there will be no 'next.' Storms don't last forever. They can materialize out of the blue and hurl their fury in fits of rain and lightning and thunder. But then they end. Acts 2:17, 'It shall come to pass.' So, too, will the turbulence of this week. The pain will remain, the sadness will continue, but—"

"What's Sheriff Sandberg covering up?" a woman said. "Eh, Stuart? You gotta know better than anyone. What are you covering up?"

My father turned and spoke loudly and sternly. "I've worked as a funeral director for the citizens of Barnstable County for more than twenty years, Mrs. Dupont. I've consulted and comforted just about everyone in this room at one point or another regarding a deceased family member. I take my responsibilities extremely seriously and have always performed them honestly and honorably. I have never participated in a 'cover-up,' and I find the accusation downright insulting."

"Is it something in the water?" someone shouted.

"Does it got something to do with the dancing?" another shouted.

"That young teacher," a third person exclaimed, "she looked possessed by the devil to me! Both she and Margaret Flatley. Nobody of sound mind goes dancing like that!"

"We need a second opinion!"

"We need to get to the bottom of this!"

"*They were murdered!*"

My father took my mother's hand and led us from the church, all of us doing our bests to ignore the taunts and threats and general craziness being flung our way.

CHAPTER 27

THE TOWER ON THE ROOF

We'd been in such a rush to flee the church that we got to the car before remembering Ralph and Steve were still in the basement in Sunday school, and I had to run back and get them. On the drive home, I'd never seen my dad in such a bad mood. He didn't say anything and he didn't need to: his invisible anger radiated off him in waves. Even my mom knew not to try to talk to him.

In the garage I changed out of my good clothes and stayed away from the house. My dad didn't get angry very often, and when he did he didn't stay that way for very long, so I figured I just had to keep out of his way until dinnertime.

I flopped down on my bed with an *Archie* comic book to kill the time before I went over to Sally's at noon. For some reason *Archie* comics always made me feel better when I was in the dumps. Maybe that was because the stories were so far removed from reality. Stuff like Betty entering a life-size macaroni statue of Archie in a state-wide art contest, or Jinx suffering separation anxiety when Hap throws out her little plush doll. I mean, have you ever heard of such fucked-up shit? But for a twelve-year-old kid that kind of goofy schlock had been perfect. I must have read through my entire collection half a dozen times during the rough stretch following Brittany's death.

There was a bang at my door. I looked up and saw Chunk peeping through the window cut into the top half. I was happy to see him up and about. The way he'd been acting yesterday, I'd figured he might have been bedbound for a week.

He swung open the door and stepped inside. "Whatcha doing, dude?" Dressed in colorful MC Hammer pants and a too-small Teenage Mutant Ninja Turtles tee-shirt busting at the seams, he looked none the worse for wear.

I sat up on the bed and tossed aside the *Archie*. "You all better now?"

He nodded. "Right as rain, fuckface."

"What does that mean anyway, 'right as rain'?"

"Dunno. But my dad always says it when he's feeling good."

After I got Chunk caught up on everything that had happened over the last twenty-four hours, I said, "I ain't never seen people go so crazy in church before."

He looked floored. "They were shouting at your *dad*?"

"It was friggin scary. Like one of those village mobs that go after the monster."

"And *three* people are dead? Holy moly, man. And you think they're all dancing themselves to death? What's making em do that?"

"Something in the water?"

"Fuck that. If it was something in the water, wouldn't everybody in town be dancing?"

"When it's flu season, not everybody gets the flu. You just gotta be unlucky."

"So anybody could catch the dancing bug and croak next? Shit, man. Maybe we should be wearing masks or something?"

"If it's a disease going around."

"What else can it be?"

"Maybe, you know...the devil?" I'd been thinking about the possibility ever since that person had mentioned it right before we were run out of the church. If you'd asked me a few days ago if the devil existed, I'd probably say no. But now with everything that was going on, I wasn't so sure.

"The devil!" Chunk said. "You mean he's *possessing* people? You mean he's *inside* Miss Forrester?"

"I dunno. Maybe. My dad told me the sheriff took Miss and the other woman we saw dancing to the hospital, so if they are possessed, at least there'll be doctors and nurses around to help them." I glanced at the clock on the table next to the bed. "Anyway, I gotta split, man."

Chunk frowned. "You said you were doing nuthin."

"I was before. But now I gotta go."

"Where?"

"None of your business."

"C'mon, dude. Tell me. I always tell you where I'm going."

You couldn't win these arguments with Chunk, so I came out with it. "Sally invited me over to hang out."

Chunk grinned. "Ooh... So you guys are *dating* now? You gonna have a *baby*?"

"Yup, and we're gonna call it Chunky," I said, going to the door. "Now scram. I'm gonna be late."

Outside, while I was locking up, he said, "You think she'll mind if I come too?"

"Yup."

"Maybe I better come and see for myself?"

"Tough luck, Chunk. You're not invited. You can't just keep inviting yourself over to people's houses." I started toward my back fence, then stopped. Chunk was following me. "You can't come."

"You can't stop me," he said defiantly. "I can follow you if I want."

"Chunk, c'mon, please? You weren't invited, and Sally's gonna think I invited you if you come."

"No, she won't. I'll just tell her I followed you."

"Go home."

"Make me."

I flexed my fists. I almost had it in me to wrestle him to the ground. But if I did that, I'd probably get dirty. I'd have to change, and then I'd really be late. Besides, Chunk might hop right up again and continue following me. When he set his mind to something, it was almost impossible to change it—and that wasn't a compliment.

"See ya, Chunk," I said. I hopped the back fence. As I crossed Sally's yard toward her house, I kept looking over my shoulder. Chunk remained on my side of the fence, silently watching me. I have to tell you, the guy might have been my best friend back in those days, but that was some strange shit. The way he just stood there, partly concealed by the bushes along the fence, his face expressionless, was straight out of Michael Myers' playbook.

I thought I was home free, but when I reached the steps to the deck and turned around a final time, he was in Sally's backyard.

Cursing, I sprinted up the steps and banged on the glass sliding door. Sally was in the kitchen. She waved at me to come inside.

I threw open the door and slid it shut behind me. I thumbed the lock.

"Ben?" Sally said, hurrying over. "Is something wrong?"

"Chunk followed me," I told her, realizing how stupid that sounded.

"He *followed* you? What for?"

"He wants to come over too."

"No way! Tell him to go home."

"Sometimes he doesn't listen."

"I'll tell him then. It's my house." We looked through the glass door at him. He stood indecisively on the porch steps. He smiled and waved at us.

"I think we should just ignore him," I said.

"And leave him out there like that?" she said.

"He'll get bored and go home."

"I guess. But that's totally weird."

$$\triangle\triangle\triangle$$

Sally took two cans of Coke from the fridge, and we carried them, along with the plate of snacks she had put together, to the sofa. It turned out she had cable TV and got gnarly channels like HBO, Showtime, ESPN, MTV, and even one that showed only movies. My dad said we might get cable next year, but he'd also said that last year.

Sally was flicking through all the channels with the remote control, asking me what I wanted to watch, when I sat straight and said, "Hold on! Go back!"

She flicked back to the previous channel. "The news?"

"Yeah, look! That's a teacher at my school!"

I couldn't believe it. Mr. Zanardo was dancing on what I presumed was the front porch of his house. His eyes were closed and his face twisted in what could have been either bliss or pain while he played an air guitar and busted moves like he was David Lee Roth or someone.

He looked like a total poser.

A female reporter with a microphone was standing in the foreground and saying, "...apparently this middle school teacher began dancing roughly two hours ago. As you can see, he seems completely oblivious to our presence. Incidentally, another teacher at Chatham Middle School named Jennifer Forrester—a teacher-in-training, I should say—was admitted to Cape Cod Hospital last night. A nurse I spoke with explained that she had to be sedated due to an episode of 'uncontrollable dancing' that had posed a danger to her health."

The screen split to show a male anchor behind a news desk. "Uncontrollable dancing that's a threat to one's health?" he said. "I've never heard of anything like that, Angie."

"I'm not sure what to make of it either, or whether it's somehow related to the...enthusiastic...dancing we're seeing here. But for the moment this man, Tony Zanardo, doesn't seem to be suffering any ill effects...and perhaps the band Men Without Hats put it best when they sang, 'We can dance if we want to.' Back to you, Dan."

△△△

"So Retardo's caught the dancing bug, huh? Couldn't have happened to a nicer guy."

Sally and I whirled around on the sofa.

Chunk stood behind us in the living room, looking for all the world like he was supposed to be there.

"How'd'ya get inside?" Sally demanded.

"How d'ya think, Sherlock? Through the door."

We looked at the sliding door. It was closed. Not to mention I'd locked it.

"The *front* door, geniuses," Chunk said.

"I didn't invite you over!" If she'd been standing, she might have stamped her foot.

"C'mon, man. What's the damage? You invited me over on Friday night."

"And you hurled in my swimming pool!"

He kicked something invisible, scuffing the bottom of his shoe on the carpeted floor. "I don't remember doing that."

"Well, you did."

"Well, I ain't gonna do it now. I ain't never drinking wine again, promise. So can I stay?"

Sally looked at me; I shrugged helplessly. I didn't want to hang out with Chunk. I wanted to be alone with Sally. But I didn't think there was anything we could do to get rid of Chunk short of calling the police.

"Jeez Louise, I guess you can stay then," she said reluctantly.

"Hell yeah!" Chunk cried. "So whatcha guys wanna do?"

"We were gonna watch TV," I said.

"What were yas gonna watch?"

"We were looking for something when we saw Retardo dancing on the news."

"I betcha there are more people around town dancing," Sally said. "Think about it. If *two* of your teachers got the dancing bug or whatever it is, it must be contagious, right?"

"I hope I don't get it," I said. "I hate dancing."

"They can always sedate you," Sally said. "Like they did to your teacher."

"What's sedated mean again?"

"Put to sleep."

"*Put to sleep?*" Chunk said. "Like, forever?"

"Not like an animal gets put to sleep, doofus. It's temporary." She stood up. "I know something we can do. Come with me upstairs."

I had forgotten what the second floor was like, and I peeked into each room we passed. I saw some things I remembered, like the glossy black piano Sally's mom had sometimes played, and I saw some new things too, like a giant aquarium filled with tropical fish, and a glass display cabinet showcasing an assortment of shiny objects.

Sally led us to her mom's office. It was mostly the same as I recalled. A computer sitting on a desk that faced a window. A bookcase that held, among many other books, a full set of encyclopedias (I'd once flicked through one of them on an especially boring day). Framed awards hanging on the walls. There was also a spiral staircase that led to a little tower on the roof. I'd never been allowed to climb it because the steps were metal and curved and steep.

Now Sally snatched a pair of binoculars off the bookcase and hurried up the staircase. Grinning excitedly, Chunk shoved ahead of me to go next.

The tower room wasn't very large, only a little wider than the staircase itself. Windows faced in every direction.

"Rad, man!" Chunk said. "I can see Main Street from here!"

"And the beach," I said.

"There's my house!"

Sally stuck the binoculars to her eyes.

"Whatcha see?" Chunk demanded.

"I'm looking for other people who might be dancing."

"Can I try? Lemme try!"

"Gimme a minute, will you? I just started."

After a few minutes Sally passed the binoculars to me, and after a few more minutes I passed them to Chunk. Neither of us had spotted any dancers. Chunk said he didn't either. But given how keenly he was searching, I had a suspicion he wasn't looking for dancers but was spying into people's windows…and

I was grateful he didn't have a house with a tower on top of it, or a pair of binoculars lying around. If he did, he would probably know what everyone's mom in town looked like naked, mine included.

△△△

When we finally pried the binoculars away from him, we went back downstairs to get something to eat. Chunk ducked into the hallway bathroom to "tinkle," as he put it. When Sally and I were alone in the kitchen, she said, "I wish he didn't hafta come over. I sorta…wanted it to be just you and me…"

I stared at the countertop. "Me too…"

"He's like bubble gum on the bottom of your shoe," she added. "You can't get rid of him."

I laughed. I'd heard Chunk get called a lot of names before, but never bubble gum on the bottom of your shoe.

Sally went to the fridge and said over her shoulder, "My parents called me. They're coming home tomorrow. Then you won't be able to come over anymore."

I frowned. I hadn't been thinking that far ahead. Now that she'd pointed out that returning to her house would be verboten, I felt like I'd been kicked in the nuts. "We can still hang out…just in other places, right?"

She set three Cokes on the counter. "Yeah, but not by *ourselves*. There will always be other people around."

"Oh…" My pulse quickened as I realized what she was getting at.

"So that means today is the last time we can hang out here. And you brought Chunk over."

"I didn't bring him over," I reminded her glumly. "He followed me. Do you—want me to make him go home?"

"He's already here. And he's like bubble gum, remember?" She popped the tab on a Coke and handed it to me. The can was ice-cube cold. "But you can come over later tonight, can't you?"

I blinked. "Tonight?"

"You can sneak out again, right?"

I managed a nod but that was all. *Sally and me alone together in her house—at nighttime!*

I was working on something to say when the toilet flushed and rattled the pipes in the walls.

Sally said, "Make sure you don't tell *him*."

"I won't."

She produced a box of Dunkin Donuts from the pantry, set it on the counter, and opened the top. I closed it again.

She looked at me in surprise. "You don't like donuts?"

"Do you know why we call Chunk 'Chunk'?"

"That's his name, isn't it?"

"His name's Chuck. Like a woodchuck. But everyone started calling him Chunk after they saw *The Goonies* because he looks like the fat kid in it."

Sally giggled. "He totally *does*. Can he do the...what was it called? When he shakes his belly?"

I shook my head. "No way, and don't ask him to. He'll go spastic. He doesn't like being fat. Anyway...the Chunk in the movie can tell the flavor of ice cream just by smelling it, and so can Chunk—"

Chunk appeared. "You guys talking about me?"

"I was telling Sally that you can tell the flavor of ice cream just by smelling it."

"Aw, shut up, Ben. I'm not that fuckin guy in *The Goonies*. He's fat."

"But you've guessed the flavor of ice cream before by smelling it. Can you do it with donuts too?"

Chunk spotted the donuts for the first time. "Oh, man! Donuts!"

Sally said, "And I'll let you keep whichever ones you guess the flavor of."

"I can take them home with me?"

"Sure."

"Deal!"

We blindfolded Chunk with a dishtowel and spun him

around three times. Sally took a chocolate donut from the box and set it on a plate. Chunk leaned forward, whiffed, and said, "Easy! Chocolate glazed."

He licked it with his tongue and set it on the counter next to him.

"Eww!" Sally shrieked. "Barf me out!"

"I don't want you guys taking it back. I won it fair and square. What's the next one?" He started to push up the blindfold before I stopped him.

"No peeking!"

Chunk guessed all the donuts we put in front of him correctly: maple, double chocolate, glazed, cinnamon, and apple fritter. He even managed to guess a vanilla one with those colorful candy sprinkles, as well as a Chocolate Long John, which was just an oddly shaped Boston Cream. How he was able to tell the difference between the two by smell alone, I had no idea.

Next to him sat his winnings, each donut slicked with saliva.

"There're only three left," I said. "One for Sally, one for me, and one more for you, if you can guess it."

All three were powdered with white sugar and looked the same, though I suspected they had different fillings.

I placed one on the plate in front of Chunk.

He bent close, sniffed, and said, "Sugar powdered!"

He made to lick it, but I got it out of the way first.

"Give it back! I guessed it right."

"You guessed the *outside*, but not the *inside*."

"Huh?"

"The filling," Sally said. "It could be lemon cream, custard, strawberry jelly..."

"Raspberry," I added, "blueberry..."

"Forget it, guys! That's cheating! I guessed it already, fair and square."

"Nope, you lose—"

"Stop! Put it back! Lemme try again."

I set the donut back on the plate. Chunk sniffed it...sniffed it again...and again—then shoved his nose right into it, trying to get as much of it into his mouth at the same time.

"Custard!" he cried, bits of cruddy pastry and filling smeared all over his face.

He looked so ridiculous that Sally and I busted a gut until tears came to our eyes.

That would be the final time I would experience that feeling that nothing seemed to matter except what you were doing in the moment and the friends you were with. It was why the memory of that afternoon remained so potent after all these years.

It was, when I think about it, the last time I was ever, truly happy.

CHAPTER 28
THE PRESENT

*S*onofawhore, I thought, looking away from the computer monitor to give my eyes a rest. *I had loved that girl, hadn't I? Sally—I'd loved her. Maybe in a naïve, young way. But I had loved her, I'm pretty sure about that.*

I picked up the tumbler of whiskey next to the keyboard and took a sip. It was warm; the ice cubes had melted long ago. I barely noticed. My mind was filled with regret and longing, reflecting on what was, and wondering about what could have been.

Eventually, reluctantly, I slipped back in time to 1988 and resumed writing.

CHAPTER 29

THE UNEXPECTED VISITOR

We watched a movie called *La Bamba*. It wasn't the kind of thing Chunk or I would normally put on. The VHS cover looked boring and the description on the back didn't sound any better. But Sally told us she had watched it in the theatre a year earlier and it was really good, so we ended up watching it—and it *was* really good. If I was by myself, I might have cried when the singer died at the end, but there was no way I was going to do that in front of other people.

When the credits started rolling, Chunk and I decided to get going. While Chunk was sealing his stash of donuts in Ziploc bags (the ones he hadn't already scarfed down), Sally said quietly, "How about eight o'clock?"

I nodded. "Good with me."

Chunk and I talked about the movie on the way back to my house. When we got there, Chunk called his mom to ask if he could stay longer (he could, until dinner), and then we went to the kitchen, where I looked in the fridge for something to eat. I cut several thick slices of cheese from a block of cheddar and gave half to Chunk. We were about to go to the garage when somebody knocked at the front door.

"I'll get it!" I called upstairs to my parents and answered the door.

I recoiled in surprise. Standing on the porch was the most beautiful woman I had ever laid eyes upon. Her pale, statuesque face seemed stolen from Greek mythology, while her lithe body curved in all the right places beneath her simple black clothes. Luminous, catlike eyes the color of emeralds held me captive with regal apathy. The faintest hint of a smile touched her lips as she said, "Hello, young one. Is your mother home?" Her accent reminded me of the Russian villains in the James Bond movies.

Nodding mutely, I went to the stairs and called, "Mom! Someone's at the door for you!"

"I'll be there in a moment!"

Chunk had joined me in the foyer, and for the first time in his life he was speechless. Both of us stared openly at the mysterious woman. It was rude, but I couldn't look away. I tried. I wanted to. I just...couldn't.

The woman found our gawking amusing as her ghost of a smile became more pronounced. She smoothed her right hand up the outer side of her thigh. Her index finger curled beneath the bottom of her black shirt. She continued to smooth her hand up her body, her shirt going with it. The skin beneath was milky pale like her face, and flawless.

The plump bottom arc of her breast appeared. From beside me Chunk made a croaky sound.

The woman dropped her hand to her side. At the next moment my mom came down the stairs.

The wooly, slow feeling in my head cleared a little, though everything still felt somehow not real.

"Hello?" my mom said to the woman curiously. "Can I help you?"

"May I speak with you for a moment...in private?"

"Ben," my mom said without looking away from the woman, "would you and Chuck give us a minute?"

We went to the kitchen, the door swinging shut behind us. Chunk grabbed my arm and was about to say something. I pressed my finger to my lips and cocked my head, trying to hear what my mom and the woman were talking about.

"*She nearly showed us her boob,*" Chunk whispered to me. "Frickin frackin fudge! If your mom didn't come..."

"*Shhh,*" I hissed. "I'm trying to hear."

But I couldn't hear them talking. I couldn't hear anything. And then the front door clunked shut. The sudden noise made me jump.

"Mom?" I said, pushing open the kitchen door. "Who was that?"

The foyer was empty.

"Mom?" I repeated, wondering if she'd gone outside.

And then I looked into the dining room, which opened off the foyer.

My mom was there.

Dancing by herself.

△△△

"Uh, oh," Chunk said from beside me.

"Mom?" I said.

She ignored me.

I backed away from the silent, horrible scene and bumped into the banister at the bottom of the stairs. "Dad?" I called, my voice cracking. I amped up the volume. "*Daaaaad?*"

Feet thumping through the ceiling. "What is it, Ben?" he demanded, appearing on the staircase landing. "What's wrong?"

I pointed a finger toward the living room. "Mom's dancing."

△△△

My dad tried to get her to stop, but she was totally out of it.

Like Miss Forrester. Like the woman on Seaview Street. Like Mr. Zanardo on the news.

It was as though the world around my mom had ceased to exist.

When my dad grabbed her arms and tried to physically hold her still, she screamed shrilly and thrashed in his grip.

"For Christ's sake, Mel, stop this—"

My mom snatched a cast-iron figure of a man on a horse from

the fireplace mantel and swung it at my dad, striking him in the side of the head. The figure flew from her hand, crashing heavily to the hardwood floor. My dad dropped to his knees, pressing a hand to the side of his head.

"Dad!" I shouted, rushing to his side.

He got to his feet and ushered me ahead of him out of the room. When we were back in the foyer with Chunk, I saw that he'd left a trail of blood across the floor and that the shoulder of his Hawaiian shirt was stained red. More blood was spurting out from between his head and hand.

Ralph and Steve had appeared on the landing above us. Their eyes were wide and frightened.

"Daddy...?" Steve said, about to burst into tears.

"Boys, go to your bedroom. Everything's fine." They obeyed, and he went to the kitchen, returning with a dish towel pressed to his head. He opened the front door. "Watch your brothers while I'm gone, Ben," he told me over his shoulder. "Keep an eye on your mother too. For God's sake, don't touch her, don't get close to her. But keep an eye on her. I'll be back shortly."

△△△

Chunk and I listened to my mom moving around in the living room, although we couldn't see her from our position on the lower steps of the staircase. That was okay with me. Watching her dance would likely drive me mental. I kept thinking about the people who had died in town and their bruised and bloodied feet. Was this going to be my mom's fate? Would she keep dancing until she collapsed from a heart attack or stroke? Was my dad going to drive her to the funeral home in the back of his van?

Chunk ate the cheese I'd given him earlier, then he ate my slices too since I no longer had an appetite. I could tell he was growing bored because he kept sighing loudly and shifting his weight. I told him he could go home if he wanted to, but he never did. I'd like to believe he was being a good friend, but he was likely only sticking around in the hopes of something morbid happening.

At one point he said, "Why'd'ya think she showed us her boob?"

I didn't know and I didn't care.

"You think she woulda let us touch it if your mom hadn't come down?"

I didn't say anything.

"She was babelicious. Like Elvira, but prettier..."

I checked my wristwatch. "Wonder what's taking my dad so long?"

"He hadda get stitched up. Your mom whacked him mad hard. Lucky he didn't bleed to death."

I was looking at the spot on the floor where the blood had been. I'd cleaned it up with a towel that I'd tossed in the laundry room sink.

"You think they're gonna hafta put your mom to sleep?" Chunk said after some silence between us.

"I don't know," I said solemnly.

"They probably are. And who knows when she's gonna wake up again? I wonder if Miss Forrester has woken up yet?"

When I heard a car pull into the driveway, I leaped to my feet. Through one of the front door side-windows I saw my dad's brown van lurch to a stop. The sheriff's car and an ambulance pulled over at the curb. My dad began talking to Sheriff Sandberg and two paramedics on the sidewalk. The paramedics took a metal stretcher from the back of the ambulance and pushed it on clacking shopping trolley wheels up the driveway.

I opened the door for them and moved back to the stairs so I didn't get in the way. My dad glanced at Chunk and me when he entered but didn't say anything. A clean white bandage wreathed his head.

Sheriff Sandberg tipped his Stetson in acknowledgment of us and said, "Don't you boys go nowhere. I want to have a word with you in a moment."

Then he and the paramedics joined my dad in the living

room. I heard them speaking in low voices. Abruptly my mom screamed. Chunk and I hustled to the living room. My dad stood behind my mom, his arms wrapped around her upper body in a bear hug. She writhed back and forth, flailing her head and kicking her legs in the air. It was no use. My dad—not a large man, but bigger than she was—held her good and tight.

One of the paramedics jabbed a needle into my mom's left arm and depressed the plunger.

She continued to scream and twist and kick, the needle poking stubbornly out of her arm like a spent tranquilizer dart in a wild animal. After about ten seconds she grew sluggish and floppy before passing out cold in my dad's arms.

The paramedics strapped her onto the stretcher and wheeled her out to the ambulance. My dad went with them.

Ralph and Steve were on the staircase landing again, both of them crying.

"Is mommy okay, Ben?" Ralph asked me in a small voice.

"Yeah, Ralphy. She's fine."

"Why was she yelling?"

"She had to have a needle. And you know how bad needles feel. But she's going to the hospital now with dad. She's gonna be fine. So you guys go on back to your room. Okay? I'll come up in a bit."

When they disappeared back up the stairs, Sheriff Sandberg said to me, "Your father mentioned that you answered the door earlier, Ben. There was someone there to see your mother. Is that right?"

I nodded. "It was a woman."

"A bitchin hot woman," Chunk added.

"Did she say why she wanted to see your mother?"

I shook my head. "She said she wanted to talk to her in private, so we went to the kitchen."

"So you didn't see anything...unusual?"

"Like what?"

"You tell me."

I started to shake my head...then paused.

"What is it, son?"

"She showed us her boob," Chunk offered.

"Excuse me?"

"She *almost* showed it to us," I said. "She lifted her shirt like she was going to show us, but then my mom came down the stairs."

The sheriff's craggy, handsome face turned skeptical. "Why do you reckon she did that?"

"Guess she liked us," Chunk said with a shrug.

The sheriff studied us for a hard moment and said, "This is serious business, boys."

"We ain't kidding," I said. "Swear to God."

"You didn't see anything in the woman's hand?"

"Like what?" I asked.

"You tell me."

"No, nuthin."

"I didn't see nuthin neither," Chunk said.

My dad returned and told the sheriff, "I'm going to follow behind the ambulance to the hospital. Is there anything you need from me before I go?"

"These boys say there was a woman at your door. I'd like to get them to describe her to a sketch artist if you don't mind?"

My dad nodded. "Ben, do you think you'd be able to describe the woman to a sketch artist?"

I nodded. Her face was crystal clear in my mind.

"Chuck?"

"Sure, Mr. Graves. Easy."

"I don't think they need to come down to the station," the sheriff said. "I can have the artist who does the freelance work come over here while you're at the hospital."

"That's fine. Ben, you heard the sheriff. He's going to send someone here while I'm gone. You and Chuck cooperate with him, you hear?"

I nodded again and said, "I just remembered something else. She had a tattoo."

"What kind of tattoo?" the sheriff asked.

"A red one, right here." I pointed to my left wrist. "It was like four or five bars in a row."

Sheriff Sandberg slapped his hands together. To my dad he said, "Doggonit! It's that *gypsy*."

"What gypsy?"

"You would have seen the lot of them in mid-August. They were in Gould Park every day for nearly two weeks, swindling tourists and all that."

"This woman with the tattoo was one of them?"

"She was one of them, all right. Had a little fortune-telling hustle of her own. Seemed to be in charge of the operation. Came to the station to get a permit for them to set up camp out in Ryders Field. Two weeks ago, she was back. Wanted another permit."

"And you gave it to her?"

"Why not? Nobody else goes out that way no more."

My dad shook his head. "I don't get it. Mel and I don't know her. Why's she knocking on our door? Why'd she…?" He bit off the last of the question.

"I have no idea, Stu. But I don't know nobody else who has a tattoo like the one your boy described."

"So what are you thinking? A gypsy *cursed* my wife? Please don't tell me you think that, Keith."

"I ain't saying that at all. Why don't you head off to the hospital? You need to be with Melinda right now. I'll head out to Ryders Field and find out what that woman was doing here. Hopefully I'll have some answers for you by tonight."

My dad hesitated, then nodded. "Boys, I'd like you not to mention any of what you've heard here for now, not until the sheriff and I know more. Will you promise me that?"

"I promise, Dad," I said.

"I promise," Chunk said.

"Ben, I don't know how long I'll be at the hospital. I might stay there overnight. You'll have to look after your brothers while I'm gone. That means making them dinner and making sure they're in bed by nine. Can you do that for me?"

I nodded. "Sure, Dad. No problem."

CHAPTER 30

THE REVOLVER

After Sheriff Sandberg and my dad left, I went straight to the basement. It wasn't furnished like Vanessa Delaney's. The floor was cemented and the walls and ceiling were unfinished, revealing the timber studs. Among the junk down there were all my dad's tools, as well as boxes filled with old *Time* and *National Geographic* and *Popular Mechanics* magazines. The Sears Craftsman lawnmower that I used to make a buck in the summer sat in a corner by itself, redolent of cut grass and gasoline.

In the furnace room I lifted a small plastic case off of the high windowsill and set it on a folding table cluttered with ice cream containers brimming with nails, screws, and other fasteners. I opened the case's lid and lifted out a heavy black handgun with wooden grips.

Chunk, who'd followed me downstairs, said, "Oh, man! What're you gonna do with *that*?"

I removed the egg foam the revolver had been resting on and collected the four brass cartridges that had been hidden beneath. I'd found them when I'd first discovered the handgun last winter.

"Seriously, man! What're you gonna do with it? You gonna shoot it?"

"I'm going to Ryders Field," I told him.

Chunk's eyes bugged. "*What?*"

"I'm gonna make the gypsy woman tell me what she did to my mom. I'm gonna make her tell me how to make my mom better again."

"Whoa, dude..." he said hesitantly.

I scowled. "People are dying, Chunk. They're dancing themselves to death, and the adults aren't doing anything about it! Now my mom's one of the people dancing. She was put to sleep, but what happens when she wakes up? We know it's that gypsy woman who cursed her—"

"And the sheriff's gonna go talk to her..."

"Yeah, talk to her. And she's just gonna tell him everything?"

"He's the sheriff. She has to."

"I don't think so. He ain't got proof. She'll just tell him she didn't do nothing wrong. She might even tell him she didn't come to my house at all. And then it's just our word against hers, and we're just kids."

"So you're gonna blow her brains out? How's she gonna tell you anything then?"

"If I have to shoot her, I'll shoot her somewhere safe, like in the leg."

Chunk frowned. "I dunno, Ben... Shooting someone is pretty major..."

I stuffed the handgun in one pocket, and the bullets in the other.

"So's making my mom dance herself to death," I said.

△△△

Out behind the garage I got on my mountain bike. "Don't tell anyone where I'm going."

"What if the gypsy woman curses *you*?" Chunk said.

"I have the gun. I won't let her get close to me."

"Sheesh, Ben. You're going for real?"

"Ryders Field ain't that far."

"But it's totally off-limits."

I knew that. Ever since the murders there four years ago, we'd been warned to stay away, even in the daytime. But I didn't have a choice if I wanted to help my mom.

"I'll call you when I get back."

"How long you gonna be?"

"I dunno. Not that long."

"Back before six?"

"I dunno. Maybe. Why?"

"Because that's what time I gotta be home for dinner, remember?"

I was surprised. "You wanna come with me?"

"Well…it's important to find out what's happening to your mom, right?"

I studied Chunk suspiciously. Offering to help with anything was very unlike him; he always had his reasons for doing what he did, and they usually involved either food or something perverted.

And that was when I realized he probably *did* have his reasons for wanting to come with me to Ryders Field. He wanted to see the gypsy woman again. He wanted to see me pointing the gun at her and making her scared, maybe making her beg and cry. He liked stuff like that in the movies, and he probably liked it in real life too. In fact, I wouldn't be surprised if he thought he might somehow get a glimpse of her boob again. That was just how his mind worked.

Nevertheless, whatever his motivation was to join me, I didn't care. I'd feel a lot better about going to Ryders Field with him tagging along than going by myself.

"Do you want me to wait here while you go get your bike?" I asked him.

"Nah. My mom might see me going into the garage, then I'll hafta s'plain where I'm going. Better if I just borrow your old one."

"It's over there," I said, pointing to where it had been stashed between the back deck and the fence. "But it's pretty small…"

Chunk pulled it out and hopped onto the old-fashioned banana seat.

"Where are you guys going?"

We looked toward the voice and saw Sally on her side of the backyard fence. She climbed over it and joined us.

"What are you doing here?" I asked her.

"I saw the ambulance at your house and got worried."

I frowned. "How'd you see it?"

"I saw it go past my house, and it made me wonder if somebody else had died from dancing. So I went up to the tower and saw the ambulance parked in front of your house, along with the sheriff's car. I didn't want to come over while they were still here, so I waited until they left. So—did something happen?"

$$\triangle\triangle\triangle$$

"You're going to *Ryders Field*?" she asked when I finished explaining everything.

"And we gotta go now if we're gonna be back by six," Chunk said.

"You're gonna *shoot* the gypsy woman?"

"Probably not," I told her. "I'm just gonna use the gun to scare her into telling me what she did to my mom."

"Is it loaded?"

"No, but I have bullets for it."

"Jeez, Ben, are you sure about this…?"

"Ben, we gotta *go*," Chunk complained. "If I'm late for dinner, my mom's gonna have a cow."

"He's right," I said. "We better get going."

"Can I come?"

"Oh, brother," Chunk said, exhaling loudly.

Sally scowled at him. "What's your damage?"

"You can't come with us. You're a *girl*."

"So what if I'm a girl?"

"You'll slow us down, and I gotta be back by six."

"Do you have a bike?" I asked, happy she'd offered to come along as well.

"Of course," she said, "and it's way faster than that one donut boy's riding."

△△△

Sally's bike was nearly brand new and had twenty-one speeds, compared to my eighteen and Chunk's six. We took Main Street to Queen Anne Road, which was a little dangerous because there were no sidewalks on parts of it, which meant we had to stick to the narrow shoulder or the grass. Sally led the way for most of the trip, with me sometimes pulling abreast. Chunk lagged behind us, and we had to wait a couple of times at street corners for him to catch up.

When Sally and I reached the turn-off into The Triangle, we stopped once again to wait for Chunk.

"Do you for real have a gun, Ben?" she asked me, brushing aside her bangs which had fallen across her eyes.

I nodded but didn't take it out of my backpack to show her. There were houses on the street and somebody might see me.

"Where'd you get it?"

"It's my dad's."

"You're not actually gonna try to shoot the gypsy woman, are you?"

"I don't think so."

"Not even in the leg?"

"I just want to scare her into thinking I'm gonna shoot her, so she fesses up about everything."

"Because if you tried shooting her, and you missed her leg, you might hit her somewhere else, like in the heart. If she died, you'd go to jail. Just so you know."

I clenched my jaw. She wasn't listening. "I'm *not* gonna shoot her, okay? I don't know why I said that. I was angry."

"Well, that's good. I'm only making sure."

Chunk finally reached us. His face was red and he was wheezing heavily.

"You okay, speedy?" Sally asked him.

"Bite me," he said. "Your bike's just better than this one, that's all. Wanna trade?"

"No way. You're all gross and sweaty. Besides, we're almost there."

She started down the two-lane road that disappeared into the dense woods.

Chunk and I followed.

CHAPTER 31

THE CAPE COD KILLER

Ryders Field was at the end of a pitted dirt road that branched off from the main one. A small clearing of land cut out of the surrounding forest, it used to be Chatham's drive-in theater. There had been a single large screen with five rows of parking in front of it, a ticket booth, a concession stand, and a small playground. My last and clearest memory of the drive-in was watching a double feature. The first movie was *The Karate Kid*. The second, *Police Academy*, was funny, especially the guy who could mimic any sound he wanted with his mouth, but I ended up falling asleep about halfway through it.

That had been at the start of the summer four years ago when I was eight. Near the end of that same summer a woman's body was discovered at the drive-in. A man working his way through a six-pack of Budweiser in his car had gone to a tree to take a leak—and realized he was pissing on a skull that had been partially unearthed in the recent rain. I'd heard that the movie that had been playing that night was John Carpenter's *The Thing*—but the discovery of the skull would have been the real fright of the evening. In the following days the police ended up finding three more skeletonized bodies. They all turned out to be females, all in their twenties. They had been chopped up with an axe into smaller pieces. For the rest of the summer it seemed all anybody was talking about were missing girls and shallow graves and dismembered bodies. The drive-in closed down and never reopened.

A TV documentary about the murders was produced last year. The killer had looked normal enough, even a bit geeky, with thick eyeglasses and a mustache. In 1984 he finished college in a different state and moved into a boarding house in Chatham. He had gotten odd jobs around town as a handyman, as well as gigs as a babysitter. Everybody who was interviewed said he seemed shy but friendly. One of the interviewees was a girl only a couple of years older than me. The man had babysat her, and she all but gushed about him, recalling how he would buy her ice cream and drive her around town in his pickup truck. She also described a time he showed her his "secret garden" in the woods. No bodies had been buried there, but fuck. What was the girl doing frolicking around in the woods with a much older male babysitter? She was lucky she was a talking head in the documentary, and not one of the dead and buried ones.

The police caught the killer soon after the first body was discovered at the drive-in, and he was in prison now. He seemed happy enough and even took pride in showing off all the correspondence with women who wanted to date him. I didn't —and still don't—get that. Didn't the women understand that if he ever got out of prison, and they went on a date, his idea of romance would likely include a visit to a dark woodshed filled with bloody instruments of death?

Nobody knew whether there were more bodies buried somewhere. At the killer's trial the judge asked him if he had anything to say about his crimes, and he replied flippantly, "Keep digging."

If you ask me, the guy should have been fried in the electric chair. Is that a cruel and unusual punishment? Sure is. But not half as cruel as what he did to those young girls three decades ago. Fortunately for him, and unfortunately for justice, Massachusetts abolished the death penalty a month before he was sentenced, and he got consecutive life sentences instead.

Halfway along the dirt road Sally and I stopped to let Chunk catch up. He had fallen so far behind that we couldn't see him anymore.

"Your friend is like mega slow," she said.

"He's faster on his own bike," I said. "He's riding my old one, and it only has six speeds."

"I don't know why you guys are such good friends."

"What'd'ya mean?"

"You're...so different."

"We've been best friends since fifth grade."

"Doesn't he bug you though?"

"Not really." I shrugged. "Sometimes, I guess. But he can be funny too."

Sally was looking down the road. Tall evergreens crowded the edges of it, along with a mix of other trees already showing spindly, dead-looking branches. The leaves that had fallen to the ground were burnt yellow and fiery red and mud brown and smelled like Halloween. On the one hand, this might have been one of the prettiest roads I'd ever seen. On the other, it was quietly scary. The silence felt heavy like it had a real presence. I couldn't help but think about the chopped-up bodies that had been buried out here, and how isolated we were from anybody else.

Sally must have been thinking along the same lines, because she said, "What kinda psychopath kills people just for the fun of it?"

"That's what psychopaths do."

"Yeah, but *why*?"

"I guess they just hate other people."

"I don't know about that. I don't think they *can* hate, just like they can't love anyone. They don't have emotions."

I tried to imagine somebody without emotions—never laughing, never crying, never smiling—and I decided that was impossible.

"Everybody has emotions," I said.

"Not psychopaths," she insisted.

"The guy who killed those women was a psychopath, and he

smiled. I saw him doing it on the TV show about him when he was talking about all the women sending him love letters."

"Psychopaths can still smile. But they're faking it. They're not happy."

I thought about it and decided she could be right. Because how could you cut off somebody's head and not feel bad about what you were doing? I wondered if the killer was fake-smiling while he murdered the women with his axe and then dug their graves.

The image made my skin crawl.

"Here comes speedy," Sally said.

Chunk was tooling up the dirt road toward us, sort of swooping from one side of it to the other, making big S's, pedaling lazily.

When he finally reached us, I said, "Thought you might have chickened out."

He made a face. "Why would I chicken out? The gypsy's not scary. She's *bodacious*."

"I wasn't talking about her. I meant Ryders Field."

He shrugged. "The sicko's in jail. What's there to be scared about? What...?"

"Nothing," I said.

"Why are you looking like that?"

"Like what?"

A big smile broke across his face. "*You're* scared."

I shook my head. "Not really."

"Scaredy-cat! Ben's a scaredy-cat!"

The truth was, the talk about psychopaths had shaken me up. Emotionless people who could pretend to be just like the rest of us while secretly dismembering others seemed a lot more frightening than guys like Freddy Krueger and Michael Myers—guys you knew were psycho just by looking at them.

"We don't hafta go, if you don't wanna, Ben," Sally said.

"*Scaredy-cat Ben's a—*"

"Zip it, Chunky!"

"That's not my name!" he exploded. "It's Chunk. C-H-U-N-K.

Got that, bimbette?"

"Keep it down, man," I told him. "You're gonna wake the dead." I thought about my mom lying in a hospital bed and maybe never being allowed to wake up because she'd start dancing again and die. I told Sally, "I ain't turning back."

"You sure?"

"Car!" Chunk bellowed.

△△△

We couldn't see it yet, but we could hear it.

"Who's that?" I asked, alarmed.

"Dunno," Chunk said. "But we better blitz."

Sally was already wheeling her bike off the road and into the trees. Chunk and I hurried after her. When we were a good way in, we dumped our bikes on their sides and dropped to our chests.

My face was right next to Sally's. I could hear her breathing quickly.

The noise of the engine grew louder, then a brown Ford appeared through the scrub. There was no doubt who it belonged to. It had a red-and-blue lightbar on the roof, a big star emblazoned on the door, and SHERIFF 1 written above the front wheel.

"It's the sheriff!" Chunk said.

"Shhhh!" Sally said.

I was positive Sheriff Sandberg would see us. He would stop his car and get out and demand to know what we were doing. He would find the gun on me and tell my dad. He might even throw me in jail for the night to teach me a lesson—

The car continued past us, and then it was gone.

I looked at Sally because I felt her looking at me.

We were so close we could touch noses if we tried.

"Close call," she said, grinning.

"Yeah," I said, also grinning, and I was overwhelmed with an urge to kiss her.

I might have if Chunk wasn't right beside us, pushing himself nosily to his knees.

"Guess Sheriff Sandberg didn't come straight here after your house, Ponch," he said.

Reluctantly, I sat up. "Guess not. He musta gone to the station first."

"Probably to pick up his deputy," Sally said. She was on her feet, brushing leaves and dirt from her knees.

Chunk and I got to our feet too, but we didn't care about the dirt. We picked our bikes up.

"Deputy?" I said.

"It looked like there were two people in the car."

"Who cares who was with him?" Chunk said, already hightailing it back to the road. "Now we're not gonna miss anything! If we hurry, we can see him give the gypsy babe shit."

I propped my bike against a tree and picked up Sally's bike and angled the handlebars toward her.

"Guys, stop farting around! We're gonna—"

"Chill, will you?" I told him. "We're coming already."

CHAPTER 32

THE PRESENT

W hen I'd finished writing for the afternoon, I slapped the laptop lid closed and said, "Halle-fucking-lujah." That was what I meant to say, at any rate. What my ears heard was something butchered and slurred. I looked at the empty tumbler next to the keyboard. How many had I had today? No idea. I did remember, however, cracking open a new bottle when I began drinking just after twelve-thirty.

I glanced over at the kitchenette, where I'd left the whiskey bottle on the counter after my last pour. It was more than half empty. I was ashamed and angry at seeing how much I'd drunk, but I wasn't surprised. Half a liter of whiskey a day had become par for the course these last couple of weeks.

You've become an alcoholic, a voice in my head told me coolly.

Yeah, maybe, I thought. *But only a temporary one.*

While writing my previous books, I'd limited myself to two standard drinks in the afternoon. Just enough to wet the ice cubes in the glass and allow me to enjoy the mellow flavor of the whiskey. *The Dancing Plague* began with the same restraint, but it wasn't long before those two drinks became three, then four. At the same time the 1.5-ounce pours were growing to two ounces, then three.

Half a liter in what? Three hours? Four?

Twelve standard drinks.

It was all the reminiscing, the reliving, the return of

memories better left buried. It was driving me batty, and booze was my coping mechanism. But that was okay, that was just fine. When the story was finished, my bingeing would be too. Maybe I'd go cold turkey for a month simply to prove to myself that I could.

I picked up one of the photographs of Brittany from next to the monitor. Wearing a white ballerina costume, tutu and all, she was pirouetting, an adorable simulacrum of the little ballerina that had sprung to life in her music box when it was opened.

I set the photo back on the desk and got to my feet, swaying slightly. I grabbed my leather jacket and left the apartment. In the hallway I hesitated. I hadn't seen Nessa in over a month now. Not since I'd clocked her husband in the lobby. I figured it was past time I apologized. Her husband might have been a first-class asshole, but he *was* her husband. I didn't have a right to punch him. In fact, he could have sued me for assault. The fact he hadn't...perhaps that was Nessa's influence? Perhaps I owed her an apology *and* a thank you.

I went to her door, told myself to act sober, then knocked. I heard someone moving inside the apartment. The chain lock jangled and the door opened.

Nessa appeared surprised to see me. "Ben?" she said. "What are you doing here?"

That wasn't exactly the greeting I'd been expecting. Before I could say anything, her husband—Rudy—appeared behind her.

"*You?*" he barked, his animus toward me clear. "What the hell are *you* doing here?"

"I'm out of sugar," I said. It sounded just as idiotic as I knew it would.

"Sugar, my ass!" He stepped aggressively forward but quickly stopped, probably remembering my right cross.

My left knee gave out. I bobbed like I was curtsying but didn't fall over. I grabbed the doorframe to steady myself and hiccuped.

"Think...I should probably go," I said, wondering why I suddenly felt so drunk. I'd been fine just a few minutes ago. I started away down the hallway, my feet heavy.

"You fucking lush!" Rudy called after me. "Stay away from my wife!"

I flicked him the bird without looking back.

The door to the apartment slammed shut. Yelling commenced on the other side of it. I jabbed the elevator button and was thankful when the doors opened immediately. I stumbled into the cab, colliding with one of the mirrored panels. The doors slid shut and the shouting receded.

I cursed, not only because I'd just made a jackass of myself, but because I'd gotten Nessa into trouble. But how was I to know the deadbeat husband would be over? Was that the reason she hadn't knocked on my door in so long? Had they rekindled their marriage? Had I just fucked it all up for them?

I realized the elevator wasn't moving.

When the buttons on the control panel stopped swimming, I hit the one for the lobby.

△△△

I took my usual route home, passing all the usual suspects: the Irish pub where I'd have a pint or two of Guinness on occasion; the Middle Eastern restaurant where I sometimes ordered takeout; the Boston Massacre Site, which was a popular meeting spot nowadays. Three teenagers absorbed in their phones were currently standing on the cobblestone commemoration, most likely oblivious to its significance.

It was late afternoon, gray and snowing, yet despite the dreary weather the streets were bustling with traffic and pedestrians and vendors. In many of the storefront windows Christmas was on full display. Colorful fairy lights decorated trees while festive wreaths adorned lampposts. For the most part I was separated from it all, my senses dulled, my mind disinterested. All I wanted to do was get home and drop into bed.

I wound through the narrow, gaslit streets of Beacon Hill down to Beacon Street. Across the road was Boston Common.

Sometimes both on the way to the apartment and on the way home I would detour through the park to see the statues and memorials and flowers. I believed the squirrels there recognized me, and so they should, as I often saved some of my hotdog bun for them. Frog Pond, where kids swam in the summer, was now frozen over and served as a skating rink. Last winter I'd skated on it twice a week. This winter I had yet to go once.

While waiting at a red traffic light, I lit a cigarette. My clumsy fingers fumbled with the lighter while trying to return it to my pocket. It dropped to the slushy sidewalk and bounced away from me. I bent over to retrieve it and ended up falling onto my side. I couldn't remember the last time I'd been so demonstrably intoxicated. I was outside a Starbucks and could feel people watching me through the windows. My face burned with embarrassment. A dad walking with his kid asked if I was all right. I nodded and pushed myself back to my feet to prove I was steady-footed. And I was. The lightheadedness from the cigarette had passed.

The light turned green. I continued. After several blocks lined with Victorian brownstones I arrived at my place. I stopped halfway up the front steps.

I didn't have my keys.

I double-checked all my pockets.

"Dammit," I mumbled, looking back down Beacon Street. Had I dropped them when I somersaulted? Or had I left them in the apartment? I thought it might have been the latter; I couldn't remember locking the door.

"*Dammit.*" There was no way I was going to walk all the way back. A cab? I dismissed that option as well. I was too tired.

I tried the front door on the off chance I hadn't locked it. I had. Rubbing my hands together to generate some warmth, I went to the alleyway that ran behind my block of townhouses and stopped in the little brick area that served as my parking lot/backyard.

Above my back door was a landing where a wrought-iron ladder led to the third-floor balcony. The door up there would be locked but the windows wouldn't be. I often opened them, even in the winter, to let in some fresh air. I was usually too lazy to lock them again.

But how would I get up on the landing?

I studied the black pipes attached to the side of the adjacent building and wondered if I could shimmy up them. It took me all of two seconds and a half-hearted attempt to realize I had no shot in hell.

Then I spotted the big recycling bin next to my SUV. I wheeled it over to the door and climbed on top of it.

Standing carefully, arms out at my side as though I were learning to surf, I was pleased to find my chest was now parallel with the landing. All I had to do was heave myself up. There was nothing to grab onto to help me, however, so I decided to throw a leg up onto the landing and then kind of roll on up.

Bad idea.

As soon as I kicked up my leg, the bin wobbled beneath my foot.

Like the time I'd fallen off the ladder while painting the crown moldings in my foyer, I experienced a split second of clarity in which I told myself I was going to fall and there was nothing I could do about it.

Sure enough, in the next moment the recycling bin disappeared beneath my foot and I dropped like a rock, landing hard on the brick ground.

Groaning and swearing and wondering whether I had broken anything, I forced myself back to my feet before anybody saw me lying there and called the police.

In frustration I drove my fist against the back door. As an afterthought I tried the handle.

The door swung inward.

Too cold and miserable to find humor in the situation, I limped inside and dropped into bed.

CHAPTER 33
RYDERS FIELD

The big white movie screen, torn in places and grimy from years of weather and neglect, stood against a dark backdrop of evergreen trees. The top right corner had folded over on itself like a dog-eared page of a paperback novel. A dozen or so vehicles (beat-up sedans and A-Team vans and brightly painted pickup trucks) were parked haphazardly before it. Two motorhomes towered above the rest. One had the bed compartment suspended up over the cab, while the other resembled a bus. A galloping unicorn was painted on the side of that one.

Three smoky fires roared and danced in stone-ringed pits. A handful of people sat in folding chairs around each, holding brown beer bottles and smoking grass and cigarettes. Their voices and laughter rose into the dreary gray afternoon, though it was difficult to hear what they were talking about from where we crouched in the trees at the edge of the clearing.

The sheriff's car, empty, was parked in front of us, next to the timber skeleton of the old ticket booth.

"They must be in that tent," Sally said, and I assumed she was talking about the sheriff and his deputy. The tent she spoke of was off to the right of the vehicles. It reminded me of a circus big top, only much smaller. The front canvas flap hung open, though the interior was lost in shadows.

"We needa get closer," Chunk said. "Can't see shit from here."

I swallowed, indecisive. When I'd decided to come out here to face off with the gypsy woman, I'd figured I'd find her and a couple of her gypsy friends. I'd show them the revolver, and they'd put up their hands and answer whatever questions I asked.

I wasn't expecting...*this*. All the cars, all the people. Booze, drugs, fires. It was *bigger* than me, if you can dig that. It made me feel more than ever that I was just a kid.

I said, "I don't know if this is such a good idea, after all."

"Don't pussy out, man!" Chunk said. "You wanna find out what's wrong with your mom, don't you?"

"If we try to get any closer, someone's gonna see us. The sheriff will find out we're here."

"No, man. We keep to the woods and circle toward the tent. When we're on the far side of it, we can sneak close and peek in with nobody seeing us."

I looked at Sally.

"Up to you, Ben," she said. "I don't mind going home if you want to. But he's right. If we sneak around to the far side of the tent, we can probably get close enough to hear what's going on inside."

"*See* what's going on inside," Chunk said. "And Ben can find out what's wrong with his mom."

I decided we had come too far to turn around. If we could overhear the sheriff grilling the gypsy woman, that would be something...enough, at least, to make this impromptu adventure worthwhile. And if the sheriff caught us somehow, well, I didn't have to tell him I had my dad's gun with me, did I? I could tell him that I was worried about my mom and wanted to learn what he'd learned from the gypsy woman, which was all true. He would probably still tell my dad I was here. But it wasn't like I was really doing anything wrong. It was still before dinnertime. I would be home in time to make Ralph and Steve some sandwiches or pancakes, or whatever they wanted. The only thing I would have done that I wasn't allowed to do was go to Ryders Field because it was off-limits...

Sally and Chunk were looking expectantly at me.

"Let's try not to make too much noise," I said.

△△△

When we stepped out from the woods behind the tent, I felt as though all the eyes in the world were upon us. Of course, that was just my overactive imagination. The tent stood between us and the fires. There was no way any of the adults could see us stealing across the grass.

Chunk darted ahead of Sally and me, bounding from tiptoes to tiptoes in a comically exaggerated way (not unlike how the agents in *Spy vs Spy* sneaked around). When he reached the tent's back flap, which mirrored the one on the front, he waved for us to join him.

We crouched next to him. I couldn't hear anybody talking. I frowned at Chunk. He shrugged back.

Then the three of us peeked around the edge of the flap, our heads stacked on top of each other like a totem pole.

Candles lit the darkness gathered inside the tent, revealing the shadowy forms of several large coolers and boxes that most likely contained perishable food and dry goods; about a dozen cases of Perrier sparkling water stacked in a tower next to an equal number of cases of Pepsi-Cola; several lidded plastic bins that could have contained anything; and a red Honda generator squatting next to four rusty jerry cans.

Sheriff Sandberg sat on the grassy ground near the center of the tent, his trousers and jockeys bunched down around his cowboy boots. The gypsy woman was buck naked and straddling him, her ashen legs hooked around his waist, her hands gripping his shoulders. She was rocking up and down rhythmically, her breasts arched out in front of her, her head tilted back so her glossy black hair trailed down her back to the top of her buttocks. The fully clothed deputy stood nearby, watching them expressionlessly.

My mind reeled.

I couldn't make sense of the bizarre scene—not only why the sheriff was having sex with the gypsy woman, but why the deputy was just standing by.

Was he waiting for his turn? Were they *raping* her?

No—they couldn't be. She was the one on top of the sheriff and seemed to be doing all the work.

So was she raping *him*?

Could women rape men? I couldn't fathom how.

I dragged my eyes away from the pseudo-orgy and nudged Sally with my elbow to get her attention.

Her cheeks had gone flamingo pink. At first I thought she might have been embarrassed by the sex, and maybe she was. Yet there was something else, a depth and intensity to her gaze, that made me think of her when we'd been dancing at her house and the song had stopped.

She'd looked like she'd wanted to be kissed then, and she looked that way now too.

Is she *horny?* I wondered in an epiphany. *Is seeing the sheriff and gypsy woman doing it turning her on?*

Shaking her head slightly, sort of in amazement, and sort of to say she didn't know what was going on either, she returned her attention to the tent.

After a glance at Chunk (his mouth hung open dumbly, a broken string of drool glued to his chin), I did too.

The gypsy woman began moving faster. With each thrust of her pelvis she issued a throaty exhalation that grew louder and louder, more guttural and savage, before culminating in an ecstatic cry that could have been mistaken for one of tremendous pain.

She slumped forward against the sheriff. For a long moment she remained unmoving except for the rise and fall of her chest as she worked to catch her breath.

Finally she stood. The sheriff didn't have an erection, but his thing was still engorged and larger than what seemed normal, making it rather obvious that he *had* had an erection (a foregone conclusion given the gypsy woman's euphoric rocking).

I stared at the curves and valleys of the gypsy woman's body. The slopes of her breasts. The roundness of her hips. The tautness of her stomach and legs.

Her nipples were strawberry pink in contrast to the creamy white of her skin. The pubic hair below her naval was the same black as the hair on her head, and the mere sight of it, something so forbidden, made me lightheaded.

"Get dressed," the gypsy woman told the sheriff, who immediately reached for his jockeys and trousers and tugged them up his hairy legs. Then she turned and looked directly at us. "Show's over, little ones. Did you enjoy it?"

CHAPTER 34

THE GYPSY WOMAN

She moved away from the sheriff and retrieved her clothes off the ground. As she walked toward us, she stepped into her black pants and pulled her black shirt over her head. She stopped when she was a few feet away and studied each of us for several long seconds.

"Chuck Archibald, Sally Bishop, and Ben Graves—yes, I know who you are. I have the sight."

"The sight...?" Chunk said. He was looking at her the way a religious person might look at a visiting angel.

"I see things that other people cannot. I know things that other people cannot. You should have not come here, young ones."

I worked up my nerve and said, "You came to my house earlier. You spoke to my mom. You made her dance. Why?"

"My reasons are my reasons, Ben Graves."

"But *why*? Why *her*? If the paramedics didn't put her to sleep, she would have danced herself to death like the other people in town!"

"Some things are worse than death," she said simply. "You will all come with me now."

"Where?" Sally asked defiantly.

"Where I bring you, that is where, little girl," the gypsy woman said. She didn't raise her voice, but it changed, became harder. She looked back at the police officers. "You will join us."

She walked briskly past us, smelling of pine needles and grasses and the deep woods. The sheriff and deputy followed. Chunk joined the line, then Sally, then me. I didn't know where the gypsy woman was taking us, but I couldn't seem to do anything but follow. I flirted with the idea of running away—grabbing Chunk and Sally and making a break for the forest—but my legs wouldn't cooperate. There was a disconnect between them and my thoughts, which didn't feel like they were mine. They felt alien and intrusive and antagonistic—a foreign mind inside a familiar one; a parasite infiltrating a host—and that scared the hell out of me.

The gypsy woman led us around the canvas tent and past the jumble of vehicles. The air there reeked of smoke and cooked meat and marijuana. The people gathered around the fires had stopped talking and watched silently as we were marched past. The gypsy woman didn't say anything to them, and they didn't say anything to her. Everything felt dreamy and menacing, which seemed to intensify with each passing second.

The gypsy woman proceeded beneath the tattered movie screen into the cheerless, shadowy forest on the other side of it. She stopped before two wooden cage wagons that had been left there, parked on a bed of dead leaves and pine needles. One was painted red, the other yellow. Black iron bars ran down the lengths of both. They sat on large wheels with white metal spokes and looked like the kind of things that had once been pulled behind horses to transport lions and tigers and other circus animals.

The gypsy woman opened a hatch at the back of the red wagon. She glanced at the sheriff and deputy, which was enough to convey her intent. They obediently mounted the metal coupling system (which had been retrofitted at some point so the wagon could be towed behind a truck) and climbed into the cage. She whacked the hatch closed with a weighty *clang!* and secured it with an old drop bar latch that had developed a greenish patina over the years.

She looked at us next and we had no choice but to scamper up and into the yellow wagon.

She closed and secured the small door behind us.

"Be prepared for a long night," she said and left.

CHAPTER 35

THE PRESENT

I stood up from my desk, lit a Marlboro, and looked around the apartment without seeing it. My mind was still in the past, playing over the surreal encounter we'd had with the gypsy woman thirty-one years ago.

First off, she hypnotized us that day. I was sure of that. I can remember very well the cold tickling that had been inside my skull. The claustrophobic crowding out of my thoughts. The paralysis of independent mental activity. I didn't understand then how she'd accomplished the hypnosis so easily, and I didn't understand now either. There had been no kicking back on a psychiatrist's couch, of course; no soft, soothing voice; no pendulating pocket watch. She had simply looked at us, and that had been enough to steal our minds.

It was possible—unlikely yet possible—that Sally, Chunk, and I had simply allowed her to lock us in the circus wagon because as children we knew our place, which was at the bottom of the totem pole. However, that didn't explain why the sheriff and deputy had allowed themselves, without protest, to be locked up also.

Moreover, during that September in 1988 several people in Chatham—my mother included—did indeed break into spontaneous and uncontrollable dance. You could go to the Chatham public library and read about it in the old paper editions of the Cape Cod *Chronicle*, preserved on microfilm. You could find references to it on the internet if you searched hard enough.

The media and politicians at the time concluded the dancing was the result of a kind of mass psychogenic disorder, or mass hysteria, in which a group of people exhibits abnormal yet similar physical symptoms. The culprit is usually a form of severe psychological stress. This is the go-to reasoning to explain the flare-ups of The Dancing Plague that have been chronicled throughout history. In the well-documented and most famous outbreak in 1518, a series of recent famines, combined with the appearance of new and deadly diseases such as smallpox and syphilis, became too much for one woman to deal with. She literally worried herself sick over getting sick and had a mental breakdown in which she resorted to dancing to calm her mind. Other citizens of Strasbourg, witnessing the woman's flamboyant and endless dancing, unwittingly tricked their bodies into manifesting the same symptoms. And there you go—a dancing mania that captured a city.

The reporters and council members in Chatham who advocated this theory pointed to the beheading of Henrickson only two weeks before. They argued that his gruesome demise reminded people of the Cape Cod Killer's murder spree four years earlier, and the twin memories were enough to trip the first domino, creating a mini twentieth-century dancing plague.

I couldn't blame any of them for adopting the harebrained idea; they had nothing else to work with. They didn't know about the gypsies. They didn't know that the gypsy woman could hypnotize a person so completely and inexorably with a glance. And if they did know, they never would have believed it possible.

But *I* knew all this. I experienced it.

And I believed the gypsy woman used that same ability to compel certain individuals in Chatham to dance until they dropped dead from exertion.

The question was...why?

Unfortunately, when Sally, Chunk, and I confronted her in

the tent in Ryders Field, she didn't wax eloquent about her motivations. She didn't embark on a rambling monologue like the villains often do in the movies to provide the paying audience with a satisfying and unambiguous denouement.

Having said that, I've had a good long while to research and reflect on why she did what she did, and as I mentioned in the prologue of my story, I've come to believe it can be traced back to Henrickson and, specifically, his murder.

Henrickson had a terrible disease—the same disease all the gypsies had, it turned out. Lin Loob, one of those afflicted by uncontrollable dancing, was a housekeeper at the Captain's Inn where Henrickson had been staying in the weeks leading up to his death. He and Lin had a sexual tryst, and this was when and how he passed on his disease to her. Lin had a prurient side, to put it nicely, and was known to be "friendly" with several single men around town. One of those men was Dale Francis, proprietor of the antique store on Main Street. Another was a man named Paul Drake, manager of the tavern at the Wayside Inn, who had a one-night fling with Jennifer Forrester, and who had been in an on-and-off-again dalliance with Margaret Flatly, the woman who had been dancing in the bay window on Seaview Street. Paul Drake and Margaret Flatly had been two of the lucky ones (along with Jennifer Forrester, Mr. Zanardo, my mother, and roughly half a dozen other people around town) who had been afflicted by the uncontrollable dancing but had survived their ordeals.

I got all this information, chapter and verse, through a series of interviews I'd conducted with the residents of Chatham who knew the individuals personally. I did not and have yet to undercover a link between Mr. Zanardo and any of the aforementioned women (or men), but I'm certain he had been sexually involved with one of them. It's the only way he could have contracted the disease, which he in turn passed on to my mother.

Again, I don't have any hard evidence of this. Zanardo had kept his private activities close to his chest, unlike many of the others in town. But looking back on certain events during the first few weeks of that autumn—Zanardo's irrational antipathy to me, his repeated and intrusive inquiries about my mother—it became quite clear that his actions were those of a scorned, jealous ex-lover. And although I can't forgive my mother for cheating on my father with the jerk, I take some consolation in the belief that she'd been the one to dump his ass, not the other way around—

My thoughts were interrupted by the sounds of tires squealing and metal crunching.

I hurried to the window and stuck my head out. Down on Atlantic Avenue a taxi driver jumped out of his cab, yelling and waving his hands at a young woman in a silver sedan who'd rear-ended him.

Pulling down the sash to block out the noise, I returned to the computer and crushed out the cigarette in a glass ashtray. I sipped my coffee. It was cold and bitter.

I resumed typing.

CHAPTER 36
LOCKED UP

O nce the gypsy woman was gone, the stuffy feeling left my head (which almost felt like my ears popping, only the popping happened in my mind), and I could think on my own again. So could everyone else, it seemed. The sheriff and deputy were moving around in their cage, searching for a way out. Sally was rattling the hatch we had climbed through. Chunk was looking at me like he was about to cry.

"What's going on, man?" he said. "Why'd she lock us up?"

"What the *hell* are you kids doing out here?" It was the sheriff. He was gripping the bars of his cage, facing us. He didn't look happy at all.

"I wanted to know what the gypsy woman told you about my mom," I said.

"Mother fuckin Mary and all the saints," he grunted, and turned away, shaking his head.

"Is she gonna let us go?" Chunk asked me, ignoring the sheriff's outburst. "What does she *want* with us? We didn't *do* nuthin."

"She's a witch," Sally said, giving up on the hatch and joining us in the center of the cage.

"She's no witch," Chunk said. "You see a broomstick anywhere?"

"Then how did she make us do what she wanted us to do like she did? I couldn't control my body."

"Sally's right," I said. "She used some sorta magic on us. I couldn't control my body either. None of us could." I looked across at Sheriff Sandberg in the other wagon. His back was to us, and he was speaking in a low voice to the deputy. I wondered if either of them remembered what had happened inside the tent. I suppose they must have. I remembered everything while being under the gypsy woman's spell.

"What are we gonna *do*?" Chunk said. "We gotta do something. What if she...?" He swallowed. His Adam's apple bobbed up and down in the fleshy folds of his throat. "You know... wants to do something bad to us?"

"Why would she want to do that?" I said, putting on a braver face than what I felt.

"Because we were spying on her, man. We saw her do it with the sheriff. She might wanna keep that under wraps."

"She won't hurt us," Sally said. "Somebody must know the sheriff and the deputy came out here. They'll come looking for them. She has to know that too."

"My dad knows the sheriff came here," I added hopefully.

"But he might be at the hospital all night," Chunk said. "Remember what he said? He might not know we're missing until tomorrow."

The three of us looked at each other, no one speaking.

"I don't wanna sleep out here tonight, guys," Chunk said finally. "Not with all those fuckfaces by the fires around. Cause sometimes weird hick fuckfaces like doing stuff to little kids when they can get away with it, you know what I mean?"

ΔΔΔ

Night came quickly in the forest. It inked over the translucent calm of dusk in big black brush strokes, and before we knew it, it was upon us, everywhere, inescapable, implacable. And it was different than the night that came to Chatham, which could be negated with the simple flick of a light switch. This night wasn't an inconvenience; it was predatory and pernicious and would get you if it could, if you let it.

At least we have the moon, I thought. It hung full and round and low in the starry sky, which was visible through breaks in the canopy towering above us. Bluish, silvered light filtered through the spindly boughs of the trees, allowing us to make out each other's pallid faces and frightened eyes in the dark.

We could make out the sheriff and deputy in the other wagon as well. The sheriff was curled in a ball on the floor, and he sounded sick. He'd been moaning constantly for the last while. Sometimes the moan would spike into a sharp cry of agony. Sometimes he would rock violently, twist and lurch on the floor, or roar in what sounded like primal rage.

I was glad Sally and Chunk and I were locked in our own wagon. The deputy probably wished he was in our wagon too. He stood as far away from the sheriff as he could.

Suddenly the sheriff screamed, his voice naked and glassy. He slammed the Cuban heel of one of his cowboy boots repeatedly against the iron bars.

When he quieted down, Chunk said, "Maybe he's got a kidney stone?"

Chunk had a kidney stone last year. The pain he experienced in his back and below his ribs was bad enough that he didn't have to attend school for two weeks.

"Or food poisoning?" I said.

"I hope it ain't that," Chunk said. "You told me you got the trots when you had it. Where's the sheriff gonna go?"

I wanted to punch him for mentioning that in front of Sally.

She said, "I don't think he has either of those things. I think the witch did something to him."

"Like what?" I asked.

"I think she put another spell on him."

"But why just him? Why not us too?"

"Maybe she did. Maybe it just hasn't kicked in yet—"

The wagon shook and we cried out in alarm.

Sally's and Chunk's eyes doubled in size as they probed the night.

Wood creaked above us.

We all tilted our heads up slowly.

Wood continued to creak.

Somebody was on top of the wagon.

Whoever it was began to sniff. Not nasally like when you have a cold. Stealthily—the way an animal sniffs when trying to pick up the scent of its prey.

A new sound joined the sniffing and creaking, a delicate clinking...almost like fingernails tapping on glass.

Or claws on wood.

I held my breath, afraid to make the slightest sound. I told myself we were safe. Whatever was up there couldn't get inside the wagon. Even so, my pulse raced and my thoughts screamed silently inside my head, conjuring different scenarios, like the creature (yes, that's what I thought was up there, a creature from nightmares) tearing off the roof in an explosion of splintered wood and liberated nails.

The wagon shook again.

Then silence.

No more creaking, no more sniffing, no more claws *tat-tat-tatting*.

The creature was gone.

ΔΔΔ

We huddled together in the center of the wagon, nobody daring to stray close to the iron bars, where a clawed hand could reach through out of the dark and maul us.

We didn't speak. We were in shock. At least, I was.

The sheriff, I noticed, had stopped moaning.

I could hear nothing except the gentle soughing of the autumn wind, the rustle of shivering leaves, our terrified, shallow breathing.

ΔΔΔ

From somewhere not too far away, the chilling, forlorn howl of a wolf shattered the quiet of the night.

CHAPTER 37
THE PRESENT

I leaned back in my chair, folded my hands behind my head, and glanced at the clock in the bottom corner of my computer monitor. It was 11:58 a.m. I got up and went to the window overlooking Atlantic Avenue. The bright sights and loud sounds and frantic activity were jarring after living inside my head, living in my memories, all morning.

I went to the small kitchen and eyed the line of whiskey bottles.

I checked my wristwatch. 11:59 a.m. I stood there and did nothing for what I thought was at least a minute. Then I checked the time once more.

Finding that it was now officially the afternoon, I selected a half-empty whiskey bottle, twisted off the cap, and took a swig. With the burn still in my throat, I filled a glass tumbler with ice and more whiskey and returned to the window with the drink.

I hiked open the lower sash, poked a cigarette between my lips, and lit up.

Sometimes my memories of that night in Ryders Field were as clear as if it had all happened yesterday. But sometimes they were opaque and obtuse, real enough...but also lacking a vital measure of clarity and veracity.

It was during these uncertain moments that doubt took root and I found myself questioning whether the memories were real or not.

After all, thirty-one years was a hell of a long time ago, and memories were not photographs of events frozen in time. They were malleable. We changed them ever so slightly each time we recalled them. Often we never realized this. But, yes, we were all guilty of playing Chinese Whispers, adding a false detail here, taking away something there...and in doing so molding the memory into something that, over time, becomes very different than the original.

This was especially true with bad or traumatic memories, and the unconscious manipulation wasn't always for the better. If we experience something frightening when we're young, the memory of that event can become more frightening each time we recall it, leading to a fear that far outgrows that experienced during the original event. A spider that bit us on the finger when we were two may evolve into a full-blown phobia of spiders in our adult years. A mob of feral, murderous gypsies camping in the woods may evolve into something much more sinister and supernatural for a young boy with an active imagination...say, a pack of bloodthirsty werewolves.

Was this what happened to me? Did I reconstruct what happened that night in Ryders Field into something much more monstrous over time, so that now I was recalling a warped facsimile of the events, and not what occurred?

In other words, did I make the fucking werewolves up?

I didn't think so. When the memories were clear, they were *clear*. The howling, I could hear it in my head, every lonesome note. The sheriff transforming, I could see it in my mind's eye, the remapping of veins and arteries, the reorganization of flesh. The werewolves themselves, more human than wolf, certainly, but still...wolf.

I stabbed out the cigarette on the brick window ledge, adding another smear of ash to all the others already there. I kept the window open, enjoying the chill of the fresh air on my skin.

Werewolves.

What were my readers going to think about that?

Fuck it, I thought. *Fuck it if they think I've gone off the rails.*

I have to tell the story. I've kept it my own for far too long. I have to get it off my chest, off my mind, and that means writing what I remember, whether it happened exactly that way or not.

Before returning to the computer, I topped up my drink.

The worst memories were yet to come.

CHAPTER 38
THE SHERIFF

"What *was* that thing?" Sally whispered.

"Shhhh!" Chunk said. "It'll hear you!"

"It's gone, I think."

"It can still hear us. It's a *werewolf*, man. It can hear us from a mile away!"

"Then stop talking so loudly!" I told him. "And you don't know it was a werewolf."

"You heard it howl."

"I heard *something* howl. It coulda been a dog."

"It wasn't a dog!"

"Then maybe an owl."

"An owl? Owls *hoot. Who-who-who.*"

"Keep it down!" The conversation was so fucked up I wasn't sure whether I wanted to laugh or cry.

"It was a werewolf," Chunk insisted. "Had to be. Cause it was a howl, and there ain't no wolves in Massachusetts."

"One might have come down from Canada."

"And wandered right into Chatham, huh?"

"It could have been a coyote," Sally said. "They howl, don't they?"

"Why are you guys being such retards?" Chunk said. "It was a werewolf. You know it was."

"Werewolves don't exist," I said.

"Wanna bet? One just jumped up onto the roof of this wagon.

And if that wasn't no werewolf up there, then what was it, huh? No way a wolf or coyote could jump that high."

He had a point, and I said, "You think the sheriff might be turning into one?"

We looked at the other cage. The sheriff was still lying in one corner. He was moaning again, softly. The deputy hadn't moved an inch and had his back flat up against the short wooden side of the wagon.

"You hafta be bitten by a werewolf to turn into a werewolf," Chunk said.

"Maybe he was bitten before we got here."

"Maybe there's *another* way you can turn into one...?" Sally said hesitantly.

Chunk and I waited for her to tell us what the other way was.

"Like, having *sex* with one," she said.

I blinked. "You think the gypsy woman's a werewolf too?"

"If one of those gypsies is a werewolf, then they all are. No way they'd live with a werewolf if they weren't werewolves too."

"And the sheriff *did* have sex with her," Chunk said. "We all saw them."

"Maybe he knows?" I said, nodding at the deputy. "He might've seen what was on the roof of our wagon."

"Ask him," Chunk said.

"You ask him."

Sally cleared her throat. "Um, Mr. Deputy?"

The man didn't answer her.

"Mr. Deputy?" she tried again.

"Why ain't he answering?" I said.

"Because Mr. Deputy's not his name," Chunk said. "You just gotta call him Deputy—"

"Would you kids *shut the fuck up*," the deputy hissed from where he crouched in the shadows. "You want it to come back?"

The raw fear in his voice surprised me and exacerbated my own fear. I had to take a moment to compose myself before saying, "Didja see it, sir?"

He didn't reply.

"Um, mister...?" Chunk said. "We just wanna know—"

The sheriff screamed, making us jump about a foot into the air. It was unlike any of his previous ones, louder, shriller, crazier. It sounded like something you might hear in the bowels of an insane asylum where the patients that people wanted to forget about went.

The sheriff tore his tan shirt from his chest, buttons popping free and pinging around on the floor of his wagon. His skin glistened with sweat and appeared to be swollen and bruised all over, a nearly uniform purple and reddish mess. He yanked off his cowboy boots one after the other, then his socks. He scratched his feet until they began to bleed. Crossing his arms against his abdomen, he moaned and rocked and sobbed, the pathetic sounds becoming louder and more miserable, the rocking becoming faster.

Abruptly he threw back his head and channeled a long-distance shriek from hell—only it wasn't a shriek, was it? It was a howl, rough and unpracticed, yet unlike any sound a human could make...a sound so terrible, so filled with wretchedness and agony, I not only pressed my hands against my ears but squeezed my eyes shut too as if that could keep his suffering at bay.

When I opened my eyes, I saw that Chunk and Sally had their hands clapped against their ears too. But they'd kept their eyes open, and they were staring at the sheriff in dumbstruck horror.

Chunk stretched one arm out. His hand stuttered. His fat index finger, the nail cut to the quick, pointed straight ahead.

I didn't want to follow that finger, but I had to see what had become of the sheriff.

I looked.

△△△

Illuminated in the icy moonlight, tilted upward toward the roof of the wagon and the black sky beyond, Sheriff Sandberg's face was unrecognizable. Where it had been whole and handsome and unblemished it was now scourges of bloodied and unripe flesh, either gouged free by his fingernails or a byproduct of his transformation—shit, folks, at this point did it matter? A roadmap of veins and arteries bulged and pulsed everywhere between his chin and hairline, some dressed in skin, some not. New growths of hair—short and dense and gray, like fur—sprouted from his forehead and cheekbones and jawline. His ears appeared larger, pointier at the tips, while his nose had broadened and flattened, the nostrils twisted into horizontal commas. His eyes were wide and wet and pleading, still his own, and that was the worst blasphemy in the desecrated face because the tatters of humanity they held underscored the tragedy of his metamorphosis into...something else.

ΔΔΔ

Someone was speaking to me. It was Chunk, yet his words weren't making sense.

"Your gun!" Sally yelled at me. "Shoot it!"

I stared at her, uncomprehending.

Chunk began pawing at my backpack, unzipping it. He produced my dad's revolver and two shells. The gun looked comically large in his hands, almost like a toy. It was shaking so badly as he loaded the shells into the chamber I thought he was going to drop it. But he got it done and cocked the hammer and aimed the barrel at the sheriff.

I gripped his wrist before he could squeeze the trigger. *"What are you doing?"* I said, and I think I was shouting, even though my voice sounded small and muted.

"We gotta kill it before it changes for good!"

"It's the sheriff!"

"It's a werewolf, Ben!" Sally cried. "Let him shoot it!"

I glanced back at the sheriff. His chin was tucked against his chest again now, making it more difficult to see the changes in his face.

"Let the kid shoot him! End his misery!"

For a moment I thought it was the sheriff yelling at me, but it was the deputy.

I removed my hand from Chunk's wrist. He shuffled forward, poked the revolver through the bars of our cage, and fired.

The report shattered the night. A tongue of fire licked from the end of the barrel. The recoil threw his arms up above his head and knocked him back a step.

The sheriff appeared unharmed.

"You missed!" Sally shouted.

"Shoot him again!" the deputy shouted. "Or pass me the damn gun and let me do it!"

Chunk hesitated, then seemed to decide it would be best to offload the responsibility to someone more qualified than himself. He stuck his arm between the iron bars and tossed the revolver through the air—only he used way too much force, and the gun sailed clear over the deputy's wagon and into the trees beyond.

I was speechless. All I could think about was his equally awful throw during fence ball when he missed the entire backstop fence. I probably would have laughed at him had I not been so terrified.

The deputy barked, "You just got me killed!"

"I didn't mean it!" Chunk wailed. "I was scared!"

I glanced at the sheriff and was dismayed to find him staring back at me, his eyes glowing red.

CHAPTER 39
THE PRESENT

I ran the heel of my hand between my eyes and up my forehead and was surprised to find my brow damp with a patina of sweat.

I stood and paced...and inevitably found myself in the kitchen, refilling my glass with whiskey.

You just got me killed.

Those five words have haunted me ever since they left the deputy's mouth. It didn't matter that they hadn't been directed at me. I felt responsible for Chunk's abysmal throw. I'd brought the revolver with us. I should have been the one to shoot the sheriff. If I hadn't frozen up, if I hadn't let Chunk take the gun, the deputy might have survived the night.

I carried my drink to the window and lit a cigarette. My head was already feeling light from the alcohol, but I wasn't yet drunk, and the writing was going well enough that I wanted to force in another hour or so before getting too fucked up to type.

I took a drag on the cigarette and flicked it, only half smoked, out the window. It wasn't helping my anxiety. I'd become acutely aware of my heart in my chest, and it felt as though it was beating faster than usual. It struck me morbidly that it could simply stop at any moment. I could drop dead right now and never finish the book.

And who would know? I wondered maudlinly. *Who would care?*

Down on the street, cars were waiting for a red light to

change. Some maintenance workers had set up a perimeter of orange pylons around a sewer manhole they were trying to open. A lady wearing a winter jacket over her dress stood in front of the street-meat vendor where I often bought a hot dog for the walk home. An elderly couple was strolling through Dewey Square Park, the man a few steps ahead of the woman.

Life as normal.

It would keep going on just as it was, whether I lived or died.

I took a long swallow of whiskey. That calmed my nerves a little, so I took another one, finishing what was left in the glass.

You just got me killed.

"Yeah, well..." I mumbled to myself.

You just got me killed.

"Fuck you," I said, and went to the kitchen and poured myself some more whiskey, emptying one bottle and opening another, so that my glass was properly full.

I had often thought about that night in Ryders Field, of course, but I'd never *written* about it, and writing was an entirely different beast than recalling. The events had never been so lucid and alive in my mind as they'd been these last few days, and I was finding it increasingly hard to believe I'd made the werewolves up. I mean—the deputy had told Chunk he'd just gotten him killed. Why would he have said that if the sheriff had only been sick? Why had he been so scared of the sheriff? Why had we all been so scared of him? We'd wanted to shoot him, after all. We wouldn't have wanted to do that if he'd simply had a bad case of the trots.

And there was something else that was making it difficult for me to dismiss my memories as corrupt.

Science was on my side.

I had done a lot of research into werewolves over the years, and although a person transforming rapidly into a hulking beast made for good drama in the movies, it was scientifically impossible. The energy needed to fuel the physiological mutations and extra body mass would require a constant supply of protein, sugar, fats, and so forth. Simply put, the person would need to eat constantly throughout the transformation, which could take weeks. Even if they were six hundred pounds to begin with, and already contained massive stores of extra body mass, transforming into a hulking beast within a matter of hours would produce so much cellular heat that it would literally cook the victim to death.

On the other hand, if werewolves weren't bear-sized monstrosities but rather emaciated wretches, if their mutations were minor additions and alterations rather than the growth of new skeletons and soft tissue—then, yes, a rapid transformation from man to...whatever...was possible.

Now, the question is: Had I as a child, in an attempt to come to grips with certain repressed trauma I'd experienced while imprisoned in Ryders Field, reimagined my captors as werewolves? That was certainly a possibility. But the other question is: Would I have reimagined them as *scientifically feasible* werewolves rather than the more traditional kinds that I would have been familiar with through popular culture?

I glanced at the computer. The Word document that housed my story was open on the screen, the cursor at the end of the last sentence I wrote blinking...waiting.

Anxiety be damned, I decided to have another cigarette, if only to put off returning to the dark place inside my head where I was spending far too much time lately.

CHAPTER 40

THE MEAL

T he sheriff's glowing red eyes weren't looking at me, I realized. They were looking at Sally. And even though there was no longer anything left of Sheriff Sandberg in those eyes, they were not cold and reptilian; they brimmed with burning hunger and—I was sure—lust.

With astounding speed, the werewolf threw itself at the confines of its prison. Its arms thrust out between the bars, its sinewy hands reaching for us, each finger terminating in a wicked, curved claw.

We cried out in alarm. I stepped protectively in front of Sally without thinking about what I was doing. Her arms wrapped around me from behind and squeezed.

As the werewolf continued its mindless efforts to reach us, I noted in a detached way the abundance of gray fur that had sprouted over much of its body, and how decrepit that body had become beneath the coarse coat. The sternum and ribcage projected against the bruised skin in ghastly relief. The hollowed stomach tapered down sickly to the pelvis, which poked above either side of the tan pants like a pair of wings. The shoulders were knobby balls, the throat sunken and mummified.

No wonder it wants to get us so bad, I thought. *It looks like it's starving to death.*

Gripping the bars of the wagon in both hands, the werewolf leaped against them with its bare feet, throwing its lower body behind each assault.

When this proved fruitless, it shoved its head between the bars, jaws snapping and saliva flinging and—

A shoe bounced off its face.

It went perfectly still for a moment—before resuming its tantrum with frenzied rage.

I gawked at Chunk. He stood next to me with only one shoe on, grinning like he did when he knew he'd done something stupid but it was worth it.

"Who cares?" he said, shrugging. "It can't get us."

"Nice aim," I said, wondering why he couldn't have had that kind of aim when he'd thrown the revolver.

"You know, if it ever gets out of that wagon," Sally told him, "it's gonna come for your first."

"How's it gonna get out?" he challenged, his false bravado faltering. "It can't, can it? It's locked up like us."

"The gypsy woman might let it out."

"Why would she do that?"

"Cause it's one of *them* now. It's on their side."

Chunk's face drained of color.

"Don't worry about it," I told him. "It would still hafta get *into* our wagon. The only way it could do that is if the gypsy woman lets it. And if she does that, then we're all goners."

"Thanks for pointing that out," Sally said, releasing her arms from around me. She pointed. "Hey, it's calming down."

The werewolf remained standing at the bars, but instead of spazzing out it was holding its nose upward and sniffing like we'd heard the one on top of our wagon doing.

Slowly it turned its head toward the deputy, who squatted in the back corner of their wagon, statue-still.

Chunk moaned. "I dunno if I wanna watch this, guys..."

△△△

I didn't know how the werewolf had overlooked the deputy until then. I suppose Chunk, Sally, and I were the first people it saw, and in its eagerness to get us, it didn't realize another person shared the wagon with it. Then again...it had wanted Sally most (before Chunk threw his shoe in its face, at least), so maybe her smell—her female scent—had overpowered the rest of us.

Whatever the reason, it didn't matter.

The werewolf was aware of the deputy now.

I expected it to leap at the trapped man with the same apoplectic fury it had thrown itself at the bars of the cage to get us.

Instead it was the *deputy* who charged *it*. Arms outstretched, he wrapped his hands around the werewolf's ropey neck and drove it into the opposite side of the wagon, smashing it up against the wood. I remembered the deputy and sheriff being about the same size. But now the deputy seemed to tower over the withered, hunched thing the sheriff had become, and I silently cheered him on, wondering why we'd ever been so frightened—

The werewolf's hands tore at the deputy's sides in a flurry of quick movement. Its claws shredded his shirt and the flesh beneath. Large dark stains bloomed on the tattered fillets of cloth. Blood spilled to the wagon's wood floor.

The deputy gasped. His knees buckled. Yet he kept his hands locked around the werewolf's neck.

It proved futile.

The werewolf buried its face in the deputy's neck. A quick jerk was followed by a spray of blood so powerful it made a dull *whump* as it splattered the roof of the wagon. The momentum of the violent bite had snapped the werewolf's face toward us, and it was impossible not to see the tubelike strips of cartilage dangling from its lupine jaws.

△△△

I whirled away and vomited, trying to aim through the bars of the wagon. I didn't know whether it was the sight and sound of me puking that compelled Sally and Chunk to do the same, or whether they'd been just as disgusted as I'd been by the spectacle of the deputy getting his throat torn out, but they dropped to their knees as well and emptied their stomachs.

When I was spent—acid searing my throat, tears stinging my eyes—I glanced over my shoulder at the other wagon.

In a grotesque parody of lovemaking, the werewolf was now astride the supine deputy, its face nuzzled in his ruined neck in what could be misconstrued as a kiss...if not for the wet and sloppy sounds of mastication.

It turned out I still had more inside me to come up.

ΔΔΔ

The wagons featured heavy velvet curtains that could be drawn across the bars. The original purpose would have been to hide whatever circus delights the cages had housed until the big reveal. Now we closed the set facing the other wagon to hide what was *outside*. And although we could no longer see the emaciated werewolf devouring the deputy, we could hear what was going on.

It wasn't a quick meal.

I was grateful when the rain began to fall because the drumming on the roof of our wagon helped to drown out the sounds of teeth gnashing flesh and chipping bone, and the slurping of liquids. However, the rain also brought a damp chill. Dressed only in jeans and a flannel shirt, I pulled my knees up against my chest and wrapped my arms around them. Chunk and Sally were doing the same.

I wanted to shuffle up behind Sally and wrap my arms around her. I knew it would help keep the both of us warm, but I wasn't sure how to instigate it. When she'd done it to me earlier, it had been natural, a frightened reaction rather than a planned action. Moreover, I didn't think it would be fair for us to cozy up in front of Chunk when he had nobody.

We didn't speak to each other for a long time. There wasn't

much to say when you had a werewolf eating a police deputy in the circus wagon next to you. Also, I didn't want to talk. I wasn't only scared but angry too. I didn't know why this was happening to us, and I sort of hated the world right then. It was how I'd felt a lot of the time in the days and weeks following Brittany's death.

I didn't want to think about Brittany, but how could I not after seeing the werewolf tear out the deputy's throat? I might not have seen the dog tear out my little sister's throat, but I saw the ruined hole it left. I wondered what she looked like now in her kid-sized coffin buried beneath an elm tree in Seaside Cemetery. I passed the cemetery every day on my way home from school. Sometimes if I was by myself, I would climb over the low three-bar fence and visit her grave. Unlike some of the other tombstones that were broken and crooked and neglected, Brit's was straight and well-kept, and there were always fresh flowers placed at the base, which made me think my mom visited her more than she told us. I never stayed in the cemetery too long. It was hard looking at Brittany's tombstone knowing she was lying beneath it because of me. No more birthdays, no more Christmases or Halloweens, no more ice cream and cake. No more anything.

Eventually I got my mind off Brittany, and to lift my mood I thought about some of the *Spy vs Spy* comics I'd read recently. At one point I made up a story myself. The werewolf was the Black Spy and I was the White Spy. I went to one of the wagon's bars and simply unscrewed it with a few twists of my wrist. Then I was outside in the rain, sneaking around our wagon to the other one, where the Black Spy was too busy interrogating the deputy to notice me. I set up a table and placed two cocktail glasses on it, one filled with nitro and one with glycerin. Then I hid behind a tree and rang a bell. The Black Spy came out of the wagon and the gypsy woman came out of the woods and the two of them sat down at the table. They raised their glasses and clinked them together in cheers...and KABOOM! They were both blown into smithereens.

I chuckled to myself, and Chunk said, "What's so funny?"

"I was thinking about blowing up the werewolf and the gypsy woman."

"How?"

"With nitroglycerin."

A peal of thunder rang through the sky somewhere in the distance. The storm was on the move toward us; I could smell it coming.

"My dad once told me that nobody deserves to die," Sally said, staring at the floor. "We were watching a movie, and the bad guy was getting away in a stagecoach, and an Indian shot him through the window with an arrow, and I said, 'Good, he deserved it.' But my dad told me that he didn't, cause there's always the possibility that a person can change for the better." She went quiet for a few moments before continuing. "I used to believe that. But I don't anymore. The gypsy woman deserves to die for turning the sheriff into a werewolf and locking him up with the deputy. She had to know what would happen."

"If we get outta here," Chunk said, "I'm gonna tell my dad what she did, and then she's really gonna get her comeuppance."

A depressing silence followed his comment.

"When," he amended, realizing what he'd said wrong. "*When* we get outta here."

"What's your dad gonna do?" I asked him, mostly just to say something.

"Shoot her through the head with a silver bullet," he said immediately. "That'll teach her."

"Your dad's an accountant," I reminded him. "Where's he going to get a silver bullet from?"

"Get bent," he said, and then added, "Hey...get it?"

"Get what?"

"Bent Ben!" he said, cranking out his honking laugh.

I pictured the Garbage Pail Kids card he'd plucked from Justin Gee's collection.

I said, "Better to be Bent Ben than Up Chuck."

"You are *so* Up Chuck!" Sally said, smiling. "You upchucked into my *swimming pool*."

"Like you're any better. You just barfed your guts out."

"You did too."

"Smelly Sally," he said tauntingly, and I saw the card in my head: a Garbage Pail-like mermaid lounging in a tin of sardines.

The rain falling on the roof of the wagon had softened. After listening to it for a full minute, and not hearing anything else, I said, "I think the werewolf's stopped eating."

Chunk and Sally concentrated on listening. Sally nodded. "I think you're right."

"Maybe you better go check," Chunk said.

I frowned. "Why?"

"To make sure it's *really* finished eating."

"Why else would it be quiet?"

"Maybe it got out of the wagon? Maybe it's sneakin up on us?"

My frown deepened. I couldn't tell whether he was ragging me or not. But I didn't like the possibility that the werewolf might have escaped its cage.

I stood up.

"Ben!" Sally said, grabbing my leg. "I don't think you should do that."

"I'll just have a peek."

"I mean, I don't think you wanna see...what's left."

"I won't be long."

Stepping away, her hand falling from my leg, I went to where the curtain met the wood end of the wagon. I moved aside the fabric and peered out. Clouds had come with the rain and scudded out the moon. The night was of a different quality of black now, deeper and thicker, more sinister.

However, my eyes had adjusted to the darkness enough over the last hour to see in the gloom. In the other wagon the deputy lay flat on his back. From neck to boots, his clothes had been peeled free and his flesh devoured to the bones. His head had been left untouched, so it just sat there, deceptively alive, atop skeletal remains.

The werewolf hadn't escaped. It was curled in a ball in a corner of the wagon, presumably sleeping.

I released the curtain.
It couldn't have fallen back in place quickly enough.

CHAPTER 41

THE STORM

There was no sleeping for me. Sally had been right. I shouldn't have looked. The image of the deputy—what had been left of him—was now burned into my mind, and I wasn't sure whether I'd ever get rid of it or ever sleep again.

On top of this the lull in the weather had ended, and a heavy metal band was now rocking out in the sky above us. The wind wailed in a banshee-like falsetto to the backup vocals of flapping tree branches and susurrant leaves. Rain drummed a staccato beat on the roof of the wagon. Thunder boomed from a cosmic bass drum. Lightning strobe-lit the black thunderheads from within, highlighting skeins of lavender and blue. Jagged golden forks blazed brightly enough to stamp themselves on my retinas.

Somehow Chunk remained oblivious to nature's rock n' roll show. He was passed out on his stomach and snoring loudly into his arms, which were folded beneath his head. Sally remained awake. She had moved next to me a while ago and had taken one of my hands in hers. It had been a simple gesture, but it had meant the world to me. We were in this together (whatever *this* was), and we would get through it together. I was sure of that.

Pretty sure, at least.

She rested her head against my shoulder now, her hair tickling my nose. I figured she was trying to get some rest, however impossible that might seem, so I wrapped my arm around her shoulder. She snuggled closer. When she couldn't seem to get comfortable, she laid down, her head in my lap.

She looked up at me. "Is this okay?" I wasn't sure if she'd spoken the words or only mouthed them; I could hear little above the rain's rapid-fire tempo.

I nodded and she closed her eyes. Soon her breathing told me she was asleep. I watched her silently, marveling at her beauty and vowing to not let anything bad happen to her.

Then I realized I was just a puny, ineffectual kid. What was I going to do against a pack of werewolves? I didn't even have my dad's revolver anymore. If I were an adult and bigger and stronger...well, would that even matter? The deputy hadn't stood a chance.

I clenched my jaw and stared through the bars on the side of the wagon we hadn't blinded with the curtain.

The storm thrashed the black night, stirring up cold air that smelled of ozone. Thin, icy raindrops splattered the wooden floorboards at the edge of the cage, pooling there in shimmering, miniature lakes. A blast of lightning turned the entire sky white, revealing the full extent of its sublime rage. The crack of thunder that followed sounded like the heavens snapping in two. I recoiled and gripped Sally tightly. The next shock of lightning was as bright and inclusive as the previous one—and in the deluge of white light I saw movement on the ground, something darting between the trees.

Then darkness returned, casting a dark cloak over the forest.

But I knew what I saw.

Hot fear stabbed me in my gut. I didn't move and didn't dare blink.

The next bout of lightning and thunder arrived simultaneously in an Armageddon of light and sound.

Deep in the woods, closer than it had been ten seconds earlier when I had first spotted it, stood a werewolf. This time, when the lightning sizzled out, I didn't lose it in the dark.

It stood stock-still for several seconds, staring back at me. Then it started toward the wagon, moving like a person on two legs, and for a hopeful and naïve moment I thought it *was* a person. But I was bullshiting myself. I knew it even before it came close enough for me to see the evil red glow of its eyes.

More lightning, more thunder; the storm was right on top of us. But right then it may as well have been in a different dimension.

The werewolf was naked and female. It sniffed the air as it approached, turning its head first one way, then the other, in jerky and lizard-like movements. It stopped when it reached the wagon. Its red eyes (which seemed to somehow glow from within) roamed over Chunk and then Sally before coming to rest on me. The abomination resembled something that might have crawled out of the anus of Satan himself. Its gargoyle face was neither human nor beast but somewhere in between, familiar yet unfamiliar, which was the worst kind of amalgamation. Its muscled, wasted body looked like roadkill come back to life, the threadbare and patchy fur plastered to skin the color of slag.

I wanted to run and scream and cry all at the same time, yet could do nothing but stare in riveted, repulsed horror.

And then in an unguarded moment lasting no longer than a heartbeat I saw beyond the demon-sheen of its eyes, *into* its eyes, into a warring maelstrom of desperation and hatred...and what might have been sorrow and longing.

The moment passed and there was only hunger in them once more.

The werewolf curled its fingers around the bars of the wagon, its claws clinking delicately against the iron. It leaned closer, its flattened, wolfish snout sniffing, its mane of black hair falling to its shoulders in wet tangles. The squished slits of its nostrils flared and exhaled a blast of warm air. Its lips peeled back from its gums and teeth and its mouth parted slightly, revealing four canines twice the lengths of any of the other teeth. A primeval sound rumbled up its throat, both hiss and growl that made gooseflesh break out all over my body.

I couldn't move, couldn't breathe, couldn't think. I was in a nightmare from which I couldn't wake, face-to-face with an impossibility that even the most depraved imagination would struggle to believe.

With an abrupt, dismissive snort, the gypsy woman loped off into the night.

△△△

"How'd you know it was her?" Chunk asked eagerly.

"I saw the tattoo on her wrist."

"What tattoo?" Sally asked.

"She has a red one there. Chunk and I saw it when she was at my house."

"And she didn't try to get you?" Chunk said.

I shook my head.

"She probably knew she couldn't," he said. "She put us in here, after all. She woulda known better than anyone she couldn't get inside."

"Maybe."

"You just told us she looked like something that had crawled out of the devil's ass, man! That sounds like something that would wanna get you, all right."

"I mean, it was like...she didn't care about me. I don't know how to explain it better than that."

"Why didn't you wake us?" Sally said.

I had wondered that myself before I *did* wake them, and I suppose it was because there hadn't been time. Although the encounter almost seemed to have happened in drawn-out slow motion, it couldn't have lasted any longer than five or six seconds in total.

"Would you have wanted me to wake you?"

"I don't know." She frowned. "I guess not. A werewolf's probably not the first thing you wannna see when you wake up."

"Yeah, well, *I* woulda liked to've seen it," Chunk said. "And if it tried anything, I woulda pelted it with my other shoe."

Sally wrinkled her nose. "I wish you never threw your first shoe. Your foot stinks."

"Not as bad as you do, shithead."

"Don't call me a *shithead*."

"Don't tell me my feet smell!"

"They do, and it's grody."

Chunk took off his other shoe, held it to his nose, and took a deep, satisfying sniff. "Ahhhh..."

"You're gonna die alone."

"Not if it happens tonight. I'll die right next to you, my feet in your face..."

Sally didn't have a comeback for that, and Chunk didn't taunt her further. They both seemed to realize, on some level, that talk about us dying hit a bit too close to home. We'd been at the age then, you see, where we understood that death happened. Grandparents and strangers and people on the news and characters in movies all died, and rather often, even little sisters that never lived long enough to blow out five candles on a birthday cake died. Nevertheless, we hadn't matured enough to get our heads around the truth that *we* would die someday too. We could think about it and joke about it, sure, but we couldn't yet internalize it to the extent needed for us to fear it. In the years between then and now, I've come to realize that the ability to deliberate nonexistence takes a surprising amount of philosophical introspection and sophistication.

So although I don't think any of us truly believed we might die that night (even though we were locked up by a pack of bloodthirsty werewolves), that didn't stop nascent, uncomfortable *what-ifs* from hijacking our thoughts.

A gust of wet wind tore through the bars of the wagon, whipping our hair and licking our clammy skin. Chunk shivered and actually said "Brrrrr..." I got up and drew the second curtain closed so we were sealed off on all four sides from the night, the darkness, and the tempestuous storm.

I sat back down next to Chunk and Sally and waited in silence...for what, I didn't think any of us knew.

ΔΔΔ

Exhaustion dragged me into a light doze in which I heard a chorus of howls rising distantly and ethereally into the night… though whether they were real or imagined, I couldn't say for certain. Eventually I sank deep enough into unconsciousness to dream. The one I remembered was graphic and incomprehensible, populated with the flying monkeys from *The Wizard of Oz* and the white luck dragon from *The Neverending Story* and a particularly nutty encounter with Hoggle from *Labyrinth* during which he chased me down a maze of dark, rat-infested alleyways.

When I woke and recognized I was not at home in bed but in the circus wagon in Ryders Field, I thought with dread of the werewolves. For a blurry moment I convinced myself I'd dreamed them too, but the hard wooden boards beneath my cheek and the cold night wrapped around my skin made it difficult to deny the reality of the situation.

Sally heard me sitting up and did the same.

"What time is it?" she asked, rubbing her eyes tiredly.

I looked at my wristwatch. "2:22," I told her.

"I hate it when the numbers are like that."

"Like what?"

"All the same. It's creepy, like the devil—666. Were you sleeping?"

"A little."

Chunk groaned and opened his eyes. "What're you guys doing?" He was on his belly again, one side of his face smushed against his forearms.

"Waking up," I said.

"I had the weirdest dream," he said, though he didn't elaborate.

I thought about my dreams, and how upon waking I couldn't immediately distinguish them from the werewolves, what was real and what was imagined, and I said, "Do you guys think we're gonna remember all of this when we're older?"

"Are you kidding?" Sally said. "We totally will. I don't know how we *couldn't*."

I wasn't so sure about that. Brittany had only died last year, and I was already finding it difficult to remember the details of the dog attack. In fact, I was finding it harder and harder to remember Brittany herself. Her face, her voice—I could call them forth whenever I wanted by closing my eyes. But I think if I ran into Brit in real life, the recollections wouldn't be as accurate as they should be. And I was pretty sure one day I wouldn't be able to recall anything about her at all except she had been my sister and I had gotten her killed. Maybe I'd even forget that last bit because it wasn't something I would want to remember.

I frowned at my hands, which were wrung together on my lap. "We should promise that we're never gonna forget what happened."

Chunk sat up now. "You wanna remember the sheriff eating the deputy?"

I shook my head. "No. But I think it's important we don't forget the werewolves. People are gonna tell us we made them up. They'll tell us that enough times we might start believing them. Because people just do what other people do, or think how other people think. And that's probably what the werewolves want. They want us to forget about them, so they can go on killing other people without anybody knowing."

"I promise," Sally said, sticking out her pinky finger.

I wrapped my pinky around hers.

"You too," I told Chunk.

His pinky finger joined ours, and we remained bonded like that for a long moment.

"Never forget," he said finally.

"Never forget," Sally said.

"Never forget," I repeated, looking from one of them to the other.

I can see them in my mind's eye right now as if it were that night in 1988. The memory of them huddled in the circus wagon while the storm blustered above us and werewolves stalked the forest around us has never eroded or changed like my memories of Brittany had. Chunk's clothes rumpled and ill-fitting; his wavy chestnut hair sticking up here and there in cowlicks; a big red mark marring his cheek where it had been pressed against his arm in sleep; his piggish eyes quizzical at what I was saying about remembering the werewolves. Sally somehow remaining attractive and fresh despite the parade of horrors we'd been subjected to; her eyes bright with fierce intelligence and resolve...and desire. Not for me, and not in the sense you're probably thinking. The desire, I believe, had been for life, for living, for the sun to rise in the morning and for everything to be okay.

Kids could be optimistic little fuckers when they wanted to be.

CHAPTER 42

THE CAVALRY

"**G**uys, come here!" Chunk said. He stood at one of the long sides of the wagon, peering through the slightly parted curtain. "I knew I heard something—look!"

Sally and I had been leaning against each other, flitting in and out of sleep. The urgency in Chunk's voice, however, was like a splash of cold water in our faces. We leaped to our feet and joined him.

"See, man!" he crowed, pointing toward Ryders Field.

Given the way the wagon was positioned, we had to press our faces to the bars to see toward the field where the fires had burned earlier. Through the trees and the giant white movie screen, I made out several beams of yellow light arcing through the darkness.

"Cars!" Sally said.

"You betcha!" Chunk crowed. "The cavalry's come to bust us out!"

The lights ceased moving. One after the other they disappeared as each vehicle shut off its engine.

I thought I could hear voices, but it was difficult to tell for certain above the heavy wash of the rain.

Chunk squeezed himself up against the bars and shouted, "HEY! HELLLOOOO! WE'RE OVER HERE!"

I stiffened, fearful the werewolves would hear him too and

come for the new arrivals. However, if we didn't call attention to ourselves, we'd likely never be discovered tucked away where we were.

Four yellow lights punched on, the sweeping beams smaller and jerkier: flashlights.

"OVER HERE!" Chunk bawled, hopping up and down. "BEHIND THE MOVIE SCREEN!"

The zigzag of lights appeared to be getting closer.

"Hello? Chuck? Where are you, boys?"

"Dad!" I cried, recognizing his voice.

"Ben!"

Then he was close enough that I heard him stomping through the mud and wet leaves.

"Mother of God…"

"What the *fuck*?" another man said.

"Oh Lord no," a third man mumbled. "That's Murphy. *Look at him*."

"Who's that other one?" a fourth man said. "Hey, you…? *Hey!*"

I hurried to the other side of the wagon and yanked back the curtain. My father wore rubber Wellingtons, a brown leather jacket, and a wide-brimmed cowboy hat. He stood alongside three policemen in knee-length navy rain slickers with reflective white stripes. All four of them had their backs to us and their flashlight beams pinned on the red wagon.

"Dad!" I said, my knees nearly giving out at the sight of him.

He whirled around. "Ben?" Shadows carved his face into sharp slabs but didn't touch the wide whites of his eyes. "What the hell's going on here?" It was almost a plea. "Who put you in that *God-fucking cage*?" He stepped back, surveyed the wagon. He went to the hatch, vanishing from view. The hatch shook and rattled but remained closed.

He reappeared, raindrops pelting the brim of his hat and gushing down his jacket and chewing the muddy ground at his feet. "Dammit, Ben, how did you get in there? *Who did this?*"

"The gypsies," I told him. "The woman who came to our house is the leader, I think. There's a whole bunch of them around. And they're werewolves, Dad! They're in the woods hunting right now, but they might come back. So you gotta get us outta here quick—"

"What in all hell *is* that?" one of the policemen blurted. The yellow cone of his flashlight beam illuminated the sheriff-turned-werewolf. Although it was curled in a ball and sleeping in the corner of its wagon, you could clearly see it wasn't all human.

"That was the sheriff," I explained. "He turned into a werewolf. He *ate* the deputy."

One of the other cops withdrew his revolver and aimed it with both hands at the sheriff. "It did that to Murphy, did it? It *ate* him, did it?" His voice was high and fainting.

"Shoot it!" Chunk said, shunting me sideways so he could press up against the bars for a front-row view. "Get it now before it wakes up! Get it good!"

The cop cocked the revolver's hammer.

"Don't!" I told him. "The others will hear!"

"The gypsies?" my dad said. "Do they all look like that thing, Ben? *Do they all look like that thing?* Answer me, goddammit!"

"I-I think so," I stammered. "One was on the roof of our wagon, but we didn't see it. But I saw another one, the leader—she looked…" I nodded my head. "Like him, like the sheriff."

"That's *not* the sheriff!" the policeman aiming the handgun said. His wild eyes were probing the black night, the towering trees. "We need to get out of here, Stu," he added.

"We got to get these kids out of that fucking wagon first!"

"You heard the boy," he said, already backing up. "There are more of them around. On the loose."

"That's my son in there, Merv!"

"We'll come back, with help."

"Merv's right, Stu," one of the other cops said, backing up as well. "We'll come back."

"I'm not leaving my son, dammit!" My dad turned to us, his face now flushed with anger. He gripped the bars of our wagon and shook them helplessly. "Shit!"

While my dad's back was turned, the cop with the unholstered revolver fled through the trees toward the vehicles. The other two cops hesitated a beat, then followed.

"HEY!" Chunk yelled. "COME BACK!"

"Quiet!" I told him. "You're gonna bring the werewolves! Dad, you needa go. We're safe in here for now—"

"HEY! COME BACK! YOU HAFTA HELP US—"

"*Shut up!*" I said, yanking Chunk away from the bars. He tripped over his feet and landed on his butt with a heavy slap.

"What the hell, man? They're *leaving* us." He titled back his head and wailed: "*COMEBACKCOMEBACKCOME*—"

A wolf's howl cut him off.

It was close, *really* close.

A different howl answered the first.

"Dad!" I cried. "Go!"

His rough hand took mine between the bars and squeezed. His face looked as though it might shatter into a thousand pieces. "By God, Ben, stay right where you are—"

The attack happened in the blink of an eye.

One moment my dad was right in front of me. The next, he was on the ground several feet away from the wagon, a werewolf on top of him.

"*Dad!*"

The werewolf went for his throat. My dad got his forearm up in time to push aside the snapping jaws. It began biting him in other places. He cried out and flailed and kicked.

Another werewolf landed on top of them. This one tore a meaty hunk out of his shoulder.

My dad recoiled like he'd been doused in flames.

A third werewolf threw itself atop the wriggling pile, then a fourth.

Scorching pain dug into my left arm, which was thrust between the bars, reaching for my dad futilely. The jaws of a werewolf had latched onto it.

Bleating a shrill cry, I jerked it back.

Sally threw the crimson curtain closed and pulled me into

the middle of the wagon.

△△△

More screams joined my dad's. A volley of gunshots. Then nothing.

The police officers were dead.

My dad was dead.

Everyone who had come to rescue us was dead.

△△△

I wanted to cry, but I couldn't. I didn't feel anything, not fully. Some anger, some sadness, some fear. But all that was trapped beneath a slab of ice.

Which was good—for the moment, at least.

Because if I had to feel any of that stuff right then, I might just go crazy.

△△△

Eventually I was aware of nothing but Sally holding me, and rocking me, and the rain that wouldn't stop.

CHAPTER 43

THE PRESENT

"T hat's it," I said to myself. "That's enough."

I stood up, wobbled, regained my balance. I was surprised to see that it was dark outside. I rarely worked into the evening.

I was stroking the white and wormy scar tissue that stretched from my left elbow to my wrist, and I promptly stopped.

Keys, I thought.

They were on the kitchen counter. I picked them up...and looked outside at the night again, then at the cot, then back outside. It was only a ten-minute walk to my house. And it would be nice to sleep in my proper bed...

Like you'd even notice.

That was true. In my current state I'd pass out as soon as my head hit the pillow and wake up in the morning, remembering nothing of the previous eight or ten hours.

Probably best to crash here on the cot, I decided. Then there would be no temptation to put off writing tomorrow. No surrendering the day to chores around the house. I would already be here and could sit down straight away at the computer.

And you're almost done with the first draft. Two or three more days and it's finished. Then it's just the second and third drafts to get through—easy as pie. More revising than writing and reliving. You'll be done picking at the scabs of your memory. How does that sound?

It sounded fantastic. I could imagine nothing more cathartic than typing those last two words: THE END. Would I instantly find peace of mind? Would everything be rainbows and unicorns? Would my shattered childhood be miraculously mended?

Of course not. But my story would be finished, my secrets shared, no longer mine alone to bear. It would be up to others to make what they will of them. Some will believe they are true; most will not. But *some* will believe, and that will be good enough for me.

I flicked off the overhead lights and moved slowly through the dark so I didn't bump into anything. When I reached the cot, I flopped down onto the hard mattress, too bothered to take off my clothes.

Sleep didn't come as promptly as I would have liked.

My body might have been drunk and exhausted, but my memories remained alive. I saw myself, the twelve-year-old boy that I had been, hair mussed, tears dried on my cheeks, my left arm swaddled in Sally's blood-stained blouse, trudging up the steps to the medical office where I had my annual check-ups. The concerned receptionist telling me my mother had never been admitted there, and later, that same receptionist driving me to the Urgent Care Hospital in Hyannis. A pair of doctors examining my injured arm. Waking up with my wound sutured and bandaged. My mother and a detective in my hospital room, asking question after question…

I hadn't felt like talking to them. My mother was no longer dancing and back to her old self, and that was all that mattered right then. I simply wanted them to go away and leave me alone. They did, for a while. I figured the cops must have talked to Chunk and Sally, and one or both of them had explained what had happened at Ryders Field because the next time my mother entered my hospital room she was hysterical and blaming me for my father's death.

Once I was discharged, I told my mom about the werewolves.

She wouldn't even look at me. After that, I never tried again. I locked myself in the garage and only left to get food from the kitchen when nobody was there. I attended my father's funeral, along with what seemed like half the town. Yet I continued to keep to myself in the days and weeks that followed. I didn't answer the telephone. I didn't return to school. I rarely went outside.

My mother sold the house and bought a new one in Pawtucket. She claimed it wasn't very big, and there wasn't a bedroom for me, so I went to live with my grandmother in Albany. I started school again in the September of 1989, I met some new friends, and I tried my best not to think about Chunk or Sally or the night in Ryders Field.

My mother died that December, two days before Christmas. She hanged herself with a rope in her bathroom, apathetic to the fact it would be either Ralph or Steve who would find her lifeless body (it was Steve). They joined me in my grandmother's bungalow, taking the bedroom I had occupied while I made do on a mattress in the basement. I took on a lot of responsibilities around the house that I wouldn't have had if our parents had been alive, and I grew up quickly. We all did, looking back on it. And I think we turned out all right in the end. Ralph operates a private dentist practice in Maine and drives a Tesla. He's married to a bubbly wife and has two girls and a golden retriever. Steve teaches science at a private high school in the suburbs of Providence. He lives with his long-term girlfriend, several hamsters, two cats, and a parrot.

And me...well, I might be a functioning (and occasionally out-of-control) alcoholic, but I'm doing all right in general. I've never spoken of Ryders Field to anyone. I've never brought it up with any of my past girlfriends, not even the two or three that had become serious. I've never ranted drunkenly about it to the guy on the barstool next to me. I've never looked up Chunk or Sally on social media to reminisce about old times. I've never said a peep to anyone.

And now I was about to announce what happened to the

world—at least the world of people who read my books.

At some point during the second draft, I was going to have to find a way to incorporate the gypsy woman's motivations for hypnotizing people. I'd so far left out this vital piece of information because I was telling the story from my first-person point-of-view, and my twelve-year-old self didn't know her motives. They would remain a mystery to me until when, in my early thirties, I conducted interviews in Chatham that led me to discover the romantic connections between Gregory Henrickson and Lin Loob and Dale Francis and the others. My conclusion then was that the gypsy woman had compelled the people infected with lycanthropy to dance themselves to death before they transformed because she needed to keep the disease under wraps. Her clan, if you wanted to call it that, wasn't very large, two dozen werewolves at most. They likely kept their numbers small so as not to draw attention to themselves, and they likely didn't infect the general population willy-nilly for that same reason. Their survival depended on anonymity, on roaming from place to place, taking a bite out of the wildlife (and perhaps the domesticated animal) population here or there and moving on again before anybody noticed. Consequently, if one of their members went rogue, retribution must be swift, and the clean-up must be immediate and thorough. Hence the gypsy woman beheading Henrickson and attempting to murder all the people he'd infected.

It was a matter of survival.

Nevertheless, while this logic was initially acceptable, it never aged well for one glaring reason. Why dancing? There are a lot more efficient ways to kill someone than by compelling them to dance for days on end until they succumbed to a heart attack or stroke—especially when you had a power like the gypsy woman. She could have made her victims drown themselves in the bathtub, overdose with sleeping pills, or any of another dozen ways that people took their lives.

Not to mention that of all the cases reported in Chatham in 1988, only three people—Lin Loob and Dale Francis and Jody

Gwynn—died. All the others survived.

And not only did they survive, but they also didn't transform during the full moon at the end of September '88, or any full moon after that. This eventually led me to believe that perhaps the gypsy woman had never been trying to murder the infected —but had rather been trying to *cure* them.

Dance rituals had been used since ancient times as a means for people to experience communion not only with one another but with the spirit world, the earth, and the universe at large. Lesser known was that dance rituals had also been used throughout the centuries as a therapy to cure mental ailments. They often involved individuals dancing themselves into a higher state of consciousness, or a trance, during which their minds shut down and their hearts opened up. Intellect and reason were suppressed while their corporeal selves took over, a swirling of raw energy that re-established the frayed or broken links to their true inner selves and thus promoted psychological healing.

Most notably, during this altered state, this crude anesthesia, there was no room for the mind to work the monstrous magic of lycanthropy on the body, to contort the body into something it was never meant to be. There was no room for anything except the movement and the moment and unthinking peace...

Sleep came finally, whisking me away to its secret, restorative world, which perhaps wasn't too far from the world I'd gone to when Sally made me dance, and by doing so, saved my life.

CHAPTER 44

THE TRANSFORMATION

T he full moon hung suspended like a ghostly button in the black, rain-washed sky. The thunderheads had moved on, taking the thunder and lightning with them, leaving behind crisp, wet air that smelled of steel and rebirth.

Immediately after I'd rescued my arm from the jaws of the werewolf, Sally had taken off her blouse and wrapped it around the wound to stem the bleeding. The pain had alternated between ice and fire. Now it had subsided to a dull, itchy ache. At the same time I was hot and headachy with a fever and sweating all over. I throbbed everywhere, especially my stomach and behind my eyes. Of course, I knew the cause. I had seen the sheriff experience the same symptoms before he'd turned into a werewolf.

I didn't think it would take long for me to follow in his footsteps. I could already feel the transformations occurring inside me, inside my cells. I could feel the chemical reactions breaking down my body to rebuild it.

And that wasn't all. I was aware of *everything*. The smell of the weathered wood and peeling paint of the circus wagon. The sap in the trees and the bacteria in the soil. I could even smell the darkness itself, and the birds and rodents and animals that hid within it.

My hearing was just as acute. New sounds infiltrated my head one after the other, an unending train of amplified noise.

The *plop!* of a droplet of water falling from leaf to ground. An industrious June bug pushing through the rotting deadfall. An owl gliding on air currents far overhead.

And my eyes—they saw the unseeable. The patterns of the seasons in the grains of the wood planks I sat on. Works of abstract art in the mill scale that coated the bars of my prison. A Frankenstein ballet in the flight of three moths navigating the night, which to me was clear as day.

It was all too much, overwhelming, nauseating, appalling. I felt bloated and ready to explode from the inside out, though I doubted even that would bring relief from my misery.

Sally and Chunk kept to the far side of the wagon. They were afraid of me. I didn't care. I didn't care that they would be my first meal. I didn't care that I would eat their meat and drink their blood. I had no choice. It was the only way to satisfy the hunger and thirst that burned at my core.

A part of me knew I was losing my mind. The cannibalistic thoughts should sicken me. They didn't. They should frighten me. They didn't. They should sadden me. They didn't. I was like the Cape Cod Killer. A psychopath. I had no emotions left. No...I was worse than the Cape Cod Killer because I couldn't even fake my emotions. I didn't have that in me. I was an animal, nothing more.

Sally was approaching me. I watched her without moving. She stopped next to me. She was scared. She was terrified. I could see her fear. I could smell it. I could taste it.

She held out a hand.

I stared balefully at it. I might have bitten it off had I the strength. But I couldn't move. I could barely keep my eyes open. Every last bit of my energy was being diverted to my metabolism to fuel the changes occurring inside me.

Sally was crouching before me now, speaking to me, telling me to stand up. Her hands touched mine. They were cool, almost cold. I felt the creases in her skin, the whorls of her fingerprints, the flexing of her muscles.

Then she was standing, pulling me up with her. I didn't think

I would move, but I rose easily, my legs powerful.

Her chest pressed against mine. Her arms wrapped around my waist. Her head rested against my shoulder. I could smell the apples in her hair that I remembered so well, but other botanicals as well. I could smell the soap she'd last used, and the sweetness of her sweat beneath. I could hear the gallop of her heartbeat and the resounding *wud-wud-wud* of her pulse and the bubbling stew of digestive juices in her stomach.

We moved in a small, clockwise circle, one step at a time, going nowhere, only turning round and round. Then her breath in my ear, like a hot hurricane, and the song, "There's a lady who's sure..."

The circus wagon disappeared. I was in Sally's living room, dancing as we were now, Led Zeppelin blaring on the sound system, thinking about kissing her, wanting to, but afraid. Becoming aroused against her—then, now, I didn't know— pressing tighter against her. Longing for nothing, never wanting the song to end.

"All that glitters with gold..."

Tears warmed my closed eyes. My parched throat tightened.

I'd had everything, and now I had nothing.

"And she's buying a stairway to heaven..."

I surrendered to Sally's voice and her touch and the incremental movements as we turned and swayed. Her living room was replaced with an endless void. For an alarming moment I thought I was alone, but I could still feel her against me, could still smell her and taste her and hear her.

Oblivious to everything outside of the moment, I let myself dance.

CHAPTER 45

THE END

W hen I opened my eyes, I saw through a gap in one of the curtains that it was early morning. The sun had risen somewhere to the east, though its light was anemic and chilly, the sky still bruised and gray from the beating it had received during the thunderstorm.

Warblers and sparrows and other birds cheeped and flitted between tree branches. Grasshoppers, cicadas, and crickets had resumed their buzzing courtship calls in earnest.

It was as if the horrors of the night before had never occurred.

I lay on my side on the hard boards of the circus wagon. I sat up slowly and stiffly. I hurt everywhere, and it wasn't from sleeping on planks. The pain was deep, as though my bones themselves were bruised.

My left arm was wrapped in Sally's blood-stained blouse.

Frowning, I looked at Sally, who lay sleeping next to me in her white bra and pink pants. Chunk slept close by, on his side, sucking his thumb.

I took off my flannel shirt and used it as a blanket to cover Sally. She opened her eyes a crack, smiled at me sleepily. Her eyes closed again—then snapped wide open.

"Ben!" She sprang awake and encased me in a hug. I groaned, feeling as though she might break something inside me.

"Sorry!" she said, releasing me. She reclaimed my shirt,

which had fallen off her, and held it against her chest. "How do you feel?"

"Like I've been shattered into a thousand pieces and glued back together." I raised my blouse-bandaged arm. "What happened?"

"You don't remember, man?" Chunk said, propping up his head with his hand. He yawned, his mouth stretching open far enough that I could see his tonsils.

I glanced through the parted curtain at the red wagon. "Yeah," I said uncomfortably. "I remember." I raised my bandaged arm again. "I mean this."

"A werewolf bit you, man! You half turned into one!"

"Fuck off," I said, at a loss for anything better as my mind reversed through the events of the previous night. The last thing that stood out was pinky-swearing with Sally and Chunk that none of us would ever forget about the werewolves. After that I had fallen asleep—and nothing until now.

I looked at Sally.

"Chunky's right—"

"Chunk!"

"It was pretty scary," she went on, ignoring him. "You were bitten and started to turn into one. But you beat it."

A lump of dread formed in the back of my throat. "How'd I do that?"

"Who knows? Guess you just fought it."

"Or *maybe* it was his *love* for you," Chunk sing-songed. "Like how the Frog Prince turns back into a handsome human prince because he loves the princess so much—only Ben ain't handsome."

"I don't remember anything at all," I said, shaking my head, the dread metastasizing.

Why can't I remember anything? And what aren't they telling me? There's something more…

"After the werewolf bit you," Sally said, "you got a fever and your skin started bruising everywhere, like what happened to the sheriff. But you weren't moaning or screaming or anything, just sitting there and staring at us."

"Your eyes glowed," Chunk said. "Sally thought you were gonna try to eat us."

"I did not!" she said. "*You* did!"

"You did too. That's why you started dancing with him."

"Huh?" I said.

"She started to dance with you to distract you from eating us. You guys looked like mega posers, just dancing there with no music."

"How long did we dance for?"

"All night," Sally said. "When it started to get light out, you fell asleep. We watched you for a bit…to make sure you weren't still going to change into a werewolf. I guess we fell asleep too."

"I have to take a leak," Chunk said.

"So go," I said.

"Do you see a toilet anywhere, dumbass?"

"Go through the bars."

"You better not look," he said, lugging himself to his feet.

"Like I'm gonna look."

"I meant Sally."

"Keep dreaming."

Chunk went to the side of the wagon with the parted curtain. He yanked it closed behind him, cocooning himself from view.

A moment later he cried, "Oh shit! Oh motherfucking shit!"

Exchanging worried glances, Sally and I got up.

She took my hand in hers. "I don't think you should look."

"Why not?"

"Ben…"

I didn't like the uneasiness in her eyes. I tugged my hand free and pulled aside the curtain.

Chunk stood against the bars, pointing at the other wagon. "Check'im out!"

My stomach surged up my throat at the sight and smell of the deputy's remains, though I managed to push it back down.

Chunk saw where I was looking and said, "Not *him*. Him! The *sheriff*! He's turned back!"

ΔΔΔ

Sheriff Sandberg had indeed turned back into his human self. He sat slumped against the wood side of the wagon opposite the dead deputy. He wore only his tan trousers, his chest and feet and head bare. He was staring blankly ahead of him.

"Think he's okay?" I mumbled, burying my nose in the crook of my good arm.

"You better ask him," Chunk said.

"Sheriff Sandberg?"

He didn't reply.

"Hey—sheriff?"

Nothing.

"He's gotta be able to hear us," Chunk said. "Unless he's gone braindead?"

"Close the curtain," Sally muttered from behind us. "Please? *Close it now.*"

"Hey," Chunk said, his gaze shifting to the forest floor. "Where'd Ben's dad go?"

ΔΔΔ

"*What?*" I said, glaring at him.

"Uhhh… you don't remember that either, huh?" He looked at Sally for help.

I looked at her too.

She was pinching her nose closed and looking green—but also heartbroken.

"I'm sorry, Ben…about your dad."

I stared at her.

"You don't remember…?"

I hadn't until that moment.

ΔΔΔ

The next thing I knew I was on my side, shriveled up in the fetal position, not even sure how I got like that. The waterworks gushed for a long time before I eventually ran out of tears. Even then, I didn't feel any better. Sally sat next to me, stroking my head and saying something now and then. I wished she'd leave me alone, but I couldn't be bothered to tell her.

It was only the arrival of the gypsy woman that kicked me out of my grief. Chunk heard her first and drew back the curtain. Sally kissed me on the cheek, got up, and joined him at the bars. After several long moments I did the same—partly out of curiosity, but mostly out of hatred. I wanted to confront the woman responsible for my dad's death.

The gypsy woman stood at the other wagon, her back to us, dressed once again in black clothes. "...the first night is by far the worst," she was saying. "It becomes easier over time. You'll have to trust me on that."

The sheriff ignored her.

"We'll be leaving soon," she went on. "I'd like you to join us. You will come to enjoy our company, our lifestyle...in time. But time is something we have in great abundance." She slipped a dagger from the waistband of her pants and placed it on the floor of the wagon. "This is the alternative. It shouldn't be a difficult decision, but the choice must be yours. You have half an hour."

She turned to leave and saw us watching.

"Are you gonna let us go now?" Chunk blurted. "We've already been here all night. I'm hungry and my mom's gonna kill me for not coming home. I won't tell her anything. We won't tell nobody nothing. We swear. So can you let us go? *Please?*"

"You talk far too much, little one," she said and left.

△△△

Sheriff Sandberg didn't need thirty minutes to decide his fate. He picked up the knife and pressed the tip of the blade to his chest, just over his heart.

"Oh, man," Chunk said, sounding both excited and dismayed.

"He's really gonna do it."

Sally and I turned away, unable to watch, but we knew by the squeamish sound that Chunk made that the sheriff had indeed done it.

△△△

When the gypsy woman returned, she appeared indifferent to Sheriff Sandberg's lifeless body. She simply unlocked and opened the hatch in the red circus wagon, climbed inside with a hacksaw in her hand, and drew the curtain facing us closed.

While she was in there doing what she was doing, a rusted green pickup truck with oversized tires reversed beneath the movie screen. Two men hitched the truck's towbar to the red wagon, then got back in the cab and drove away, pulling the groaning and creaking wagon behind them.

A short time later a different pickup truck—blue with a white shell over the bed—backed beneath the movie screen. It vanished from sight as it lined itself up with our wagon. Doors opened and banged closed. A key rattled in the hatch's lock, then the small door opened. The gypsy woman looked in at us.

"Time to come out, young ones," she said.

△△△

I stood closest to the hatch but didn't move. It was a trap. It had to be. She was going to stick us with a dagger as soon as we exited the wagon.

"I'm not going to harm you," she said, reading my mind.

"You're really gonna let us go?" Chunk asked hopefully.

"If I wanted you dead, you would be dead already, wouldn't you agree?"

Knowing this was true, we climbed out through the hatch and stood aside while she helped a man wearing a mesh trucker's cap hitch the blue pickup truck to the circus wagon.

I watched the gypsy woman silently, my emotionless face

masking the malevolence inside me. The only thing that stopped me from attacking her with tooth and nail—actions that would likely result in my death—was a promise I made repeatedly to myself that I would get my revenge one day. I would kill her. I would do it with my bare hands and watch the life drain from her eyes so she knew it was me who was responsible for her undoing.

With the truck and wagon hitched, the gypsy woman turned to us. Her emerald-green eyes met each of ours, and I suddenly feared she was going to hypnotize us again, only this time she would make us dance to death right there in the woods.

I didn't fear death, not then; I feared I would be cheated of my revenge.

"I wasn't kidding earlier," Chunk blabbed. "We ain't gonna tell no one you're a werewolf. We promise. Cross our hearts and hope —"

"I care little about what you tell others, Chuck Archibald," she said. "They would never believe what you tell them."

"So...can we go?"

"After we've departed, you are free to go wherever you wish."

△△△

We followed the blue pickup truck and yellow circus wagon from the trees, where they joined the parade of vehicles crossing Ryders Field and turning onto the pitted dirt road.

Soon only the sheriff's Ford, a blue-and-white police car, and my dad's brown van remained behind in the empty field, glaring reminders of what had happened to their owners.

Oblivious to the automotive tombstones, Chunk grinned at Sally and me and said, "Home free, guys! I always knew we had nuthin to worry bout—"

I punched him in the face.

△△△

"Why'd'ya hafta go and do that?" he whined, holding a hand to his bleeding lip.

"I told you to be quiet," I said, my hands still balled into fists, my body trembling. "But you just kept yelling."

"Huh?"

"Last night when my dad was trying to help us. If you woulda shut up, the werewolves wouldn't've come and got him."

Chunk appeared ashamed but defiant. "You don't know that. Maybe they heard the cars arrive? They have real good hearing. They probably heard the cars. That's why they came."

"Your shouting didn't help. They only started howling after you started yelling your head off."

"I was scared, man. I couldn't help it. The cops were *leaving* us."

"My dad's dead, Chunk, and it's your fault."

I started walking away.

"Ben!" Sally said, grabbing my wrist.

I tugged it away and kept walking.

"Ben! Where're you going?"

I kept walking.

"Ben! Wait!"

"I want to be alone."

"But I *don't* want to be alone."

I didn't stop, didn't look back. When I reached the spot where we'd stashed our bikes in the trees, I picked up mine and pushed it onto the dirt road. I climbed onto the seat and began pedaling.

I never saw Sally or Chunk again.

EPILOGUE
THE PRESENT

I was late for my own party.

I stopped outside The Rizzoli Bookstore on Broadway in New York City's NoMad neighborhood. Looking in through the glass front door, I found the book launch already in full swing, everyone dressed in gray or black, the colors of sophistication.

I entered and made my way through the milling crowd, smiling, nodding, shaking hands, hating all of it. Rizzoli's was one of the last classy bookstores left in the city, featuring high ceilings supported by towering black pillars, Italian frescos on the walls, iron chandeliers, and grand oak bookcases.

I spotted my literary agent, Tim Booker, by a bookcase labeled NEW FICTION. Dressed sharply in a black jacket over a black polo shirt, he was chatting with Joan Rangel, an associate editor who'd worked on my last two books. She wore a little black dress and gold heels and held a clipboard under one arm.

"Ben!" Tim said, raising a glass of red wine. "Didn't know whether you were going to make it or not."

We shook. "I walked from the hotel. Forgot how big Manhattan blocks are. Hi, Joan."

She gave me an air kiss and said, "Donald's been looking all over for you. I think he wants to get things underway."

I nodded. "We'll chat in a bit."

I continued through the crowd to the spacious back room

where Donald Blumstein, the editor-in-chief at my publishing house, was holding court with some of his staff. He was a large man, in both height and girth, and always impeccably groomed. The gleaming gold buttons on his charcoal blazer matched a gold tie clip.

Seeing me approach, his broad, bearded face broke into a smile. "Dammit, Ben, you know all this is for you, right? We don't go to these lengths for any old author. The least you can do is show up on time."

"I thought it kicked off at six."

"Bullshit you did. I'll introduce you now. Meredith? Get Ben one of his books to read."

A bird-like assistant publicist with silver-blonde hair fetched one of my books from a stack on a nearby table and handed it to me, while Donald stepped onto a makeshift podium. He clinked his silver wedding band against his champagne flute until the chatter died down and someone turned off the music that had been playing. Surveying the crowd with a pretentious uptilt of his chin, he raised his glass. "Please join me in welcoming one of our *New York Times* bestselling authors, Ben Graves. His latest novel, *The Dancing Plague*, is unlike anything he's written before, and he's here—late, but here—to share a scene from it with us. Please put your hands together for him. Ben? Come on up."

I exchanged places with Donald on the podium and placed my book on the lectern. I cracked it open and read slowly, matching my voice to the rhythm of the prose. I'd selected the scene in which Chunk and I were sneaking off to the beach and ran into Sally in her backyard.

At one point when I looked up I saw her—Sally, my childhood friend—among the people that had packed tightly into the room.

My heart skipped a beat and I lost my place on the page. I cleared my throat, found where I had left off, and resumed reading. I didn't look up again until I finished the scene—and Sally wasn't where she'd been.

Had she really been there?

I stepped off the podium, barely hearing the polite applause.

I picked up a flute of champagne, brushed off Donald, and circulated through the crowd, alert and watchful.

I found Sally leaning against one of the black pillars. She had a copy of my book in her hands and was reading the back cover. I took the moment to study her, the contours of her face, the tilt of her head. Her chestnut hair was slightly shorter than I remembered.

Was it Sally? I hadn't seen her for thirty-one years, after all.

She looked up from the book and her eyes met mine.

I stepped forward, trying a smile. "Sally?" I said, and for a moment I was convinced I'd gotten it wrong. She didn't look anything like the Sally I'd known. "Sally Levine?"

"Ben Graves," she said, and no matter how else she'd changed, the voice was hers.

"Jesus, it *is* you." I hesitated, unsure whether to shake her hand or kiss her cheek or attempt a hug. I settled on a kiss.

"You've made me famous," she said, smiling.

I felt myself blush. I'd never before based my characters on people I knew. I might use something here or there, a personality quirk or a physical description, but nothing too obvious. *The Dancing Plague*, however, was an exception. The book was autobiographical. And even though it was billed as fiction, I'd wanted to keep it as authentic as possible—I'd wanted to keep Chunk and Sally as authentic as possible. To help, I wrote the first draft using their real given names. I'd planned on changing them in a later draft...but I could never bring myself to do it. The story wouldn't have been the same.

"It's been over thirty years," I said. "I didn't think you'd mind. I mean...I didn't think... I never thought you'd ever hear about the book."

She flicked the book open to the copyright page and read, "This is a work of fiction." She raised an eyebrow at me and continued, "Names, characters, places, and incidents are products of the author's imagination or are used fictitiously and are not to be construed as real." Another raised eyebrow. "Any resemblance to actual events, locales, organizations, or persons, living or dead, is entirely coincidental."

"I changed your last name," I said. "Bishop."

"Oh, you mean that Sally with the big-screen TV was *me*?" she said coquettishly.

I frowned. "You've read the book?"

"Of course."

"It's not on sale yet…" I was confused. "I mean…you didn't pick up that copy tonight?"

"I wrote to your publisher a few months ago and asked for a galley." She showed me the cover, which was clearly labeled as an advanced reader's copy.

"And they just sent one to you?" I said, surprised.

"I told them I was a reviewer for the *New York Journal of Books*."

"How did you even know about it?"

"I've read all your books, Ben. You might have forgotten about me…but I never forgot about you."

"I never forgot about you," I said quietly. "I just wrote an entire book about you, didn't I?"

"And I'm flattered."

"So you're not going to sue me?"

"I'm still consulting my lawyers."

We laughed, and I took a sip of champagne. It felt unreal to be talking to Sally—unreal and electrifying.

She said, "So what's it like to have your name on the cover of a book?"

"You get used to it after the first one."

"But the first one must have been pretty neat."

I nodded. "It was tubular."

She blinked. "Are you serious?"

"Yeah, I mean, it was a totally tubular experience."

She grinned. "You're so joking."

"What are you talking about?"

"You don't still use that word?"

"Sure, I do."

"I'm not buying it."

Now I grinned. "You remembered when I said it at your place?"

"Not until I read it in here." She waggled the book. "And that was a pretty good retelling of the party we had."

"I'm happy to hear that. I wasn't sure. It all happened so long ago, I doubted my memory at times."

"No, everything in the book was pretty spot on. Except for your take on the gypsies, of course. But that worked out well in the end."

I wasn't sure I'd heard her right. "My *take*?"

"The werewolves."

I was staring at her in puzzlement when Donald Blumstein appeared at my shoulder. "Here you are, Ben. And who might your lovely companion be?"

"I'm an old friend of Ben's," Sally said.

"Watch what you say to him. You know how authors are. He might just quote you in one of his next books."

"Only quote? I think I could handle that."

"I'm Donald. I never got your name."

"Sally," she said, shaking his hand.

"Ah ha! There you go! He's already stolen your name. Sally, you see, is a character in his latest novel."

"I'm aware," she said, raising the book she held.

"You've got yourself a copy. Wonderful. I do hope you enjoy it."

"Um, Donald..." I said. "Sally and I were just discussing something of a personal nature—"

"You don't have to tell me twice! I'll leave you two alone. I simply wanted to let you know, Ben, that Meredith has added another stop to your book tour. Camp Verde, Arizona."

"Don't I already have a stop in Phoenix?"

"Sure, and Camp Verde's a dot on the map. But here's the rub —it's having a dancing plague of its very own!" He nodded his head enthusiastically. "That's right. Several people have taken to dancing in a wild delirium for the last several days. A woman even dropped dead before anyone could intervene—which was what got the story into the news. So Meredith and I were thinking, if you do a signing in Camp Verde, you'll get yourself in the news too. Nothing better than free publicity, am I right? And if we're lucky and more people dance themselves into their graves, we're talking about national exposure..."

ΔΔΔ

I was pacing outside the bookstore on Broadway, Sally peppering me with questions I barely heard.

"It's got nothing to do with *them*, Ben."

That got my attention. "You mean the gypsies? Of course it does! It has to." I recalled what she'd mentioned to me before Donald interrupted us. "What did you mean when you said my 'take' on the gypsies."

She shrugged. "How you made them into actual werewolves."

"Sally, they *were* werewolves."

She laughed. "Oh, come on, Ben. Not this again."

"Not what again?"

"You're pulling my leg."

"What do you think happened in Ryders Field?"

"You got it mostly right, the sequence of events. But the gypsies weren't *werewolves*. They were just a bunch of sickos who *thought* they were werewolves."

"*What?*"

"You know, lycanthropy. The illness?"

I knew what lycanthropy was, of course. It was a form of madness involving the delusion of being an animal, usually a wolf, with correspondingly altered behavior.

I reeled, wondering if she could be right and knowing at the same time that she wasn't.

"I saw them, Sally," I said. "You saw them too. Those weren't people playing dress-up, for God's sake."

"They were wearing wolf skins and headpieces. The drugs made us see the rest."

I frowned. "The *drugs*?"

"The drugs the gypsies were on to enhance whatever it was they were doing. The drugs they gave the sheriff that made him go crazy. The drugs they gave us—"

"Us?"

"That's why we tripped out so badly, Ben. You the most. You thought you were turning into a real-life werewolf!"

I was shaking my head. "No way, Sally. No way. That's not what happened."

"Werewolves *don't exist*, Ben."

I was grateful we were in New York City. The people passing us on the busy street could no doubt overhear snippets of our conversation, but not one of them gave us a second glance.

"Who told you all this?" I asked.

"All what?" she said.

"What you're telling me! That the gypsies were a bunch of nutcases! That they drugged us!"

"My parents. Your mother didn't tell you?"

I shook my head. "She didn't talk to me after that night. She blamed me for my father's death."

"Why would she blame you?"

"Because we went to Ryders Field in the first place. If we didn't go, my father wouldn't have come looking for us…"

"Oh, Ben…" She reached out to take my hand, reconsidered, and let it be. "Well, she knew. She had to. Everybody in town knew. You never came back to school, and then you moved away… I guess…well, I guess if your mother never told you, you just never heard what people were saying. If you asked her now —"

"She's dead. And you're wrong, Sally. I know what I saw. We weren't on drugs." I clenched my jaw. It felt as though my reality was slipping away from me. "What about all the dancing in town? How do you explain—"

"That was a kind of mass hysteria—"

"The hell it was!"

"It was. It was covered extensively in the Chatham news. Mass hysteria is real. It's a clinical thing, Ben. And it had nothing to do with the gypsies."

"She came to my house, Sally. The gypsy woman. She hypnotized my mom. She made her dance. I was there. I saw it happen."

"Ben..."

Why do you think we went to Ryders Field in the first place? I wanted to confront the gypsy woman."

"I know that. I'm not saying she didn't go to your house. I don't know what relationship she had with your mother. But she didn't make her dance. That doesn't make sense. You must have misinterpreted why she was there."

"It *does* make sense, and I didn't misinterpret anything. You've read the book. She was trying to cure the people that Gregory Henrickson had infected."

"Ben..."

"Stop it! Stop saying my name like that." I held up my hands, palms outward. I didn't want to hear anymore. "I need to get going," I said, finding it suddenly hard to look Sally in the eyes.

"Oh, Ben, don't go. I don't want us to end on another...bad note."

"No bad note," I lied. "It was good seeing you again, Sally. But I need to go."

"Then take this," she said, producing a business card from her handbag and holding it out for me. "Call me sometime, okay? We can get a coffee or something?"

I tucked the card into a pocket without looking at it. "I live in Boston," I said noncommittedly.

"Call me next time you're in New York then?"

I said I would, gave her a tight smile, and left.

△△△

I spent the rest of the evening in my hotel room, raiding the mini-bar and reading everything I could on the internet about the dancing going on in Camp Verde, Arizona. By the time I'd gotten through all the miniature liquor bottles, I had a flight booked from LaGuardia to Flagstaff, which was less than an hour's drive from Camp Verde.

Before crashing out on the bed, I went to the window to have a much-deserved cigarette. Up in the clear night sky the spectral moon was fat and roundish, well into its waxing gibbous phase.

In a few days it would be full.

AFTERWORD

Thank you for reading *The Dancing Plague*. This was Book 1. Book 2 concludes the story thirty-one years later when Ben, Sally, and Chunk are adults.

ABOUT THE AUTHOR

Jeremy Bates

 USA TODAY and #1 AMAZON bestselling author Jeremy Bates has published more than twenty novels and novellas. They have sold more than one million copies, been translated into several languages, and been optioned for film and TV by major studios. Midwest Book Review compares his work to "Stephen King, Joe Lansdale, and other masters of the art." He has won both an Australian Shadows Award and a Canadian Arthur Ellis Award. He was also a finalist in the Goodreads Choice Awards, the only major book awards decided by readers.

31646345R00166